# THE RIPPLE
## EFFECT

ISBN-13 Paperback        978-1-967903-38-2
        eBook        978-1-967903-37-5

Library of Congress Control Number: 2025912485

# THE RIPPLE EFFECT

ROBIN CLARK ANDERSON

# THE CHAPTER 1

HE HAD SPENT MOST OF his life after the military wondering what to do with himself. He had tried just about every job there was, from garbage collector to real estate sales. He had married, divorced, re-married, and had live-ins, but somehow, he couldn't get it together long enough to make any relationship or job work for longer than a few months. So now he had yet another decision to make.

As Valient Washington sat in his armchair trying to get his thoughts to make some kind of sense, he felt a foreboding as never before. Something had to give.

Once upon a time he had hope: hope of a successful life, love, and future. Now it looked like he would continue to fail at everything. What did he have to do that he hadn't already done? Should he move again? He had moved into his parent's house after his mom died. It was his and it was paid for, so he'd kept it. Should he try going back to school again? He already had two bachelor's degrees and a master's in literature. Valient's thought twirled around and around until he felt the inevitable headache blasting the back of his brain. As he fell asleep feeling sorry for himself, a fleeting thought came to him: Get off your butt and get a life!

Simple, right?

# CHAPTER 2

SINCE HIS SOUL-SEARCHING EPIPHANY ALL those weeks ago, life continued in a roller coast of more ups and downs. But he had formed a plan and tried to stick with it. A few, actually more than just a few, stutter steps were finally paying off.

He started to make a list:

A. Clean my house
B. Join something
C. Decide on one job you would really like to do
D. Research what is necessary to qualify for that job
E. Enroll in school/training to get that qualification
F. Get a dog

The last happened first. He saw a dog on a local T.V. news program that very morning. Deciding he needed something in his life to take care of and give him some kind of responsibility, he went straight to the shelter and adopted a two-month-old mutt. No one seemed sure of what its breeding was, but she sure was ugly. She was black, had hair that stuck out at every angle no matter what he did, and was fat, just what he needed to have a reason to get out of bed in the morning. Valient named her Buddy. Go figure. That was three months ago.

Now she sat near his feet as he struggled with what to do today. He had managed to clean most of the house. Maybe he should finish the back rooms? He still was researching what kind of job he would like to do that he hadn't already tried and discarded, but the Internet was down today, so he'd have to wait for that. That left joining something.

"What to join, girl? Any ideas?" he asked Buddy. She looked up at him with a twinkle in her eye. She barked out her answer, wagging her tail like it was going to fall off. He got the feeling she could really communicate with him. It scared him a little as he looked into those big, blue eyes. He swore she wanted him to go to the shelter, the homeless shelter. He sat looking at her and the feeling got stronger. Weird.

He got up and poured himself another cup of coffee. He stood by the sink sipping from his cup, staring at the back yard and could feel the mutt staring at him. It didn't make sense. He didn't even know where the homeless shelter was. There had to be one somewhere. There always was right? It was a large town after all. Besides, dogs couldn't communicate with people, could they? And why the homeless shelter? It was never even on his radar on the worst of days. And the only way to join a homeless shelter was to be homeless, right? He was being stupid.

# CHAPTER 3

HE TRAIPSED INTO THE BACK room and got started pulling books off the shelves and dusting the dirt off the jackets. It had been a very long time since he ventured back here. The books had been here since his parents owned the house years ago. Some of them came from his grandparent's house before he was even born. There sure were a lot of them; four walls, floor to ceiling, shelves and shelves.

As Valient handled each one, he tried to separate what he wanted to keep and what should go. It was proving far harder than he thought; childhood memories of his mother reading this one or that one to him at bedtime; quiet afternoons by a fire, reading on his own as he grew, his dad's favorite volume of Shakespeare, the first book he bought with his own pennies when he was eight. This was going to be a bigger job than he felt ready for today.

He thought about abandoning his quest. He'd done a few shelves. That should be enough for today. If he cleaned a section each time it would be less overwhelming. He had one small box to give away or sell.

As he looked around and saw the amount of work to be done, he gave a great sigh. He couldn't give up so easily. The whole idea was to change his ways, right? He pulled off a few more books, dusting them off and separating them into piles on the floor.

The next time he looked up the hallway was dark. He had worked his way through the first wall of bookshelves. It was beginning to smell better in there. Furniture polish from the cleaned shelves made the room smell like lemons.

He had four piles of books; three to keep and one to go. The three were separated into types of books. The first was children's books. Those he might donate to some charity for kids, maybe a hospital. The second were books his mom loved the most. He wasn't sure if he could ever part with them. The third was a pile of his own favorites. He would go through the many more times before this task would be truly complete.

The last were book he never saw before. Since he wasn't sure what their origins were, he felt no attachment to them so they could go. At least that was his plan.

Buddy was pushing her way through the door with her leash in her mouth. She obviously had to go out. Now! He put down the book in his hand and attached the leash to her collar. With a last look around, he took her for a quick walk down the street. She did her business at the first patch of dead grass. He must have worked longer than he thought. She really had to go!

When she had finished her business she pulled him along the sidewalk to the next block. There she slowed and let him catch his breath. Looking at him, she seemed to want him to do something. What? He wasn't getting it.

They walked the next block just for the sake of walking the kinks of the day from his poor legs. At the beginning of the next block a little boy was sitting on a stoop watching them. Buddy pulled toward him and he smiled wide. "Can I pet your dog mister?"

"Sure. I think she wants you to." As he watched Buddy, he realized the boy was out kind of late by himself. While it was a pretty safe neighborhood, he still should have not been outside at this hour. Where were his parents?

"Do you live here?" Valient asked the boy.

"Just for tonight, I guess." the boy replied.

"What do you mean, 'just for tonight'? Where do you live normally? Are you visiting someone here?"

"Na, I don't have a home My mom and I stay wherever we can. This is a shelter house. She's inside helping clean up from the dinner tonight."

"Does she know where you are? Should you be out here alone?"

"I asked her if I could sit outside. I promised not to go off the steps. I have to go in in a minute. My two minutes are over now. Thank you for letting me pet your dog. She's soft."

With that he jumped up and scampered into the house, closing the door soundly behind him.

Valient and Buddy headed home, but Valent was thinking about the boy. He didn't appear to be homeless. He was clean and well mannered; didn't look undernourished like those kids you see on T.V. Maybe he hadn't been homeless that long. The kid mentioned a mom but not dad. He wondered about that too. Valient wondered about the house. It didn't look like the shelters he'd imagined, store front churches with rows of cots with dirty blankets. The house was in a nice neighborhood; clean on the outside at least. The boy said they served dinner. This was not an ordinary shelter that he ever heard of. Was this normal? Probably not he decided. But since it wasn't his problem anyway, he wasn't going to have to think about it anymore. He wouldn't see the kid again.

# CHAPTER 4

A FEW DAYS LATER AFTER HE and Buddy did their morning constitutional and had cleaned up after breakfast, he got back to work on the library. The piles got bigger, the shelves got shinier, and his mood got happier. Valient didn't realize that the mere act of cleaning would give him the lift he had been lacking.

He began organizing the shelves he had cleaned. One wall he deemed the children's section, although there were no children to read the books and probably would never be. He just couldn't bring himself to even think about giving away his childhood memories. The books from the other piles were arranged tentatively into shelves by author.

As he was putting the bookcases in order, he thought again of the boy from yesterday. Did he like to read? Could he read? Was he in school? Would the kid like the kind of books that Valient liked? Why was he even thinking about this?

After the first two walls and the current piles of books were organized, he looked around the room with satisfaction. There were still two more to go, but he felt he had a great start.

Buddy was whining in the doorway to go out. He didn't realize it had been hours since breakfast, and it was getting dark. He leashed her and went for a long walk. They walked in the opposite direction from the shelter house because he didn't like to be too predictable. He had read somewhere that bad guys who case some of the better neighborhoods depend on people having a routine. Since he was currently unemployed and had nowhere to go most of the time, he certainly didn't have a routine. He didn't walk the dog on a regular timetable either. Whenever she showed signs of distress, he took her out. He didn't eat his meals at regular time or go to bed or get up at the same times either. So he figured he would be safe from anyone out there. Besides, who was Valient Washington to think anyone cared enough to case him out anyway?

# CHAPTER 5

He and Buddy walked toward the downtown area where the streets were bustling with people on their way home from their daily activities. He found himself outside their favorite outdoor bistro and decided they would get their supper instead of trying to cook something at home. He was tired after all the work of the last couple of days anyway.

He ordered a pita with beef and pork sandwich and a beer for himself and a Shepard's pie and water for Buddy. Buddy was such a regular that she had her own dishes along with some of the other dogs who frequented the outside tables. The owner, Micco, served them himself. They had been friends since Valient's parents used to bring him here when both men were in grade school. Micco sat with him as they ate, talking about how the business was going and what he was not doing with himself these days.

Years ago the men's mothers had traveled together. Every year or so they would travel to some exotic location, leaving the men behind to mind both the store and the kids. Valient's dad was a dealer in antique books and owned a store a few doors from Micco's restaurant. The families became good friends, and the men have continued that friendship even after the parents all passed on. Micco kept the restaurant, but Valient sold the bookstore to his father's partner for a good profit.

Micco excused himself to get back to the kitchen as Valent and Buddy finished eating. They were leaving the patio when Buddy spotted the little boy from the shelter house across the street. She pulled on her leash, trying to get to him as Valient strained to get her under control through the traffic. They caught up to the little boy and his mom, Buddy jumping around them, barking and wagging her tail in greeting. The boy hugged the dog while she licked him. Valient apologized for behavior, but the mom nervously laughed at the antics. He introduced himself and Buddy and began to explain that they had met the boy on the steps of the house while out walking a day or so ago. She said the boy's name was Irving and she was Jessie. The talked a few minutes about the dog. What was her breed? How old was she? How long she lived with Valient. Irving asked where he lived and if it was near the shelter house. He whispered when he said the words "shelter house", looking at his mom. She looked embarrassed and suddenly very nervous. Valient wasn't sure what to say, but Jessie said they had to get going so he didn't say anything. Taking his cue, they said their goodbyes and walked away in opposite direction. He wondered where they were going.

# CHAPTER 6

J ESSIE WAS PARANOID. WHO WAS this guy? Was he a threat? He seemed harmless, but she couldn't be sure. She would have to be more careful when letting Irving out of her sight, even for a minute. Maybe time was making her careless. She had thought the new house was safe, being in the kind of neighborhood where people minded their own business. It was more of a boarding house than the kind of shelter s normally associated with being homeless, so anyone looking for her and the boy wouldn't likely think of looking there. She didn't have to register and paid for the things they needed in cash, so there'd be no record anyway.

They had been moving around for a couple months. Her husband, Matt, was dead, killed by the people she was hiding from. They would have killed her and Irving too, but Matt got them out of the house before the people came. Her husband was to meet them after making his deal with some mysterious contact that was going to make them disappear with enough money and identities no one could trace. Since Matt never told her who this contact was and wouldn't let her meet him (or her?), she had no idea who or what she was hiding from. She didn't even know why. Matt never confided in her as to what the reason they had to disappear! He had only said that he saw something he wasn't supposed to, and they needed to get away before anyone found out. He wouldn't go to the police. He just said they needed to go. When she begged him that last night for an answer, he promised to explain everything once they were settled someplace safe.

She and the boy had waited at the little restaurant for two hours before she realized her husband wasn't coming. Jessie had called Matt's phone numerous times getting voicemail. When a female stranger picked up she got scared. All she really knew was Matt would never willingly give up his phone when the call was from her. As she was leaving the restaurant, a Jeep-looking car screeched to a stop at the curb, and a man and woman rushed in. They talked to the hostess, and Jessie saw her point out the door in her direction. She picked up the boy and ran into the first store she came to After running out the back door of that one and into an open door to another she took off down a narrow street to an alley. Hoping she lost whoever was in the Jeep she went to the corner to figure out where she was.

She was really confused. Never in a million years would she have thought she and Matt would be in this kind of mess. What was going on? Where was Matt? Who were those people? What the blazes was she going to do? Where could she go? How was she going to get anywhere? She had no transportation, very little money, no clothes. She had left her phone in the restaurant. She slid down the side of the building in the alley and tried to think. Irving was looking at her like she had lost her mind. Maybe she had. She had to contact the police. They were supposed to help people in her kind of trouble, right? But she didn't even know what kind of trouble she was in! Okay, find police station.

She looked out of the alley and thought she saw the Jeep coming down the street. She quickly ducked back into the shadows and put a hand over Irving's mouth to keep him quiet. He looked up at her questioningly but seemed to know to keep quiet. She could feel her heart beating and Irving's too. After what seemed like forever, she dared to take another look. The street was empty. She spied a gas station on the nest corner and headed to it.

There was a lady behind the counter but no one else in the store area. She asked to use a telephone. The lady asked why she didn't just use her own phone. Every adult and most kids had cell phones, didn't they? After convincing her that she was really in need of a phone, the lady let her into the office to use the land line there. Jessie called 9-1-1 and tried to explain her situation to the operator. Finally, the operator said they would send an officer to take a report.

The patrolman they sent seemed to think Jessie was some kind of nut case. He didn't take her seriously at first. While questioning her about what was going on, a report came over his radio of a homicide. The address was Jessie's! When she heard the address, she nearly fainted. The officer put her and the boy in the back of his patrol car and called in to his superior.

The patrolman drove to Jessie's house but wouldn't let her out of the car. The detective on scene came out to question her. She told him what she could, but he didn't seem to believe she knew nothing of the details of her husband's death. Where had she been? Why did her husband make her leave the house? Who would have done this? Who was he meeting?

Since she wasn't very forthcoming, they decided she had to go to the stationhouse. They put her and Irving into an interrogation room and made her wait until the detective came back from her house. It seemed like hours. Irving was tired and irritable. They tried to take him away from her during the interview, but he had such a fit they decided to leave him where he could see she was all right. She could see him through a window, and he could still see her. A policewoman was trying to keep him occupied. After a couple more hours of the same questions and answers, they let her leave.

Problem was she didn't know where to go. As she was standing by the door trying to decide, the Jeep she saw earlier in the afternoon pulled up the street. Screaming for the detective, she ran back into the station. By the time she got him and back out to the street, the Jeep was long gone. Needless to say, he was less than impressed with her hysterics. Jessie couldn't understand why he didn't believe someone may be looking for her an Irving. Hadn't her husband just been murdered? He had told her after all his questions that he felt it was a burglary gone bad. Detective Shot gave her one of his cards, asked if she wanted to be taken somewhere, and left after giving instructions to the desk sergeant to get her a ride anywhere she needed to go.

Leaving the police station, she had them take her to her sister's house. She wouldn't stay there, but she had nowhere else to go right then. Dorothy was less than thrilled to see her as she knew it would be. They hadn't gotten along in a very long time, since their parents had died, in fact. Their parents had left so many bills, and the girls had been sued by one of the homes for the balance the insurance didn't pay for their mom's care. Dorothy didn't think she should have to pay for the attorney's fees because Jessie had handled Mom's placement. Didn't matter they won the lawsuit, and the home ended up with all the expenses to pay. Nothing made a difference to her sister, she just continued to blame Jessie for all the inconvenience.

Dorothy did listen to Jessie when she asked for help though. As Jessie explained what had been going on the last few days and about Matt being murdered, her sister's eyes got wide, and she started to cry. That was the last thing Jessie expected. Bottom line was she let Jessie and Irving stay overnight, sent someone to the house to pick up clothes in the middle of the night, and went the next morning to set up a prepay card account with her personal banker so Jessie could access money with no strings. Jessie didn't ask how it was done or how her sister know to be so clandestine. She just said thank you. The only stipulation was that Jessie was not to come back to her house. But any contact would be through the banker. She didn't want her family to be put in any danger because of Jessie's troubles. She didn't want to know where she was or anything else. When she left for work, Dorothy gave her some extra cash and then told Jessie not to be there when she got home. So much for sisterly love and concern.

That was three months ago. Jessie and Irving had first stayed in cheap hotels in town. But after she thought she had seen the Jeep again (actually several times), she started moving around from hotels to shelters and sometimes on the street. She was scared and alone with a child to care for. Somehow, she kept in touch with the detective working Matt's murder, and he had filled her in on what he thought were some details of Matt's reason for wanting to disappear. He had wanted to put her in protective custody, but Jessie wasn't sure it would be any safer than her on her own. She thought the detective would press the issue, but he didn't. She still wasn't sure who she could really trust, or for that matter, why they were still after her when Matt was dead and she knew nothing!

# CHAPTER 7

Valient had accomplished exactly one- and one-half points on his list. He had gotten a dog and cleaned all but two rooms in his house. He still didn't know what kind of job he'd like to do or how to go about figuring that out. He had no desire to go back to school at thirty-something, he was getting too old for that If he couldn't do something with what he already had, then he'd do nothing. He had enough money to support himself without scrimping, so it was an option. But he was bored. Maybe he just needed a hobby instead. He could do two things at once by joining a group for a hobby.

His thoughts kept going back to the woman and her son. Why were they homeless? What about the boy? It was driving him to distraction, more because it seemed his bloody dog was so bent on making friends with the kid. What was the attraction? Buddy kept looking a Valient with expectancy. It seemed to be she wanted to go find the boy. Valient could feel her thoughts and was seeing pictures. It sounded stupid even to him. But he would swear to it.

"Okay girl, we will go walk toward the house and see if the kid is still there." Buddy turned the baby blues on him and actually looked like she smiled as she got her leash from the chair near the door.

Now he's having a conversation with a dog. "I'm losing what's left of my mind," he said out loud.

They walked the three blocks to the house where they first saw the boy on the steps. Valient stood looking up at the door, trying to decide if he should go up and knock or turn around and go home.

He saw someone looking out a side window, but the curtain fell when he looked that way. He waited to see if anyone came to the door, but no one did. "Well girl, I guess they aren't all that sociable to strangers. Wonder how they select their tenants?" He felt kind of foolish standing there staring, especially now that someone knew he was out there. So up the stairs he went and pushed the bell.

To his surprise, a child about six opened the door almost before the bell stopped ringing. She did a little curtsey and told him to wait in the foyer. What the? This was not what he expected, especially these days. And certainly not in what he thought was a homeless shelter.

He heard a woman scold the child as she made her way from the back of the house.

"Sarah, haven't I told you over and over not to go near that door? One of these days someone is going to take you clean away from here! Go to your room! We will deal with this when I get finished with whoever you let in here!" As the little girl ran up the stairs as fast as her little legs would carry her, the woman turned to him. "What do you want and who are you? And who said you could bring that animal into my home?" she scowled at him.

"Sorry, I didn't think about it. She goes wherever I go usually. I will tie her on the porch if you like." Valient stammered, not sure what to do.

The woman looked like she was going to throw him out without giving him a chance to tell her what he was doing there. "Don't worry now, damage is done. So, what do you want...Mr?"

"Oh, sorry, Valient Washington. I live a few blocks from here."

"So? Again, what are you doing in my house?" She was very suspicious and not at all friendly.

"I was talking to a little boy who was sitting on your front steps a couple days or so ago, and I saw him again after that downtown. I was wondering if they were still here. Their names were Jessie and Irving. I didn't get a last name. Are they still here?"

"I have no idea who or what you are talking about, young man. No one here by those names; now or ever. You must have the wrong place. Now take your-I guess it's a dog-out of here, and don't come back!" With that she opened the door and motioned for them to leave.

Buddy looked up at the door as they made it to the sidewalk and gave a low growl. Weird, he'd never heard her growl before! This was getting more and more strange. He knew he had the right house. He could feel Buddy telling him they were in there somewhere. Why would the woman deny they were here? There was something going on that now had his attention. He can't stand a mystery. Apparently neither could Buddy, she was still staring up at the door.

"Well girl? What do we do now? Should we give it up or do a little sleuthing on our own?" he asked the dog. Right! Now he's looking for guidance from a dog. He was losing it for sure.

On the way back to the house, Valient decided to call his dad's old friend, Jake, from the bookstore. He had lots of friends and contacts. He could also ask Micco. He talked to everyone in the area. Maybe he could get some information from them about his mysterious new acquaintances. And that house.

# CHAPTER 8

J ESSIE WATCHED VALIENT WALK DOWN the street from the window in her room. Thankfully it was Sarah who had answered the door and not Irving. They would have had to move if he had, but Mrs. James had gotten rid of him, and Irving was none the wiser. Both children had been told not to go near the door, but Sarah still insisted it was her job. Hopefully the spanking Mrs. James had given her would bring home the lesson. Not that she condoned such punishment, but sometimes drastic measures were called for. She had done the same to Irving when she found out he had been out front without her.

She went downstairs to the kitchen to see Mrs. James, leaving Irving sleeping in their room. "Did he say anything? Like why he was looking for us?" she asked the landlady.

"Only that he had met you and Irving: first here, then downtown. He wanted to know if you were still here. Just what you heard. Didn't give him a chance to say much else. Just got rid of him. Why did you even talk to him that day? Why on earth did you let Irving sit outside? And by himself! What if someone else had spotted him? It seems you made an impression—or Irving did," she growled. Changing the subject, she asked, "How long do you plan on staying here? I need to get more food if it's going to be long." She reached for her paper and pen to make a grocery list.

"I'm not sure. We like it here, and your cooking is fattening up Irving. Besides that, Sarah is good company for him. I feel bad about him not having any friends. It depends on what I find out today." She sat pensively for a minute. "I need to call Detective Shot. We have to stop this running sometime, and I have to figure out what to do. I can't do this much longer. You're right, I should never have let Irving outside by himself. I thought he had gone out back. I talked to this guy out of common courtesy; habits from childhood. I don't know what I was thinking. I guess I just forgot myself for a minute." Jessie looked around the comfortable kitchen and sighed. She had to get some help. And answers.

"A minute is all it would take to kill you. You can't let your guard down. Ever. Until your husband's killer is found you have to stay on your toes. We don't need any trouble here," Mrs. James admonished her.

Jessie went to the front room where she used the house phone to call Detective Shot. Having to leave a message, she asked that he call her using the code name because she may have a problem. She didn't leave any particulars hoping he'd call quickly. He didn't need the number because he was the one who brought her to this place. Turns out it was a place he had hid witnesses in the past. Mrs. James was a cop's widow and a former cop herself. Sarah was her granddaughter who lived with her. Sarah's parents had been killed in kind of accident when she was just a baby.

# CHAPTER 9

DETECTIVE SHOT CALLED THE NEXT morning, mad as the devil because someone had left the message on his desk instead of letting him know right away. Jessie told him what had happened and asked him what she should do. He told her to hold tight, and he'd be over soon. He knew Mrs. James would have let hm know if there was an emergency situation, but he should have been called by the dope who took Jessie's message.

He got to the house around nine o'clock that evening. He never wanted to be seen in the daytime, if possible, in case someone was watching. He always used the back door where there were no outside lights. Mrs. James was great, and he never wanted to put her in more danger than was necessary. He had never put anyone there that he believed was an imminent threat. She was an ex-cop and could handle herself, but she did have that kid with her. Shot had worked briefly with her husband and knew she was no slouch.

After he had spoken to Jessie that morning on the phone, he had run the name Jessie had given him through the various computer programs designed by government agencies and called in some favors for information. He got an address from DMV. He found out this Valient Washington guy had no criminal record locally or nationally.

He didn't bother with international databases. Washington did serve in the military. He was an Army mechanic for five years and had served in Germany for two of that. Honorable discharge, no disciplinary records, Good Conduct medal, multiple commendations, and a Sharpshooter medal for marksmanship. Since the military, he had moved around, had various nowhere jobs, has an impressive education, and now lived in his parent's house and was currently unemployed. He had a small inheritance and money in the bank. Sounded like the guy you'd want your daughter to marry, except for the job thing anyway. No obvious threat as far as Shot could see. So why was he so interested in Jessie and Irving? Was there something there that didn't show up on the database? Shot would have to talk to this guy and find out.

Detective Shot, Jessie, and Mrs. James were sitting in the kitchen. The coffee and cake were forgotten as the women explained what little they knew to Detective Shot. Jessie was sure she had never seen or heard of Valent Washington before last week. Irving had told the detective what had happened on the stoop. Nothing seemed amiss there; just a friendly guy with his dog. Shot would have to look deeper to make sure that was all it was.

They agreed that Detective Shot would ask around at the restaurant where Jessie thought Washington had been before seeing him downtown. Then go talk to him face to face.

Jessie asked about her husband's case. Any new leads? How long was she going to be hiding? How long could she stay here? The only thing Dectitive Shot could tell her is it looked to be gang related. And there was someone he was interested in but nothing concrete yet. Jessie could think of absolutely nothing that would link her wonderful husband to anything gang related. Matt came from upper class family, lived in a gated community growing up, college educated, wouldn't know a drug that didn't come from a pharmacy, worked out religiously and worked at a paper factory as a production supervisor. What could a gang possibly be interested in?

It had been determined that nothing had been taken from the house, so burglary was all but ruled out as a motive for Matt's murder. No forced entry, no defensive marks on his body. One gunshot to the head and one to the heart. Double tap, as one of the patrolmen had described it. A mark of a professional hit? Matt had been lying on the kitchen floor; coffee pot shattered near him and three cups untouched on the island. He obviously had not felt threatened by whoever was there. No fingerprints and no evidence. Nothing made sense. All they had to go on was what Matt had said about seeing something he wasn't supposed to. What could he have seen that would have gotten him killed? And why were they still after Jessie and Irving?

She was sure they still were after them as she had seen the woman, she thought anyway, downtown. She hadn't seen the Jeep for over a week. Maybe she was just being crazy. Detective Shot didn't think so. He wanted her to stay hidden until he could get some answers. Unfortunately, he had no idea if and when that would be.

# CHAPTER 10

J AKE WAS SHELVING BOOKS IN the science section when Valient and Buddy came in the bookstore. When he heard the jingle of the little bells above the door Jake moved to meet them in the aisle. Hugging Valient and petting Buddy, he invited them to the counter to have some refreshment.

Unlike the big bookstores everyone came to JWBooks not just to buy a book, but to see the owners. Since his dad had died—right here in this store as a matter of fact—of a heart attack, Jake had carried on as before. Everyone was welcomed with a smile and was offered tea, coffee, water, and cookies. There was a grouping of couches and another four chairs in the side area of the store. Every employee was carefully picked to fit into that mindset.

Today Ceila was working the cash register, but no one was in the store at this early hour.

They moved to the chairs and got settled with coffee and chocolate chip cookies. Jake asked to what he owed this honor. Valient laughed at that description and then got down to the small talk. How was business? Fine. How was Jake? Fine. How was Valient? Pretty good. How was Buddy? Spooky. Jake laughed at that and rubbed Buddy's head.

"Now that we got that all out of the way, why are you really here?" Jake finally asked. He knew Valient wouldn't come here unless it was important. He hadn't been here much since they had found his dad stretched out on the couch, dead from a heart attack, going on four years ago. He had lain down after lunch one day and never woke up. Valient, being home on leave from Germany, had found him. His mom had sent him to fetch his dad for a family dinner. He never really recovered from that. Now Valient sat, not looking at that couch.

"I have a mystery I want to solve," the young man replied. He then proceeded to explain about the woman and the little boy. Jake listened to the story and then asked, "Why do you care?"

"I'm not sure, truthfully. Buddy here seems to want to be friends with the kid. I know that sounds lame, but it's all I got" Valient answered.

Jake looked at the two of them and shook his head. "Well, I've heard worse, I guess. Are you sure you're just not falling in love here?"

"I knew you'd think I was nuts. But I had to ask anyway. Buddy says she is in trouble. Maybe I can help." Valient knew he should not have said that. Now he *did* sound nuts!

"Buddy says?" Jake's eyebrows went up in question and he chuckled at that. "You talk dog now?"

"No, I don't. But it's a feeling I have, and I'm not sure why." Valient tried to cover his behind. Why had he said that? Buddy was looking at him happily and telling him he was right. Oh brother! He had to be going nutso!

"All right what was the address you said you saw the kid at?" He wrote it in his little notebook he always kept in his pocket. "I'll ask around—discreetly, I know—and let you know if I find out anything," Jake agreed.

"Buddy, you ok with that?" The dog wagged her tail in reply.

They finished their coffee, and Jake gave Valient a new edition of one of his dad's favorite classics. Just what he needed; another book!

He thanked his old friend and left the store, feeling a little nostalgic. He knew Jake would come through for him; always did, always will, he thought.

From the bookstore, he and Buddy stopped by Micco's place. The restaurant was not busy, and Micco was upstairs for his afternoon break. Valient and Buddy made their way up to the apartment Micco had lived in most of his life and knocked. Micco answered by hollering, "Come in!"

They went in through the hallway to the living room where Micco was stretched out watching T.V. When Buddy jumped up on to the couch, Micco sat up before he was dumped off his own furniture. He ruffed up the mutt and then stood to shake hands with Valient. "What brings you up here at this time of day, my friend?"

"I need some help with a dilemma I have. Buddy and I have met someone I need some info on, and I don't know how to go about it."

"And you come to me? What can I do?" Micco wanted to know.

"Not sure why. Maybe just throw around some ideas. Or tell me I'm nuts and forget about it. Help me out here."

"Okay. Tell me the story. I like impossible dreams. Who is she? How did you meet?" At least he looked interested.

Valient repeated what he had told Jake but left out Buddy's input of course. When he had finished, Micco just smiled.

"I knew it was a woman. Sounds like something you should steer clear of though. You really think a woman with a kid is something you need in your life? A homeless one at that? What are you thinking of doing, saving her from the world?" Micco looked dubious.

"I know. Nuts, right? I should walk away and forget about it. Not like I don't have issues of my own to deal with. I can't even hold a job since the military, and my love life sucks. If it weren't for the dog I would be still sitting in my chair, doing absolutely nothing. As least Buddy gives me a reason to get up in the morning. Something to think about besides myself. But there is something I can't put my finger on going on here. It's driving me crazy. I've got to figure out what it is." Valient looked a Micco imploringly.

"Okay. I'm not sure what to do either. I am not a detective, just a lowly cook. What was your first idea?"

"Ask questions in the neighborhood? You would have to be really quiet about it though. I wouldn't want to get her into more trouble, if she is in trouble in the first place. Do you have any ideas?"

Micco looked thoughtful. He sat petting Buddy absently. Suddenly Buddy shot out of the room and down the stairs, barking and growling again!

The two men took off after her, almost falling down the stairs in their haste. Buddy just didn't growl! What the blue blazes was going on here?

When they got to the bottom of the stairs, Buddy had a man pinned up against the wall opposite of the door to the upstairs. She was growling and showing her teeth at him. Valient grabbed her by the collar and made her sit. She obeyed but kept a low growl going. Who was this guy? Why was Buddy so upset by him?

"Who ae you? What are you doing in this part of the place?" Micco snarled at the man.

"Looking for the guy with the dog. I want to ask him a few questions." the guy snarled right back.

"What do you want me for?" Valient was just as angry sounding as the other two. "What is going on here?"

"That woman and kid you talked to last week, where are they?" The guy started to come closer to Valient menacingly. Buddy stood and got between them and all but took a piece of the man. He backed up slightly but made it clear he meant business.

"I have no idea! She's just a person on the street. My dog happened to like the looks of the kid. What is it to you, anyway?" Valient didn't back up or back down from the guy. They stared at each other like prizefighters. The other guy blinked first.

"My boss wants her found. I think you know where she is. I'll give you a day to think about it. Then I'll be back. Oh, yeah, I know where you live so don't think I can't find you. You should keep that mutt locked up. It's a menace." With that he shook himself and stomped out of the restaurant. He stole a candy bar from the register on the way out and held it up for them to see. Nice touch!

"What the hell was that about?" Micco roared!

"I have no bloody idea! I told you I thought that woman was in trouble. I guess I don't need any more proof, do I?"

Micco and Valient decided they needed a drink. While Valient went back upstairs with Buddy, Micco went to the bar and procured a bottle Regal and a couple glasses. He kept very little other than water glasses in the apartment as he spent most of his time and took most meals in the restaurant anyway. He made a side trip to the kitchen and asked the cook to have a tray sent up. After telling him what to put on it, Micco went back upstairs. Owning a restaurant has its perks, he thought absently.

They tried to make some sense of the man and his threats. Valient had no idea how he got to this point. He was trying to get his life on track, trying to have a future other than T.V. and himself. Then he got this spooky dog! All he did was talk to a kid and a pretty woman. Story of his life! Women! Who could figure them out? And all he knew of this one was her name! That was probably false too! He had another drink.

# CHAPTER 11

VALIENT DIDN'T GO HOME UNTIL the next morning after all he had
to drink. When he got there, he locked the door, put on the
chain, locked the dead bolt, checked all the windows and set the
alarm. Paranoid? Yup! But he wanted to make sure he knew if someone was coming for him. The guy at Micco's spooked him big time.

He was so hung over all he wanted was to sleep. So he and Buddy
spent the day just hanging around. Valient slept on the couch in
front of the T.V. He ate soup and drank tea. He let Buddy into the
yard instead of walking her. She wasn't happy about it. She kept
going to the front door and getting her leash from the chair. She let
him know she wasn't happy. For a dog, she had some pretty dirty
looks!

The day was quiet until around six o'clock. Someone was banging on the door! Not banging! Pounding! When Valient looked out,
it was the guy from Micco's with some woman. "Open the damn
door! I'll break it down if I have to! I know you are in there! Open
up! Now!"

Valient had his dad's Glock in his hand, and the phone dialing
9-1-1 in the other.

As the operator came on the line, the window shattered. The woman had thrown the porch vase through it. The alarm started screeching. The guy broke out the rest of the glass and started through the window. Valient yelled for him to stop, that he had a gun. The 9-1-1 operator was still on the phone that Valient had dropped when the window broke. He had both hands on the Glock and was taking aim when the guy put his foot through the window. Valient fired next to him as a warning, but he kept coming. Valient fired again, this time hitting him in the leg as he put his foot on the floor. The guy didn't even flinch. Valient fired a third time, this time hitting him in the chest. The guy went down hard! The police pulled up with sirens blasting. The woman had run at the first sound of sirens. She was turning the corner as the police cut their engines.

Valient ran to the door and, after a lot of fumbling, got the door open. But he forgot he had the gun still in his hand. "Drop the gun! On the floor!" Is what he heard from the cop with the gun pointed at his head.

"What? No! Sorry! I'm the victim here!" Valient screamed back slipping the gun to the floor. He backed up and raised his hands giving room so the cops could come in. It took a lot of explaining, but they finally figured out Valient was the victim of an attempted break-in by a guy two times his size and armed as well. It was all self-defense. Valient did not tell them about the real reason the guy was after him. He figured he would never be able to explain about Jessie, since he didn't know any more anyway.

In all the confusion, Valient didn't realize Buddy was gone! What now? Where in the blue blazes was the dog? When did she get out?

While the police were busy looking around, questioning the neighbors, and whatever other police stuff they were doing, Valient started searching the house for Buddy. She wasn't there. He checked the yard, no place to hide out there. He went out to the front and looked under the porch. No dog. Where was she?

He was standing on the porch when another car pulled up. The patrolman seemed to know who it was because he waved the car on to the lawn. Thanks a lot! Valient hoped the had yard repair in the budget. Did home insurance cover this sort of thing? Where had that come from? Valient was tired. He needed some coffee.

He was in the kitchen, putting water into the coffee maker when the new guy came in. He stood looking at Valient. "What was that guy looking for Mr. Washington?" the guy asked.

"Don't know. I have nothing of real value here. Unless he was looking for an old book. Who are you? You don't look like a cop." Valient answered him while continuing to make the coffee. "Want some?"

"I am Detective Shot and, yes, I'd love some. It's been a long day." he replied taking out his badge and I.D. to show Valient.

"I shot that guy in self-defense you know. "

"Yes, I do. What I don't know is what you have to do with Jessie and Irving. Does this guy have anything to do with them?"

"How do you know about them?" Valient was wary. What was going on here?

"You first. Why are you interested in them?"

"I guess just human curiosity. I was out walking my dog one evening and saw the boy, Irving, on a stoop. He asked to pet my dog. Then on another day, he and his mom were on the street near a restaurant I went to for supper. The boy petted the dog, the adults said hello. All went their respective ways. End of story."

"Not quite. You went back to the house asking for them. Why?"

"Truthfully, I'm not sure. The woman seemed troubled, and the boy is kinda cute. I wanted to find out more about them. I really don't know why."

"No other reason?" Shot asked him.

"Why are you so interested in some homeless mom and kid? How are they involved with a police detective?" Valient was really intrigued now.

"I can't tell you anything about that. I can tell you to stay away from them and leave them be."

"That would be easier if there wasn't a dead guy in my window." Valient mumbled. "By the way, he wasn't alone. There was a woman with him. She took off when she heard the sirens."

"Why didn't you say something before now? She's probably halfway to China by now!" Shot bellowed for the patrol officers.

Two patrolmen who had been in the front room came running at the noise. Detective Shot looked at Valient. "Description of the woman? If it isn't too much trouble." he asked sarcastically.

Valient did his best to describe the woman to the detective and patrolman. He didn't have much because the man had been in front of her most of the time. Height, weight, hair color, clothes--that was about all he could remember. He really was a bit busy trying to save his own backside.

Where was that stupid dog?! "Have any of you seen a really ugly dog around here?"

"Dog? What dog? There's been no dog since we've been here." All the patrolmen were talking at once. Detective Shot told them to look around. Valient told them he had checked the house and yard a few minutes ago, but he'd appreciate it if they'd keep an eye out for her.

The coroner was there finally. Detective Shot went back out into the front room to talk to him. They looked over the scene and photos were taken; the techs were bagging up glass and the shells from Valient's gun. Detective Shot had the Glock in a plastic bag and the man's gun in another one. In all the excitement Valient never realized the guy had a gun in his hand! Why hadn't he shot back? He had time. More questions. Valient looked at Detective Shot with wide eyes.

"What? Did you see something? What?" Shot asked suspiciously.

"Why didn't the guy shoot back?"

"What do you mean?"

"I shot *at* him once; shot him in the leg and then shot him in the chest. The whole time he had a gun in his hand, loaded. Why didn't he shoot?" Valient was incredulous. Why? It didn't make sense.

"Good question. Did you shoot quickly, like, bang, bang, bang? Or was there a pause in between?" Shot asked him.

"A pause. I was hoping he would just leave. Dumb, I know. One warning shot, into the wall. See?" Valient pointed to the hole in the wall under the window, about six inches from where the body had been. "Second, a couple seconds later when he kept coming. You saw his leg, right? And then the third to the chest after he cleared the windowsill. So all in all, it had to be ten or fifteen seconds. I think so anyway." Valient looked bewildered.

"What hand did he have the gun in?" the coroner asked.

"What?" Both Valient and Detective Shot turned to him.

"What hand?"

"Left, I think. At least that's what the patrolman said on the evidence bag. Why?" the Detective answered.

"Because this guy was right-handed. He probably would have had to change hands to shoot. He broke out the remaining glass with the gun before he tried climbing in. See?" He held out the gun in the bag for them to look at. "Glass in the slide and a cut on his left hand. No cuts on the right." He held up the hands in turn. "Didn't want to cut his shooting hand? Possibly didn't see Mr. Washington's gun until he started firing? Maybe he figured he'd shoot back after the got in here. Or that he could take the gun from this guy." Gesturing to Valient, he said "Mr. Washington here doesn't look all that menacing. After missing him once, then shooting him in the leg, maybe the guy figured he'd be too chicken to shoot him dead. I guess he figured wrong" The coroner looked satisfied with his own rendition of the event.

"How do you know he was right-handed?" Valient asked the coroner.

"Because it is had better definition and more calluses. It has been used more. Besides, his watch is on the left wrist." was the smug reply.

Valient wasn't sure if he believed him or not. But he couldn't prove or disprove what he was being told so he let it go.

The technicians packed the guy into the body bag and took him away on the stretcher. The coroner packed up his vials and whatever else he had into his big tackle box-looking thing, and they all left the house.

The patrolmen carried out the paper bags they had put the glass pieces and guns into and left right behind them. Valient had to sign the bag containing his own gun. When he asked why, he was told it was procedure. Asking when he'd get it back, he was told to ask Detective Shot.

After everyone else had left, Valient and Detective Shot stood in the kitchen finishing the coffee.

"Why did you say it would be easier to leave Jessie alone if there wasn't a body in your window?" Shot asked Valient.

Valient was surprised at the question. He didn't think the detective had heard the remark.

"Because the guy in the window came looking for me at my friend's restaurant yesterday. He wanted to know where the woman and kid were. Apparently, someone had seen us talking on the street last week. I don't know how he found me, but he threatened me in front of my friend Micco and told me to think about my answer, and he'd come back today. I spent the night at my friend's apartment because we got too drunk to go anywhere. I got home this morning and lounged around all day, nursing a hangover. About six or so, this guy and the woman came pounding on my door. When I didn't open it, she broke the window with the vase you saw on the floor, and he came through the broken glass. That's pretty much the whole story in a nutshell. 9-1-1 should have most of it on tape. The operator was on the phone the whole time. Your patrolman talked to her, I think."

"I'll check on that. I will need you to come to the station tomorrow and make a formal statement. Do you have someplace to stay tonight? That window doesn't look too secure just now."

"No. I'll get a board from the back and nail it up. I still have to find my crazy dog. She probably got spooked with all the commotion and took off somewhere."

# CHAPTER 12

Detective Shot didn't want to leave until he was sure Valient was secure, so he went out back with him to get a board and nails to fix the window.

They were putting the finishing touches on the window when Buddy came trotting down the sidewalk. "Is that your mutt?" Shot asked.

"Hey Buddy! Where have you been? Did all the noise scare you off?" Valient squatted down and hugged her tight. He didn't want to admit it, but he was terrified she had gone forever. All the excitement of the night hit him like a ton of bricks. He started shaking and couldn't even stand back up. He sat there, holding on to the dog and trying to calm himself.

Detective Shot saw what was happening and stepped back into the house to give the man and dog a few minutes to regain some composure. He'd seen this reaction too many times and knew the guy needed a minute to regroup. Just as he was about to go see if he could help, Valient and the dog came inside. "Got anything stronger than coffee in this place?" he asked Valient.

"Yeah, I think there's some brandy left over from some holiday in the kitchen under the sink. I do think I could use a drink. All that excitement can't be good for a body." Valient tried to laugh but it came out more like a croak. "Make mine a double."

"Do you have someone you could call to come stay tonight at least?"

"I think I'll call my friend, Micco. The restaurant should be about closed by now. See if he will come and maybe bring another bottle." Valient smiled at his own wit.

After calling Micco, Valient felt much better. Micco was on his way, so Detective Shot took his leave after getting Valient's assurance he would come in the morning to give his statement.

"Okay, Buddy, what is going on? Where did you go?" To his surprise, he felt Buddy showing him a house. "What? Are you telling me something? I must be drunk or really tired. I'm seeing things here."

In his mind, he saw the house again in more detail. The woman was standing in front of it. He looked at Buddy. "Are you really doing this girl? I'm freaking out here."

Buddy wagged her tail like it was on fire and tried to jump up on Valient. "You followed that woman, didn't you? Can you find this place again? He felt really stupid talking to the dog like this, but he could swear she was communicating with him. He saw the house again like a Polaroid picture in his mind. He guessed that was a *yes* from the dog. He really needed a drink. Buddy must have been able to read his mind because she looked at the empty brandy bottle on the table.

Thankfully Micco rang the bell just then.

# CHAPTER 13

HE WAS IN AN INTERVIEW room at the police station writing out his statement of last night's events. It seemed so straightforward. So why was he having so much trouble putting it on paper? He was shaking and having problems concentration this morning. Two days of alcohol and people threatening him, not to mention he killed a guy in his own home last night, was taking its toll on his brain.

Finally, he was done. He signed the paper after a clerk had typed out what he had written and was getting ready to leave. He wanted to get home to Buddy to see if she could really bring him to the house he saw in his mind last night. He knew it was nuts, but something told him he had to give it a shot. If he could find it and maybe see the woman (hopefully without *her* seeing *him*), then he could let Detective Shot know about it. Valient hadn't figured out how he was going to explain to the detective how he had found it, but he would worry about that if it actually came to past.

Detective Shot came into the room just as the clerk put the statement into a file. He smiled at the boy as he left. Valient asked if he'd wanted to read the statement. Shot said no, he'd wait until later. He was going to talk to Valient's friend, Micco, about what had happened at the restaurant the other day.

"What do you expect to find out that I haven't already told you?" Valient wanted to know.

"Nothing really, just wanted his take on things. I know you've told me all you know. You don't seem like the kind of person who would hold back or lie. It's just a feeling I have about you. I'm a pretty good judge of character after all these years on the police force. Don't worry about it."

Valient wasn't sure about that. But he'd taken him at his word. Micco was a witness after all, and the man was now dead thanks to Valient shooting him. He figured it couldn't hurt to have some backup to his story. He also realized just then that he never asked who the guy was or about the woman.

"Do you have any idea who the guy was I shot? I don't know why I didn't ask sooner. Seems that would have been one of the first questions we all would want to know the answer to." Valient finally said out loud. "Maybe it is my military training. We never needed to know the names of our kills."

"His prints and pictures have been sent to the lab. We have computer programs to match fingerprints here. If nothing comes up, we'll send his picture to the FBI for face recognition. It sometimes takes a while depending on the backlog. Since he's dead and not an immediate danger to anyone, it isn't top priority, I'm afraid."

"What about the woman? She's still out there, alive and well." Valient asked.

"Since we don't have any description from either you or Jessie, we have nothing to match, now do we?"

"I guess not. Sorry, I wish I had seen her better. Didn't even see her face and couldn't even make a guess as to how old she might be. Not very much help, am I?"

"Jessie guessed she was in her late thirties maybe. That's the best she had to offer. Don't feel bad about that. Killing a guy up close and personal, even in self-defense, is enough to deal with. Which remind me, I have a card here of a counselor if you want to talk to someone. It's the same person we cops go to after a shooting. She's pretty good, listens without judgment." Shot offered the card and stood up. "Been to her myself once. I would strongly recommend it."

"How would Jessie know this woman?" Valient's brain just woke up. "What does she have to do with anything?"

"I guess I better tell you the truth. We think this woman has something to do with Jessie's husband. He was murdered a few months ago. We think they want to finish the job." Detective Shot said grudgingly.

"What happens now?" Valient asked. Shot just shrugged his shoulders.

"You go home, try to relax, and get back to your life. There might be a few more questions down the line, but I doubt it. I'll let you know if there is any word on the woman who was with that guy, but other than that, things should be done."

"What about my gun?" Valient wanted to know.

"There is a problem there. It seems you don't have a permit. We only found a registration for your dad. Where did you get that thing anyway?"

"The patrolman asked me that last night. It has always been in the hall closet in a hatbox. Dad used to carry it when he made bank deposits from the bookstore. I was so spooked when I got back that morning, I got it out and put it on the table by the couch. It just made me feel better having it near, I guess. He had a permit, I think. I just never thought about it. Am I in trouble?"

"Not with me, but I"ll talk to the powers that be to see about getting you legal. I have a friend who is a judge who might be willing to sign off on you application quickly. With your squeaky-clean record and military background, it shouldn't be a problem. But you can't have the gun back until you get a permit. Wait here a minute and I'll see if I can find some paperwork to get you started."

Shot left the room and Valient dropped into the chair he had been sitting in. What a mess! He really did know better. He had put off getting the gun permit when he moved into his house because he was too broken up about his mom's death. *Details, details, the devil is in the details* his dad used to say. Now he knew what that really meant. Then he just plain forgot about it until that guy threatened him.

# CHAPTER 14

Detective Shot was hungry. He had helped Washington with the gun paperwork and then had to run out on another case. Some woman had shot her ex-husband over custody of a cat! Really! If it weren't so sad, it would be funny.

He found himself downtown near Micco's place. Since he was hungry and it was as good a time as any, he figured he'd go there for a late lunch.

As he sat near the bar where he could see the comings and goings of the patrons, he thought about Jessie. He needed to go see her from here to let her know what had gone on last night. The man was dead, but the woman was still out there. Hopefully Jessie would remember more of her description and they could get to looking for her and finish this thing.

He ordered a steak hoagie and Greek salad and asked for Micco. He was told he was upstairs and not expected to come back down until five, which was his usual routine. "Send him a message for me, please. I am Detective Shot, and I need to talk to him about the guy who came in here the other day looking for his friend. He can come down here, or I can go up to see him. But I need to talk to him before I leave."

The waiter took Shot's card and went upstairs to deliver the message. A few minutes later, he came back. "Micco said he'll be down as soon as he gets dressed. It shouldn't be more than fifteen minutes."

"Thanks, that gives me enough time to finish eating. This is great, by the way, my compliments to the cook."

The waiter sauntered away smiling. The cook loved compliments, even for a lowly sandwich. Maybe he'd stop growling for a while.

Micco sat down with the detective as he was drinking his coffee. "Can I interest you in some dessert?" Micco asked him.

"No, but thanks. Gotta watch the belt getting too tight. Eat here too many times, and I'd have to buy a new one," Shot grinned.

"What can I do for you, Detective? I understand from Valient you had some questions for me about the corpse in his window."

"Washington said the guy was here asking about a woman and kid and was pretty belligerent about it. What do you know about all this?"

"Not much. Valient had come to ask me to help him find out about them. We were trying to figure out how to go about it, when the dog went nuts and bounded down the stairs. We followed and saw her backing this guy up against the wall at the bottom of the stairs. I can tell you Buddy didn't like the guy. She seemed to want to eat him. He tried to get in Valient's face and intimidate him. Didn't work though. Valient never backed down from anything in his life. He threatened Valient and then left. He stole a candy bar off the counter on his way out. Parting shot, I guess. All he said worth repeating is that his boss wanted to know where the woman was. That's about it." Micco motioned to the waiter. "Want more coffee, Detective?"

"Yeah, thanks."

Micco said to the waiter, "more coffee for the detective, and bring me a cup too, please Jeno. Thanks."

"Are you sure that was what he said, 'his boss wanted to know'?" Shot wanted to clarify that point.

"Yup, that was it. The he left."

The men finished their coffee with Shot asking about the restaurant business. Then he left to get back to work.

# CHAPTER 15

Jessie hung up the phone. She was wondering what could have happened that Detective Shot was coming before dark. Did they have to leave? Should she pack? Was it over? Why wouldn't he tell her over the phone? She shook her head in frustration.

She went back to the kitchen to help Mrs. James get dinner ready. The children had been playing outside today. It almost seemed normal. The yard had an eight-foot wood fence that no one could see over and a loud buzzer on the gate that went off if the gate was open. There was a peek hole disguised like a knot hole that opened only on the inside of the fence. A keypad was hidden in the finial for the code that disabled the alarm, like for when Detective Shot came. Mrs. James had a beautiful backyard garden and a separate area where there was and old swing set and sand box for them to play. Even so, one of the adults was on the porch, watching at all times.

They were going to have a picnic on the porch. Mrs. James had put a blanket on the floor for the kids. A small table was set up for the adults. The kids were in the half bath, supposedly getting cleaned up to eat. From the sounds coming from that direction, they were making a bigger mess than they were cleaning.

Jessie went to check on them. Sure enough, there was water splashed everywhere. She opened the door and the kids froze! Jessie couldn't help laughing at the looks on their faces! All she could do was hand them both a towel and tell them to clean it up before Mrs. James saw the mess. They scrambled to wipe up the muddy water as Jessie turned off the tap.

A few minutes later, Mrs. James came to see what was going on. She stood in the doorway smiling. "Reminds me of my kid's messes. I never had a clean bathroom until they moved out." she said absently. "Dinner's ready. Get going now." she said as she walked away.

Jessie wondered at the woman. Mrs. James seemed so strict on some things and so understanding on others. Problem was you couldn't figure from one to the next how she would react. It had been almost two weeks. And Jessie was beginning to think her gruff act was just that-an act. She obviously loved her granddaughter and did her best for her. Mrs. James was a kind person but a cautious one. Detective Shot said he trusted her with his own life. Jessie took him at his word. So far, he was right. At least she could sleep at night, not worrying about their safety. Jessie also suspected the woman was armed. She saw the little bulge at her ankle and knew police sometimes wore guns on their ankles.

Detective Shot showed up as they were finishing their picnic. The kids were churning ice cream in the bucket as he opened the gate. "That looks like hard work." he said to Sarah.

She was turning the handle for all she was worth. "You wanna try?" she asked hopefully. "Irving and me are getting tired, but Grannie says we can't stop or it won't get to be ice cream."

"Irving and *I*," her grandmother corrected her.

Sarah just frowned and said "Irving and I are tired" and then looked at Detective Shot.

"Sure, let me see. Do you turn it like this?" Shot sat down on the steps next to the little girl.

"Yes, sir. You done this before?"

"My mom had one just like this when I was a little boy." Shot told her. "I had to make it all by myself. I didn't have a helper."

A few more minutes and the ice cream was declared ready to eat. Mrs. James took the bucket and children inside to scoop it into bowls.

"Brings back memories watching those kids." Shot said to Jessie as she made room for him on one of the chairs.

"I hope Irving remembers the good times here. Mrs. James has been very kind to us, even though I'm sure she wishes we were anywhere but here. They sat in silence for a few minutes. "Can you tell me what is going on? The suspense is killing me."

"Been some new developments. I'm not sure exactly what it means for the immediate future for you, though."

Just then the children and Mrs. James appeared with their ice cream. She had put chocolate chips and whip cream on it. "Looks wonderful, Mrs. James. You are certainly spoiling us today." Shot said with a mouthful and a wink at the woman. All he got was a scowl back, but he knew she was pleased.

After the ice cream had been demolished, Mrs. James took the kids inside to get ready for bed. Detective Shot and Jessie had some quiet time to finally talk. He told her about the break-in at Valient Washington's house and how Washington had killed the man who was looking for her and Irving. He told her about the woman getting away.

# CHAPTER 16

VALIENT FINALLY GOT HOME AROUND midafternoon and found Buddy sitting by the door with the leash in her mouth. "Sorry it took so long, girl. Turns out I had to write the statement over three times before I could get the words right. Then Detective Shot had me making out an application for a permit for that gun of Dad's. I swear that took longer than the statement. Let me get a sandwich and we'll go search for the house you went to last night. Okay?"

Buddy looked at him like she would bite him. "I'm hungry girl! I haven't eaten since this morning. I'm about to keel over! Give me a break. "Now I'm explaining my life to a dog! Heaven help me! Valient thought tiredly. He was still in shock and a bit hung over from all the activities of the past few days. How had he gotten involved in this mess? All he really wanted to do was lie down and sleep for a week.

Valient had eaten his sandwich and put an apple in his pocket to eat on the way. He would stop by Micco's and get some of his special coffee later he thought.

Buddy took him to a neighborhood about six blocks from their house. It looked older and settled. There were brownstones, some converted into apartments, and all well cared for. It was near a new shopping area and the main road through town. She stopped at the third house from the corner and growled. Valient looked up and didn't see anything out of the ordinary. Now what? Was he just going to stand there and stare at the house waiting for it to give him a sign? He didn't think this through very well. Buddy was looking at him like she expected some kind of action.

It didn't appear that there was a lot of traffic at this time of day. He felt a bit exposed, just standing in front of the place. If anyone saw them, they would be sure to remember the dog. She was definitely one of a kind. Well, now that he knew where the woman had run off to, he would tell Detective Shot and let him handle it. It wasn't Valient's job after all. He would just have to think of a plausible explanation as to how he got the information. He didn't think 'Buddy told me' would be too believable.

Valient really needed to get a cell phone. He never felt the need for one before. He hardly every left his house. He would have to wait until he got home to call Detective Shot.

He started off going in the direction he hoped was downtown to go to Micco's. As he turned the corner by the shopping center, he saw a woman coming his way. He tried to turn away quickly, hoping she didn't see him. Too late!

"Hey! YOU! STOP!" The woman was screaming at him. Valient started running as fast as his legs would take him. The woman kept screaming at him, but he just ignored her. She followed him as far as the end of the block, but he ducked into a store to hide. He saw her looking up and down the street trying to spot him then she turned back to where she had come from. He roamed around the store looking for another door. One of the store clerks came up to him and told him to get out of there with the mutt!

"No dogs allowed in here." She glared at him. She escorted him out the back door as it was closer than going out the front. He didn't bother to tell her that was what he was looking for anyway. Fortunately no one was in the alley. Getting to the end of the row of stores he looked cautiously around. He had no idea what to do. He just knew he needed to get out of there. And NOW!

He started walking in the direction of home. That was too close. What was he thinking? Buddy was telling him to get to Detective Shot. At least he was seeing his picture in his mind. He looked down at the dog and swore she shook her head like to say 'yes'. Good grief! Buddy didn't want to go home. Valient was getting pictures of the strange woman and felt danger. He kept staring at the dog and the feeling got so strong he started shaking. "Okay! Where should we go? You got any ideas on that? He asked the dog. Buddy looked up at him and barked. Valient got another picture in his head of Micco. "Not sure that's a good idea. Wouldn't that be the second place any-one would look for us?" He got yet another picture of Detective Shot. "How do we find him?" Now he was seeing a police car in his mind.

This was ridiculous! A dog is giving telepathic messages and he was believing it! He had to be imagining this. He was tired, hung over, and overwrought. He needed some sleep. Things would look better in the morning. He'd call Detective Shot tomorrow and then get on with cleaning the library.

He headed toward his house and bed.

# CHAPTER 17

V ALIENT WOKE UP LATE THE next morning. He opened the back door to let Buddy do her business in the yard while he made his breakfast. Buddy wasn't happy. She wanted to go for a walk. She got the leash and brought it to Valient. He saw a picture of Detective Shot in his mind. "Stop that, Buddy! I will call him at the police station after I've had some coffee." This was too weird for words! He took the leash from her and pointed out the back door.

After he ate, he called Detective Shot. He left a message that he had information about the man that he had shot. He set the alarm and then got back to his bookshelves.

About an hour later the doorbell rang. Cautiously Valient approached the door. It was the woman with another man! With no gun, he wasn't sure how well he'd defend himself. He didn't think they had seen him. They wouldn't break in in broad daylight, would they?

As if in answer to his question, the handle on the door rattled. Valient could hear scratching. It wasn't from Buddy, who was standing with him, growling quietly obviously sensing danger and getting ready to lunge at the first person through the door.

Valient ran to the back of the house and out the kitchen door. He heard his alarm system screeching as he hit the bottom of the steps. Buddy was already past him to the gate. They ran down the service road and out toward downtown. He had no idea where to go. Were they following? Had they gotten into the house?

He got to Micco's in record time. He busted through the door and made straight for the apartment. Once there he finally stopped to breathe. Micco came running up the stairs after him. "What's going on now?" he shouted. "You look like you've seen a ghost!"

"Call the cops! I need to see Detective Shot! They're after me!"

"Okay, calm down. Tell me what happened now." Micco looked as scared as Valient was. "Who's after you? I thought you killed the guy. This has to be someone new, right?"

"There was a woman with him. Remember I told you about her that night? Buddy had followed her, and yesterday she took me to where the woman had run to. The woman spotted me on the street, at least it must have been her. I didn't get a good look at her the first time. She yelled at me, but I took off. This afternoon she and another guy were at my door. I think they were trying to break in. I didn't hang around to find out."

"Oh, man! They could have followed me here! I am so sorry, Micco. I had nowhere else to go. I should get out of here!" Valient got up from the chair and started to leave.

"Don't be stupid. Where would you go anyway? No one is going to get up here without my guys seeing them. I'll go down and let them know what's going on. I'll be right back. Use the phone to call Detective Shot while I'm gone." With that Micco left to talk to the employees downstairs.

Valient did call the detective again. This time he was there, thank goodness. Shop told him to sit tight, that there was a patrol car at his house already in response to the alarm. The patrolman would see if the couple was still there.

Micco came back a few minutes later and brought coffee with him. He had alerted the employees and told them to call the cops if anyone tried to get up to the apartment. He had the pistol from the cash register tucked in the back of his pants. They sat waiting for the police to get there.

The Detective got to Valient's house ten minutes later. The front door was open. He drew his gun and stepped inside. The place was trashed. The front room looked like a hurricane had hit it. Someone was looking for something or sending a message. They apparently didn't care much about the alarm going off and they worked fast! He checked the rest of the house, but the front room was the only room destroyed. A message, he figured. He called the alarm company, gave them his badge number and name and had them turn the alarm off.

He went back and looked at the front door. There were scratches in the lock opening, like picks had been used. The patrolman who had answered the call said he thought the people were still in the house when he drove up. He had been out back searching the yard when Detective Shot had gotten there. He had not actually seen anyone, just shadows going out the yard. The alley gate was opened.

They called the Crime Scene Unit and Shot left the patrolman there to wait for them. He went to find Valient Washington.

# CHAPTER 18

Micco and Valient had finished the coffee. Micco had gone back downstairs to check on how business had done for the lunch period. He had been gone for less than an hour when he came back with Detective Shot.

Valient jumped up from the chair as they walked in the door. "What did you find out?" he asked anxiously.

"Well, you have a bit more housekeeping to do. Your front room is trashed. The lamps are broken, and the table was smashed. The couch and chairs ripped up. That was the only room touched though. Can't figure that. The woman and man were long gone when I got there. The patrolman thought he had seen at least their backsides going through the yard. Couldn't catch up with anyone, though. I'll need you to go back with me to see if anything is missing." Shot looked more than annoyed. Three months and this case just keeps getting bigger and better, he said to himself.

"I don't think it's a good idea for you to stay at your house tonight. The Crime Scene Unit will be there going over everything for at least the next few hours. And you need to get new locks for your door. The one they picked is ruined." Shot advised Valient.

They both looked at Micco. "Well, where else would he go? Of course he's staying here. Between the two of us, we can watch our backs."

"I'll get surveillance set up to keep an eye on things here. It will be difficult to do during business hours, but at least at night you'll have some protection." the detective told them.

"It makes no difference during the day. My people will be looking out for anyone suspicious in the restaurant. They've already been told about what's going on, and some of them were here when the guy came after Valient. All of them said not to worry. I trust them to do what has to be done." Micco said proudly.

Valient was seeing a picture of the woman and the brownstone in his mind. Buddy again? "Um, Detective, in all the excitement I forgot to tell you why I had called in the first place this morning." Valient said tentatively.

"What? When did you call?" Now Shot was looking confused. "I got no messages from you today, other than when we actually talked."

"The night I shot the guy, the dog took off, remember?" he said, not answering the detective's question. "Well, somehow, she followed the woman to a brownstone near that new shopping center. Yesterday she led me back there. It's on Drake Street; third one from the corner on the side away from the shopping center. I didn't think about getting the house number. I was too freaked out."

"When did you leave your message?" Shot asked again.

"About noon. Why is that important?" Valient wanted to know.

"For some reason, I'm not getting my messages at the office, from you or from Jessie. I have to find out why." Shot said looking annoyed.

"Okay, you found a brownstone she went to. The dog took you there. Seriously? Smart dog. How are you sure it was the right place?

Did you see anyone? Did you see her?" Shot had switched gears again.

"As we were headed back home a woman saw us. She started screaming for me to stop. I took off running as fast as I could." Valient felt the fear all over again even in this safe place. "Buddy started growling when we were in front of the house. I can't say 100 percent it was the woman's place. I just think it based on Buddy's behavior. She only started growling when we got involved with this mess. I never heard her growling before."

"Please tell me you got a good look at her this time. There or at your house? It was the same woman, right?" Shot asked hopefully.

"Actually, yes to both. I'm pretty sure I could describe her this time. And it was the same woman both places."

"Wonderful!" Detective Shot finally felt a sliver of hope of solving this thing. "I'll get an artist over here and you can describe her. The sooner the better! We can go back to your house after that. If something is missing, it will still be missing in a few hours."

The artist showed up an hour later. Detective Shot had left, after getting a call, telling Valient they'd go back to his house later. Valient was supposed to call him when the artist was done.

In the meantime, Valient had taken a short nap. Buddy was curled up on the end of the couch napping too. They were both beyond exhausted, mentally and physically.

Micco had come up with the police artist to make sure Valient didn't freak out at the sight of a stranger. The way things were going he wouldn't blame him. It wasn't Valient's way but, under the circumstances, who knew. After they were settled in the front room, Micco left them to their business with the promise of coffee and his special cake. Valent's mouth was already watering.

It took a little over an hour for the artist to get the portrait done to Valient's satisfaction. It was remarkable, even with Valient's directions and Buddy's guidance, of which the artist had no clue, thank goodness. Valient saw the picture of woman in his mind from Buddy and described it to the artist. He knew that because when he tried to recall what she looked like, all he could see was a blur. He was beginning to believe in Buddy. Heaven Help him!

# CHAPTER 19

Detective Shot was driving to Drake Street. He had picked up Washington from the restaurant, intending to take him to his house to check things out, which they had done. But Washington, instead of going straight back, wanted to show him where the dog had trailed the woman. They had the picture of her on Shot's cell phone in case they came across her.

So, with Washington sitting in the front seat and the dog shedding hair all over his back seat, they headed out.

When they turned the corner near the house, Buddy started barking. There was a man walking toward the brownstone they were looking for. Valient thought he looked like the guy who was with the woman at his house this afternoon.

"What do we do? Can we stop him? Do we have, what do you call it? Probable cause?" Valient was shaking with anticipation.

Shot pulled the car over to the curb and told Valient to stay in the car. Buddy was barking and turning in circles in the back. She made so much noise the guy looked over. Seeing Shot getting out of the car, he started running. He headed for the brownstone and ducked in the door, slamming it behind him.

Detective Shot called in for some backup and took off through a small pathway that led around to the back of the building. He yelled at Valient to watch for the backup and not to move.

No more than five minutes later, Valient heard, and then saw, three police cars speeding into the street. They screeched to a stop in front of the brownstone. Two of the policemen ran up the steps and cautiously went through the door. Two others followed the same path Detective Shot had run down, while the other two stayed near the cars with guns drawn and pointed toward the house. They must have been communicating via radio. Valient saw them talking into their shoulders.

Detective Shot came back out through the front door. He was motioning to someone behind him. He ran down the steps to the first police car, and Valient saw him talking on the radio. Then he ran back up the stairs and inside.

For a while, nothing else happened. The police kept their watch on the house. Another police car had joined the others, and the occupants went to the houses on either side. In a few minutes, people ran out of each of them and down the street. The police were evacuating people from the surrounding brownstones! What did Shot find inside?

Valient was dying of curiosity. Buddy had finally settled down when the patrol cars had showed up. Valient kept seeing a picture of the woman in his head. Was Buddy asking if Shot had found her? "Don't know any more then you do girl. We just have to stay here and wait. There are guns out there, and bad guys are in that house. We sit here and let the police do what they are paid for."

At that moment, Valient heard gun shots! He instinctively scrunched down as for into the floor well as he could. Buddy started barking, and Valient got a picture of Detective Shot in his head. "Down!" he shouted at the dog. Buddy dove to the floor and whined. "Hush!" Buddy stopped whining.

Detective Shot came out of the front door with the man in handcuffs about ten minutes later. The two patrolmen were behind him, and another man was with them. Who was he? The police put them in separate cars. Shot came over to the car to talk to Valient.

"They were holed up in the kitchen. I was afraid he'd run out the back and then I saw the guy walk by a back window. The patrolmen and I went in the back way, and one of them shot at us. The other patrolmen went in through the living room. They gave up when they saw how many cops there were." Shot explained.

Valient asked if everyone was okay and asked about the woman. Shot assured him no one was injured, and they were taking everyone to the station to question them. The woman wasn't in the house. A woman lived there though. There were clothes and woman's personal things in a bathroom.

"I'll have the patrol take you back to Micco's. Stay there until you hear from me. Don't go back to your house. We're not sure who all is involved in this yet, and I don't want to have to find you. Understand?" Shot said.

"I got it. Wait for you. Got it." Valient agreed grudgingly. He saw a picture of Jessie in his head. "You going to tell Jessie about this?"

"Not until we know more. We're still not sure how far this goes, and I don't really know what to tell her." the detective replied with a faraway look. He was thinking ahead of himself, Valient thought.

He went back to the patrol cars and told one of them to take Valient away. He then posted a car on the corner to wait to see if the woman showed up. He'd keep surveillance on the brownstone until she did. He was hoping to get an unmarked car to take over after he talked to his boss.

# CHAPTER 20

Detective Shot was relieved. He had arrested his suspects and did not need the S.W.A.T. people to do it. For a short time, he thought it would get really ugly. But when the guy started shooting his cops kept their heads. Now all he needed to do was get some answers.

He tried the guy from Valient's house first. "Mr. Yats, Murray Yats, is that right? I'm Detective Shot."

"Yeah, and that's all you're going to get from me. I don't know nothing about nothing that would have to do with the police." Yats leaned back on his chair and stared at the detective.

It's going to be a long night, Shot thought. Out loud he said, "Mr. Yats, you were with a woman at the home of a Mr. Washington yesterday afternoon. You picked the lock on the front door and ransacked his front room before hightailing it out the back door when the patrol pulled up. We know this because you were identified by the victim." He waited for some kind of response. What he got was more staring. "Any comment?"

"Wasn't there. Don't know what you are talking about."

"Who are you working for Mr. Yats? Is it the woman? Care to give me a name?" Shot went on.

"I'm retired."

"Really. You seem awfully young for retirement. What did you retire from?"

"None of your business."

"Everything is my business in here. I have your record." Shot opened the file in front of him. "You have been a busy boy. Breaking and entering, assault, battery, real tough guy stuff Beat up on women. Nice guy. You should practice more with the picks. You made a mess of that lock. So, is that what you retired from?"

Yats just glared.

"What were you doing with woman, and what did you two want with Mr. Washington?"

More glaring.

"Why do you work with the woman if you think so little of them? I bet you love taking orders from her." Shot waited to see some reaction.

"She don't give me no orders! She knows better. I'd give her what I gave them other bitches. No skirt tells me what to do. She asks me nice. She pays real good, too. Or I walk." Yats said smugly.

Detective Shot sighed. He was getting a headache. He needed a cup of coffee. He left the interrogation room and went to his desk. He saw his boss in her office and went to talk to her. He let Yats sit for a while. He had nowhere to go. He hoped his colleague had some luck with the other guy.

He filled in his boss on his case and explained he wanted surveillance set up on the brownstone. To his surprise he got no argument from the captain. Wonders never cease!

He left instructions to book Mr. Yats and then went home. He was tired and frustrated he didn't get the woman. He needed to eat and get some sleep. He's start again tomorrow.

The next morning started out better. Detective Gillman, who had interviewed the other suspect from the brownstone, had some news. The guy's name was Leeh Attics, a low life from the neighborhood looking to make a name for himself. Turns out he doesn't have the stomach for it. One night in lockup and he got religion. He had a lot to say according to Gillman. He told the detective he had been hired by a Carla Shultz to find Jessie and Irving. That was a month ago. He had traced them to a homeless shelter three weeks ago, but they never went back there to stay. Attics had hung around the shelter and the area surrounding it for about a week to no avail. When one of his buddies had seen them on the street talking to Washington, he thought he was lucky. The guy didn't follow either of them but a waiter at the restaurant across the street gave him a name. Attics gave the name to Shultz. She took the guy who got shot, his name was Doug Stepshick, and went to convince Washington to give them Jessie's whereabouts.

According to Attics, Shultz was the ringleader here. Yats was the one who broke into Washington's with Shultz. His job was to hang around downtown in case Jessie showed up there and follow her to where she was staying. Shultz wanted both her and the boy. She said they had something of hers and she wanted it back. Badly!

The two men looked enough alike that Shot was at first concerned Washington had made a mistake when they saw the guy on the street. It didn't matter now anyway.

Okay, so now Shot had a place to start. He felt another spark of hope. He had Yats brought back to the interrogation room.

"Well Mr. Yats, you aren't a very good stalker, are you? The woman you've been looking for had managed to avoid running into you. For what, three weeks now? How did you manage to beat up those women if you can't get close to them?" Shot started right in on the guy. He had read the report on Yats again. He had a violent past but nothing on the record in North Carolina for the last five years. Shot wondered what he had been up to in that time.

"So much you know flatfoot. Those women where a bunch of no accounts. They deserved what they got. All of them aggravating bitches! They didn't even follow through with the charges. The one in Georgia that did left town before I could find her. Good thing, too! She better hope I don't never see her again. She cost me jail time." Yats looked like he wanted to eat nails. That explained why no charges in the past five years.

"Tell me why you're working for a woman now, if you feel the way you do about them in general. I bet you love it when she starts bossing you around." Shot was baiting him.

"Like I told you, she pays *real* good, and she knows better than to give me orders. She asks me real nice! Otherwise, I 'd do the same to her, money or no. No bitch gives me orders." Yats snarled. "Besides, she promised I could have that woman when she got what she wanted back. Then I could have some real fun."

Shot didn't let the disgust show on his face, but he wanted to give this clown a taste of his own medicine. God! There were times Shot wished he'd been a cop in the good old days. Nowadays he had to play nice. Suspects had rights.

"How long you been working for her?" Shot sat back and looked at the guy.

"We met up a few months ago."

Managing to keep his voice even, Shot continued. "What do you do for her exactly?"

"I do errands for some of her friends." Yats smiled.

"What kind of errands? Groceries? Laundry? What?"

"I convince people to pay their bills." he said, still smiling.

"So you're an enforcer. That right?" the Detective was getting nowhere.

Yats just shook his head. "Don't know what that is."

"What is it Carla Shultz has you do?" Shot tried again.

Yats looked sick. "How do you know her name!? Her old man will kill whoever told you that! You sure didn't get it from me!!"

"Who's her old man? Why would he care we know her name?" Shot sat up at the man's panic.

"You know her name, but not the old man's? Man! I'm dead now! I shoulda kept my mouth shut!" Yats was near a full out panic attack.

Detective Shot watched him for a few minutes. He was clearly terrified of the woman's father. Shot would have to check this out. He excused himself and went to his desk to look the father up in the databases.

He thought the name was familiar. He had worked a couple murder-for-hire cases. The first was ten years ago. The last one was three years ago. Luke Shultz was a name that had come up in connection with both those cases. But there was nothing to definitively tie him to any evidence.

Shot went back to the interrogation room. "Mr. Yats, if you agree to help us out here, we may be able to keep Mr. Shultz away from you."

"He's gonna kill me and whoever gave you her real name. No place is good enough to hide from him!" Yats was thoroughly terrified.

"Do you know anything about the murder of Mrs. Stevens' husband?" Detective Shot thought he might as well go fishing. He might get lucky.

Yats looked like he swallowed a poison pill. He just sat there. Detective Shot could tell he was having a fight with his self and his self-preservation. Shot just watched to see which one came out on top.

"I'm a dead man either way, so I might as well die for something rather than nothing." he finally said dejectedly. "Carla shot him. Her and that guy, Stepshick, and me went to his house. They went inside, and I stayed outside to keep an eye out for nosy neighbors. I pretended to be a bug sprayer so nobody would notice me. They were in there about half an hour. We went to look for his wife and the kid, but she got away."

"Did the Shultz woman get whatever it was she thought the dead man had?"

"I don't know. Maybe that's why she still wants the wife."

"So let me get this right. This Carla Shultz hired you to muscle the woman into giving up whatever it is that Shoultz thinks she has. What is it she's looking for?" Shot managed to keep his voice even.

"Some pictures, I think. Seems this woman's husband took some pictures that can get Carla into trouble with some very nasty people. Carla killed him before he'd given them up. We've been looking for the wife ever since."

"You realize you just confessed, on tape, that you were an accessory to murder and conspiracy to commit murder? So, you can testify you were there and know who killed Matt Stevens? And you were supposed to muscle the wife into telling what the woman wanted to know? That right?"

There was more glaring. This guy was an idiot!

Yats turned a not-so-pretty green color. "Yeah, I worked for her once in a while, when she needed some heavy work done. She didn't think the guy would be any trouble because she had Stepshick with her. She took me along anyway to keep a look out outside. I didn't kill him. Just so you got the straight. You said you would keep me alive. How you gonna do that?"

Detective Shot took Yats back to the cells and into isolation. He was sick to think this jerk would get anywhere near Jessie and Irving. He was glad they were safe at the moment.

A couple of pieces of information intrigued him. Why was Carla Shultz really after Jessie? And what did she think Jessie had? He needed to do some research on the Shultz woman.

Attics and Yats were due in court tomorrow. If Shot didn't get something concrete by then, he may lose them. Attics didn't have a record they could find, but Yats was a repeater. Hopefully the DA could get bail denied and give him some extra time.

He needed to talk to Jessie.

# CHAPTER 21

S HE WAS SITTING ON THE bed, folding clothes when Detective Shot came through the gate. Mrs. James sent Irving up to get her.

"We heard you had arrested some people yesterday. Are they the ones after Jessie?" Mrs. James asked after she had sent the boy off.

"Yes, they are, but not the woman." Shot told her. "Problem is there are still too many questions. I'm not convinced they are the only players here."

"Is it over? Do you have the murderers?' Jessie asked, breathless from running down the stairs.

"No, and I'm not sure. There are a few loose ends I'm not comfortable with. The woman wasn't there. There are lots of questions I still have. The woman's name is Carla Shultz. Ring any bells with you?" Shot looked at Jessie expectantly.

She furrowed her brow trying to think if she'd ever heard that name. "Not that I can think of. She may have been a client of the printer Matt worked for possibly. You could check with them."

"I know a lady named Mrs. Shultz."

Everyone turned to look at Irving. Jessie held out her arms to him. He jumped up on her lap. "How do you know her, Irving?" Detective Shot asked him.

"She was talking to Daddy at the ice cream place. They were whispering and I couldn't hear them. But then she asked me my name and told me hers. Daddy wasn't happy. We had to go home without finishing my ice cream." Irving said, frowning at the memory of unfinished treats.

"When did this happen, sweetheart?" Jessie asked him.

"On Tuesday. Remember Daddy always took me for ice cream when you went out on Tuesday. It was the last time I had ice cream with Daddy." Irving started to cry. "I want Daddy to take me for ice cream again." he sobbed.

"I know, darling. But maybe when Detective Shot says it's safe again you and I can go have ice cream. Would that be okay?" Jessie tried to soothe the child. Her heart was breaking for him and she wanted to cry right along with him.

"Irving, I need you to think real hard about something for me. Do you think you can do that?" Shot tried to get the boy's attention back.

Irving wiped his eyes on the napkin Mrs. James had given him and looked at the detective. "Yes sir, I can try. What do I have to think about?"

Shot smiled at the kid. "Do you remember if Daddy and Mrs. Shultz were mad at each other, or just talking?"

"I think they were mad. Daddy made me leave without eating all my ice cream. He never did that before. I cried because it was my favorite." Irving said sadly.

"Okay, one more thing. Was the lady by herself, or did she have a friend with her? Think hard." Shot asked him.

Irving looked at his mom and then at Detective Shot. After a minute or so, he finally said, "I think there was a man with her. He didn't talk to Daddy, but he was standing by us. Daddy took my ice cream and moved it, so I had to move closer to Daddy while he talked to the lady. I don't think he liked that guy. He was real big."

"Thank you, Irving. You remembered real good. When the bad people go away maybe I'll join you and Mommy for your favorite ice cream. Would that be okay with you?" Shot smiled at the expression on the boy's face. He had to think about the idea for minute.

"Can Sarah and Mrs. James come too? They've been real nice to us." Irving looked so hopeful all the adults laughed.

"Sure thing kid." Shot told him.

Jessie sent Irving up to play with Sarah in the playroom. Now the adults could talk freely.

"So, is it over or what?" Jessie wanted a straight answer.

"Something isn't fitting for me yet. The men confessed to their parts in your husband's murder and chasing you. The Shultz woman wasn't caught. She's afraid of something, and it's not the police. One of the men said your husband took some pictures that would get Shultz into trouble with someone. I'm not sure if that means he actually *took the* picture or stole some snapshots. I was hoping you'd know something about it." Shot looked at her hopefully.

"I don't remember anything like that. Sorry. That doesn't mean he didn't have something. He could have hidden it anywhere. He did that with money sometimes. He said it was so he could buy the presents without me knowing how much he spent. He was sweet like that." Jessie almost whispered that last part. She had a lump in her throat thinking about Matt. A tear fell and she wiped it away.

"Do you have a safe deposit box anywhere? Or a safe at your house?" Shot was grasping at straws and he knew it. He searched the house himself during the initial investigation of Matt's murder. The people who killed him also searched, and they were none too careful about it. A lot of damage had been done there. He hoped Jessie didn't go back. No safe had been found. The bank accounts had been checked to make sure no unaccountable monies changed hands. No one had found evidence of a safe deposit box. But that didn't mean he didn't have one they hadn't found yet.

"Did Matt have any friends he could trust with something he wouldn't want anyone to find?" That was an angle he hadn't explored yet. He had talked to the neighbors, family, and some of his co-workers in the days and weeks after the murder but no one mentioned any secrets.

"The only friend Matt would trust like that would be his brother, Kenny. They shared everything but me. Sometimes it drove me crazy. I liked my brother-in-law, but he knew more of our business than I did I thought sometimes. I could call him tomorrow if I have to."

"No, I'll take care of it. Give me his number and address. I have it in the file, but I don't want to go back to the station to get it. Why didn't you go to your brother-in-law when all this started?"

"I would have but he was out of the country on businesss. When he returned, I contacted him. He seemed to think now that Matt was dead, I was his next wife. He made me very uncomfortable, the things he said on the phone. I thought it best to stay away from him. Jessie shivered at the memory of that conversation.

"In any case, I don't want you out there yet. I'm still not convinced you're safe. Remember Shultz is still out there. Give me a little while longer, okay?"

Jessie gave an exasperated sigh. She was getting impatient not having anything to do. The banker had arranged for the house bills to be paid from the monies her sister gave her, so she had no worries there yet. She was getting concerned as to how long her sister would keep making deposits for her, though. She also worried about where that money was coming from. They were comfortable but not rich. How long would she keep it up.? How was she ever going to be able to repay her? "Okay. Any idea how much longer? This living in limbo is beginning to get old, especially since those people are locked up."

"They could make bail or even be released at the arraignment tomorrow. So please just hang on a little while longer. If you get impatient, you might get hurt." Detective Shot knew how she felt. His patience was wearing a bit thin, too.

# CHAPTER 22

VALIENT HAD BEEN HANGING OUT at Micco's for four days now. Detective Shot had come by yesterday just to tell him practically nothing. He just wanted to go home.

Jake had come through for him. He found out the house where Jessie was staying belonged to an ex-cop. She was a widow of a cop and had her six-year-old granddaughter living with her. And she was friends with that detective. Why Jessie was there was a matter of speculation. He thought maybe Shot used it as a safe house. Years ago the widow used to take in battered women hiding from spouses. It would make sense. He was still trying to find out about Jessie. With no last name it was proving a bit difficult.

Valient had snuck through the back yards like he did when they were children to see Jake. He didn't remember the fences being so hard to climb! He vowed to start exercising again. One more thing to put on his list.

To give Valient something to do, Jake suggested he try finding some information from the Internet. Why didn't Valient think about that? So that is why he was sitting with Micco's laptop surfing the net.

He typed in "Murders in 2014, Parkville, NC." The computer came up with five possibilities He clicked on each one in turn.

The first one was an old woman whose husband killed her so she wouldn't suffer from last stages of cancer. I say, God bless him, Valient thought.

The second one was some kid who killed his girlfriend in a rage. He was in a mental institution. He must have had a good lawyer.

The third one was interesting. A guy was killed in his driveway by a drive by shooter. His wife and kid had found him when they got home from shopping. Right ages, anyway. He saved that site. The article didn't give the names of the wife and kid. He'd look for an obituary later.

The fourth one was domestic violence. The guy beat his wife so bad they couldn't recognize a face. The bastard got life. Finally, some justice to the world, Valient said to himself.

The fifth one was a guy killed in his kitchen. Shot to death. Valient tried to find out more about that one. He found an obituary. It said the guy was survived by a wife, a son, and a brother. Parents were deceased, and he worked at a printing company. Wife's name was Jessie. It didn't give the kid's name. That sounded promising.

So now that he had this information, what did he do with it? He could ask Detective Shot, but he doubted he'd get an answer. He could go back to the house and see if Jessie would talk to him. Providing she was still there. Shot would have a fit. He did tell Valient to stay away from her.

But under the circumstances, wouldn't it be justified? He'd been attacked, run out of his home and scared out of his mind, all because he talked to her. The sooner they got this cleared up, the better for him *and* Jessie. Right? He made up his mind to go see her tomorrow. Enough hiding like a fugitive. He was going home.

He had dinner with Micco at the restaurant. During dinner he told Micco his plans. After suggesting he clear it with the detective, Micco begrudgingly said to be extremely careful and call if he was needed. Valient and Buddy left after dinner.

Valient had stopped at a hardware store for new locks. He spent two hours changing all the locks on the doors and windows. He had an appointment for tomorrow to get the front window replaced. He called the twenty-four –hour number for the alarm company to have video cameras installed in the front and back porches. Maybe he was being excessive, but he didn't care.

He found the baseball bat he had played little league with in what seemed like a century ago. Valient took it upstairs to his bedroom, along with the bottle of wine Micco had supplied. He watched T.V. while sipping the wine for about an hour. He'd been so stressed these past few days that just being at home felt like heaven. He couldn't keep his eyes open.

# CHAPTER 23

JESSIE AND IRVING WERE IN the front room reading. Jessie thought she'd do as much as she could with Irving, so he didn't fall behind in school. With all that was going on he would not be able to start school on schedule. He would have started kindergarten in a few weeks. It didn't look like that was going to happen now.

She didn't even know if they had a home when this was over. She didn't think she could stay in the house where Matt was killed. She'd see him in every room. How could she handle that? They had loved each other so much and had so many wonderful memories in that place. They had bought it when she was pregnant for Irving. They had agonized over the color of the paints, argued over wallpaper in the kitchen, and almost got electrocuted trying to put a ceiling fan in their bedroom. They had chased each other with the hose in the summers, with every family member squealing like children. They had made love in front of the fireplace on cold winter nights. How could she go back there? She started to cry.

Irving felt his mother crying behind him. She put her arms around his little body and sobbed. "Don't cry Mommy! I'll be good, I promise! Don't cry, please." Irving started to cry too.

"Oh, darling, I am just missing Daddy. You are always a good boy. You could never make me cry." Jessie tried to compose herself. She hadn't broken down since Matt's funeral. She had hidden in the back of the church and cried her heart out. She was terrified the people who had killed Matt would be there looking for her.

Mrs. James heard Irving crying and came into the living room. "Everything okay in here?" She looked concerned when she saw Jessie crying too.

"We're fine, Mrs. James. Just a weak moment is all." Jessie tried to smile.

Mrs. James left the room only to return a few minutes later with some washcloths wet with her special lavender water, a cup of tea for Jessie, and chocolate for Irving. She didn't say anything. She just looked at Jessie with a smile then went back to the kitchen to finish lunch.

"Are we ever going home, Mommy?" Irving's eyes were still wet with his tears. ?

"How would you feel about a new house, Irving?" Jessie looked into his eyes. He was so innocent. How could this be happening to them?

"I like our own house. All my toys are there. My swing set is in the backyard. I want my own stuff back. I don't want to play with Sarah's anymore. They are girl's stuff. And I'm a boy!" Irving was getting mad. She had to diffuse this before it got out of hand.

"We could move all our stuff to the new place. Would that be okay with you?" Jessie was trying to put a good face on this.

"Even my swing set?" Irving asked hopefully.

"Even your swing set. And then maybe Sarah could come play with your boy toys with you. Would you like that?"

"Okay, but she better not break them! And I'm not pushing a girl on the swings. She'll have to learn to swing like me." Irving looked defiant.

With that he jumped up from the couch, books forgotten, and ran up to the playroom. Jessie heard him start yelling before he hit the top stair. "Sarah! You wanna play at my house? Mommy said you could when we get a new one!"

Jessie smiled and took the tray of dishes out to the kitchen.

"You all right?" Mrs. James asked her.

"I haven't talked much to Irving about all this. I thought to protect him from the reality of the situation. I'm not sure I'm right anymore." Jessie said sadly.

"We all do what we think is best for our kids. Sometimes we get it right and sometimes we don't. You just pray you get more right than wrong. Then they grow up and have kids of their own. That's when you can tell if you did right. It's in how they treat their own kids you see yourself. Not likely they would admit that, though. It's the best we got. In your place, with Irving's age, I would be just like you I would hope. He's a good boy and smart. This tragedy, of course, makes a huge impression on how you live your life in the aftermath, but it seems like you're doing the right thing, under these circumstances. There will be plenty of time to talk to Irving later, when he's old enough to handle it. You are letting him be a kid. That's a very good thing." Mrs. James said sagely.

Jessie just stared at her. She was so compassionate and kind. Jessie hoped she could be a little like her. Except for the gruff exterior, Jessie chuckled to herself.

"What? Mrs. James was looking at her.

"Don't take this wrong, but how can you be so hard and so loving at the same time?"

"It takes practice." Mrs. James laughed. "Don't tell anyone my secret, okay?"

This time Jessie did hug her.

# CHAPTER 24

Detective Shot was furious! Didn't Washington know he was still in danger? The two men had stayed locked up with no bail. But that woman was still out there! And she could be recruiting more idiots! If he wanted to put his own neck on the block, so be it! But if he led anyone to Jessie and the kid, Shot would shoot him himself! Shot half hoped he fell off the earth.

He needed to get a grip on himself. He couldn't control what anyone did. But he sure was going to let Washington have it for not letting him know where he went!

It wasn't that hard. Washington only had one place to go. Home. Shot was on his way there now.

He pulled up to a flurry of activity in front of the house. The people from the glass company were replacing the window. And to Shop's surprise, what looked like an army was working hard to repair the front lawn where the police vehicles had run all over the place. Washington came out toward him.

"What's all this?" the detective growled.

"They were here before I got up this morning. These are all friends from the neighborhood. My family has lived here since before I was born. They pitched in to clean up the mess you guys made of my yard." Valient said, wiping the dirt off his hands on his rag.

"Can't have young Valient here living in a crappy looking house. It's bad for the neighborhood. Property values will go down, ya know." one of the men offered.

"I think it will look better than it ever did after today. My dad wasn't much of a gardener, and my mom was allergic to flowers. I take after my dad. I'm lucky I get out to mow it once in a while. I guess they felt sorry for me. Care for a cold one?" Valient led him into the house to the kitchen. The front room of his house was still a mess.

"Look, Detective, I was bored out of my skull waiting there at Micco's. I wanted to sleep in a bed. My own bed. I'm a big boy and can take care of myself. I always have. So I took my tail out from between my legs and came home." Valient said trying to defend himself from the fury in Shot's eyes. "I never backed down from a fight before, and I'm ashamed of myself for doing it now." He said as he handed Shot a beer.

"Yeah, but this isn't a high school bully you're up against here. These people mean business. Two people are dead, and I don't want any more to follow, even you. And if they get to Jessie and the kid because you lead them there. You could get everyone killed."

"I know that. I will be careful. But I have a question for you. Since I'm in the thick of this mess now, can I have the story? What is this about? People are after me because I talked to a woman and her kid for five seconds. And I killed one of these bozos in my own home. I think I deserve to know the deal." Valient looked at him expectantly.

Detective Shot groaned. Washington was right. He should be told why he was being targeted. So he told the story. It didn't take long. There really wasn't much to tell.

"So, Jessie doesn't know anything about any pictures? Or where her husband may have hidden anything? Have you talked to the brother yet?" Valient asked when Shot finished a few minutes later.

"No. Jessie has no clue. And I haven't talked to the brother yet. I was going to see him later."

Buddy had been lying in the corner of the kitchen on her bed. During the conversation between the men, she watched them intently. She took in their conversation with interest. She sent a picture of the woman to Valient.

Valient saw the woman in his head and glared at Buddy. She barked and wagged her tail in response. He swore she was smiling. Bloody dog.

Out loud he said, "What about the woman? Any more information?"

"No sightings, if that's what you mean. We have a team sitting on the brownstone. We know her name, thanks to those two lame brains we have locked up. It's Carla Shultz. Other than that, nothing" Shot sounded frustrated.

# CHAPTER 25

CARLA SHULTZ HID BEHIND THE dumpster on the corner watching the cop trying not to look like one behind her house. She needed to get in there to get some clothes and her money that was hidden there. She didn't think the cops were smart enough to figure out where her hiding place was. It was brilliant, really. She had VISA gift cards she had loaded with $50,000. It had taken a year to get them a few at a time from different places. No name and no restrictions, other than a daily limit. She would live on that for a long time. Of course, if they ever got lost, she'd be without, but she was confident that wouldn't happen. Yats and Attics had even been paid with some. Carla thought she was clever because she hid them in the freezer, inside the cavity of a chicken in a small can. She had about ten of them. That way she could pull the baggie out and not have to defrost the bird. She smiled at her own ingenuity. Now all she had to do was get to them.

With cops out front in the black unmarked *you can't see me car* and the one lurking in the bushes out back, she had no way in. She would have to wait until the neighborhood kids came home from school in about an hour and try to blend in with them. In her jeans and hoodie, she could pull it off if the cops weren't looking too close. She could sneak in the house next door with the kid and crawl through the windows to her bedroom. That kid was always bringing friends home so it wouldn't be out of the ordinary. Carla had gotten the kid drugs from time to time so she knew she wouldn't turn her in. She would go out in the morning the same way.

As she waited, she thought of the Stevens woman. Where was she? How could she not be found? The closest she had gotten was the guy who shot Stepshick. Carla was getting desperate. If she didn't get that woman soon, her life wasn't worth dirt.

That idiot Stevens had heard Carla and her contact from the accounting firm talking at the restaurant. He was standing near their table waiting for take-out of all things. He had heard part of their conversation and saw the money change hands. Carla was sure he didn't have a clue as to what it all meant, but her contact wouldn't listen to reason. NO loose ends. That's what he had said. It was her first professional hit on her own, and if she were to survive, she would do what was necessary to please the client. She had already screwed up by letting those two idiots into her life. Now they were in jail and she was on the run. And she still had a job to do.

A few days later she saw Stevens again at the restaurant having ice cream with the kid. She had approached him. He was waiting for more take-out, so they stood and chatted for a few minutes. A waiter walked by them and bumped her arm. That's when her purse fell and spilled out on the floor. The gun she carried and a picture of her target were in plain sight. Stevens had helped her pickup the contents and apologized for the waiter. When he commented on the picture, she told him it was her uncle, and the gun was because she was out late at night, and her husband wanted her to protect herself. He just looked at her nervously.

She followed him from the restaurant. It was easy to track him. The next day she called him from the corner, getting his number from the directory. She gave him a story that Mafia hit men were after him because he saw her at the restaurant. She convinced him he was in mortal danger and that she could help him. How gullible! After what he had overheard, he was nervous already. Whatever she said to him he decided to have her 'help' him. She set up a meeting at his home.

The next afternoon when she and Shepstick showed up at his house, he let them in and had even made coffee. He wsn't quite as trusting as she had thought though because he had sent the wife and kid away. She asked him about what he had heard and if he told anyone about it. He insisted he didn't know what she was talking about. He asked why he was in danger. The answer he got was a bullet to the head and one to the chest of good measure.

The kid from next door was coming down the street. Carla stepped out of where she was waiting as she came close. "Hey, Sally, mind if I walk home with you? I locked myself out of the house and need to use the window route."

The girl looked at her for a minute, dressed in jeans and a hoodie she didn't look like her usual self. Then she realized it really was Carla and said "Sure, as long as my mom's not home. I don't want her to know how I sneak out at night."

"I haven't seen any lights in the house since I've been waiting so she'll never know, okay?"

"Yeah, cool. You've never narc'd on me, so I guess it's okay." Sally smiled at her.

They walked toward the house and Carla tried to sneak a look at the unmarked car. They were watching the kids but didn't seem to see anything different than they had seen the past few days.

Sally, hitching her chin toward the car, said, "Thoses guys have been watching your house since they took those guys away. Is that why you have to sneak in? You in some kind of trouble from the cops?"

"Nothing for you to concern yourself about. The less you know the better. Don't ask questions I can't or won't answer and we'll all be happy." Carla looked at the kid.

"How are you getting out once you get what you want?" Sally was smarter than she let on.

"I had hoped to go back out the same way. I will meet you in the morning in your room. We avoid you mom, and no one will be the wiser. We can walk out together, and the cops won't know it was me." Carla admitted.

"Good plan. I feel like a spy. Too cool!"

"You can't tell anyone about this! Not a friend, not nobody! You could be arrested for helping me, you know." Carla didn't tell her she could be dead because of this either. No point in scaring her when she thought this was such fun.

"I'm not stupid you know." Sally pouted.

By then they were in Sally's room. She opened the window and was putting the board across the gap. All Carla had to do was shimmy across it and open her bedroom window. She kept it unlocked for Sally, so it went off without a hitch. She waved at Sally and pulled the board into her bedroom.

Once there Carla went to her closet and got some clothes packed. With that done, she took a shower and changed into clean clothes. She was hungry, but instead of turning on lights or risking opening the refrigerator, she found the pantry in the dark and made a peanut butter sandwich. Ther was warm soda there too, so she drank that.

She would wait until morning to get the cards when the sun ws shining into the kitchen. The freezer light wouldn't be noticed then. Tonight she'd sleep in her own bed.

Carla got away from the house the same way she got in. She had dressed in jeans and a hoodie again, and she had Sally carry the duffle bag until they were out of sight of the cops. Then, after reminding Sally she would be in big time trouble for helping her, they separated. Sally wished her luck and told her she owed her some weed for her troubles.

Now she had to figure out her next move. Where should she go?

Okay, that guy was her only lead to the woman. Go sit on his house and see if he goes anywhere. She had another guy watching the cop. One of them should be contacting Stevens soon, she figured.

# CHAPTER 26

VALIENT COULDN'T BELIEVE HIS EYES! There she was! Where was Shot's card? He had to call him. He rummaged around the phone table and found the card. It took him two tries to dial the number because his hands were shaking.

"Detective Shot, she's here! She's across the street! Standing behind Mr. Statt's porch! What should I do?" Valient was sweating with excitement. Buddy was jumping all over the place.

"Don't do anything! Stay away from the windows and keep sharp. I'm on my way." Shot said into the phone, trying to stay calm. The woman had cheek, he'd give her that. Showing up again! And in broad daylight! God save us from idiots, Shot thought as he got in the car. He called the detail from her house to get over to Washington's. Now!

Both cars cleared the opposite corners at the same time. Carla watched them stop and the occupants converge toward her. She turned and ran as fast as she could. She got to her car just as they cleared the trees beyond the yard. That damn dog was closing on her fast. She made it into the car just as it got to her. She managed to get it started and moving before the policemen caught up. She floored it and escaped just in time.

Carla was shaking as she drove away. The police had to run back to their cars, so it gave her a moment to lose them. She took a cleansing breath and tried to calm down enough to get a plan. They knew her car. Okay. Ditch this one and find another.

Up ahead was a used car dealership. Avoid stealing a new ride and leaving a trail. Right! She pulled into it and drove into the service area behind the building. Getting out of the car she walked up to a smiling salesman. "What will you give me for it?" she asked sweetly. She looked past him out the window seeing th cops fly by. It would be at least a few hours before they got around to asking about her here, if at all. In record time she had paid cash, or rather VISA, for an old clunker. It served its purpose and she was back out on the road within the hour. She had given them one of the identifications and address her dad had faked for her when he left for Europe. Apparently they didn't check too closely. She had three more backups. Dad was a mastermind. He thought of everything. He was going to wring her neck when he found out what a mess she had made of everything. It was a good thing he was on his yacht in the Mediterranean. Hopefully he wouldn't find out too soon.

She drove to a rundown hotel down the highway and checked in. They didn't even ask for I.D. when she paid for the room with a VISA. She gave the name Sarah Smith. How dumb was that? She chuckled as she walked to her room.

Valient opened the front door as the police cars stopped in front of his house. Buddy bolted toward where the woman had been hiding. She shot across the street just as the policemen started running from their cars. Men and dog disappeared from view behind Mr. Statt's house. A few minutes later they all came running back. The men jumped into the cars and took off int the direction of the highway, sirens blaring.

Buddy came back, barking like a maniac. Valient took her back in the house to wait for Detective Shot and the results of the chase. He wished he was with them. This was nerve wracking and terrifying. He didn't know what to do so he made coffee, then he sat down to wait.

Shot radioed the make and model of the car and told dispatch they were in pursuit. He and two patrol cars raced along the road to the main highway. They searched frantically for the woman and her car. Nothing. He sent the patrol cars east and west to see if they could catch sight of her. After an hour of searching, he called it off. She had gotten away---again! He put out an all-points bulletin and went back to Washington's house.

Valient had been sitting outside on the back porch when Detective Shot rang the doorbell. He answered the door, hoping they had the Shultz woman in custody and everyone could get on with their lives. From the look on the detective's face, he knew it wasn't to be today.

"No luck?" Valient stated the obvious.

"Right." Shot looked like he wanted to eat nails. "Got anything stronger than that coffee?"

"Micco left the rest of the bottle of Regals here. It's under the sink. I'll pour us both some."

# CHAPTER 27

Carla still had a job to do. The client was getting impatient. She had spent so much time chasing down the Stevens woman and kid, and her window of opportunity was closing on her prime target. They were threatening to replace her---permanently. He father would never have let things get to this point. It would serve her right if she were caught. She was sloppy.

The target was a forty-year-old accountant. He had worked for the client's firm for fifteen years. It had recently come to their attention he had embezzled more than a million dollars over that time. While they could have pressed charges with the authorities, it would have caused more than a little embarrassment. This particular firm had some not-so-understanding clients mixed in with their legitimate ones. Shielding drug cartels and mob bosses from government questions was their specialty. If any of them found out the company had let someone steal from them, especially for that long, it would be fatal for all involved.

She needed to finish her main objective before she did anything else. The file was open on her computer. She studied his face until she could close her eyes and see it in her mind. His address, make and model of car, and his schedule had been supplied by the client in great detail. He was a creature of habit, leaving the house at nearly the same time every morning to run a six-mile circuit, home to shower and left the house for work within minutes of the same time. He took the same route every day. Too easy. Really stupid for a wannabe criminal. She needed to study his running route. That would be when he was most exposed. First thing tomorrow she would follow him on his run.

The accountant was true to form. Six o'clock and he was on his way. Carla drove a half mile and parked to wait for him to come into view. When she saw him in the rear-view mirror she started up and drove another half mile. She did this for the whole run. He never seemed to notice and kept his eyes on the road. She had spied a stand of bushes near a vacant lot about halfway through his route. That's where she would ambush him. Today was Wednesday, she would follow him again tomorrow. If all was well, she decided Friday was his dying day.

Leaving him as he pulled into work she stopped at a diner for some breakfast and much needed coffee. She would spend the next forty-eight hours resting and preparing. She needed to get her rifle from her dad's place. While she was there, she'd do some practicing in the range her dad had built in the tunnel under the barn. She knew the caretaker was still there and could help her set it up. Now that she was back on track and Dad wasn't there, she figured she would stay at the farm in her old room. She was raised there and groomed to follow in her father's footsteps. They had horses and ran a rescue for pit bulls. Her father had made her shoot the dogs they couldn't rehabilitate. She killed the first one when she was ten. He said he was proud of her when she didn't hesitate or cry afterwards. From then on, he taught her to handle different kinds of guns. As she got older, she went on local jobs with him. He never missed and never even came close to getting caught. He was the absolute best.

She didn't stay there when her dad was in residence because she just plain hated his latest wife. That's why she had the house in town.

Thursday dawned dark, dreary, and wet. Carla was parked four houses from the accountant's house. It was almost six thirty and no one was stirring. The rain had started in earnest a few minutes ago, and there was a leak in the driver's door seal. No wonder the car was so cheap. She was getting soaked on her lower leg and shoe. She really should leave. Obviously something was wrong. According to the bio, he ran rain or shine, every day.

Carla pulled herself up to start the car and spotted the accountant pulling out of the driveway. He drove down the street in the opposite direction from his office. Where was he going? She pulled behind him and followed the car downtown. He pulled into a gas station and went inside, where he talked to the man behind the counter as he paid for coffee. That's when she saw he was not alone. A woman, whom Carla assumed was his wife, was with him, so that meant the kids were probably in the car seats. Crap! What was this about?

She continued to follow him as he pulled onto the highway. He drove into Charlotte. She almost lost him when he pulled into a parking garage. She turned around and entered the same lot. As she did, she realized it was the government building parking lot. What the hell?

The accountant pulled up by the fourth-floor elevator and was met by three official-looking guys. They spirited them into the elevator and another guy took the car to a parking spot. This was not good! What the hell just happened?

There were cops and suits of all descriptions coming and going. She couldn't just sit there. She moved to a parking spot a couple rows over from the elevator and turned off the car, At this point all she could do was wait and see if they came back out anytime soon. If she kept down and looked like she was gathering her thing should anyone came near, she might not look too suspicious. She wondered suddenly if the security cameras would pick up the car and if they could see the driver! In a panic, she got out of there.

CRAP! CRAP! CRAP! Now what to do? She would have to call the client and tell him what had happened. How long would it be before the client put out a hit on her? Her wasting time chasing her tail with the Stevens problem cost her job and probably her life. She had to call her dad. He might just kill her himself she thought dejectedly. All his effort and years to train her and she screwed up on the very first job. He was so not going to like this.

Carla drove back to the farm. She needed to get rid of the car and then call her dad. As she pulled up to the house, Mr. Craft, the caretaker, met her at the door. "How did things go?" he asked her.

"Where do I start?" she answered sarcastically. "My dad is going to kill me himself"

"That bad?"

"Worse. Will you get rid of the car? I need to call Dad. I think the target is in custody." Carla gave him the highlights as she walked to her dad's study.

"Until he can get a plan, I don't think you should leave the compound. This is bad. In thirty years, your father never had this happen. Call him now." Mr. Craft shook his head. He wondered as he went out to the car if he would have to kill her and how soon. Mr. Shultz did not condone failure of any kind. Too bad.

The time difference from the States to----she thought he was near Greece somewhere----would put him seven hours ahead at about supper time. Wonderful! This keeps getting better she thought resignedly.

She dialed the satellite phone with shaking fingers. It took several minutes for a connection. When her dad picked up the line she started to cry just hearing his voice. "Dad, I am in so much trouble. I don't know how to start." she whispered.

"Hey, babe, it's great to hear your voice. You must be having man problems again? You pregnant?" he laughed.

"No, Dad, I missed my assignment, big time." She went on to try to explain all that had happened, from being overheard setting up the job and how the thugs she had hired to take care of the Stevens' job failed and got arrested, to how she took too long to carry out the job and how, when she finally got to it, the target had gone to the government building. She told him everything.

There was silence on the line.

"Dad, are you still there?" She was scared now.

"I'm here. Stay put. I need to make some calls. You disappoint me. I don't even know you. How could you let this happen after all the training I gave you?" He hung up on her.

Carla sat at the desk and just cried. Disappointing her father was a dangerous proposition. She didn't know how far he'd go. She poured herself some of her father's brandy. Shaking like she was it was a miracle any got into the glass. She took the bottle of brandy and her now-empty glass to her room. If this was going to be her last night, she might as well get drunk. It was an indulgence she never let herself have. There may be many indulgences she won't get if her dad couldn't get her out of this mess.

Mr. Craft came back a couple hours later. The car was taken care of. No trace of it would ever be found. He looked in on her to let her know but she was beyond caring. All he could do for her now was cover her and let her sleep it off. He took the bottle back to the study. Tomorrow would be an interesting day.

# CHAPTER 28

J ESSIE WAS HAVING BREAKFAST WHEN the cell phone the banker had given her vibrated. She answered it and looked at Mr. James incredulously.

"What's wrong?" Mrs. James was instantly wary.

"My sister and her family are in FBI custody! He couldn't tell me why. Just that the monies in my account were all there was going to be. The FBI had frozen all their money and assets. He would try to keep mine out of it as long as he could. I don't understand any of this! What the hell has happened?" Jessie was beside herself. What now?

"I need to call Detective Shot. Hopefully he can find out something. This is insane! My sister Dorothy can be a pain in the backside, but she's no criminal! Her husband is an accountant for heaven's sake! How much trouble could he get into?" She was pacing the kitchen. Mrs. James just sat watching her get more and more upset.

"I'll call Shot. You sit back down here and have another cup of coffee. I'll get him to see what he can find out. In the meantime, I have a contact in the FBI. I'll call her and see what she has. Someone should be able to give us some kind of information. Just calm yourself. I'll be back in a few minutes." Mrs. James said as she left the room.

As she was picking up the phone, the doorbell rang. In the window she could see Detective Shot's car at the curb. Sarah came running down the stairs. When she saw her grandmother she stopped short and took off back up the way she came. "Good thing young lady! You know what would happen if you got to this door!" Mrs. James shook her head as she shouted. That child was just like her father! Hardheaded!

"Come on in, Detective. I was just calling you." She said as she opened the door. "What brings you here so early?"

"I have to talk to Jessie. Her sister is in protective custody with the FBI. She asked them to call Jessie. I got a call when they tried to find her. Why are you calling me?"

"She got a call from that banker fellow. Told her all the assets were frozen and there'd be no more money. She's beside herself with worry about her sister. What's going on?"

"I'm really not sure, but I'm sure as hell going to find out. Where's Jessie?".

"She's in the kitchen. I was going to call Sheilla after I called you. I'll go do that now. See if she has anything to say." Mrs. James walked off so the front room while Shot continued into the kitchen.

"Detective Shot! What's going on? Why is my sister in custody? Tell me something! Please!" Jessie was crying.

Shot went to her and took her in his arms while she sobbed. "I wish I knew what to say. But right now I don't know anything. Mrs. James is calling someone we know who might be able to shed some light on this."

Sheilla Able was a friend of Mrs. James from her police days. Detective Shot and her husband had worked a couple cases with Sheilla when she joined the FBI and got to know her pretty well. The had all remained friends. Mrs. James just hoped the woman was back in the area. Rumor control had it she had been undercover in Florida and hadn't returned to North Carolina yet.

Sheilla wasn't in. Mrs. James asked if the agent in charge was available. She identified herself and asked for information on Jessie's sister and family. He wouldn't tell her anything. He knew about Jessie's husband and wanted her to come in and talk to his agents.

Mrs. James returned to the kitchen. "They want to see you, Jessie. The A.C. wants to know if the situations could be related. We have an appointment for tomorrow at one. I'll get Cathy from next door to watch the little ones. If she takes them over there, it shouldn't be a problem."

"This is all too much. First Matt, now this. When did the aliens come and take over the world?" Jessie smiled a wan smile.

"What aliens, Mommy?" Irving ran into the kitchen.

"There are aliens here? Grammie, don't let them get us!" Sarah squealed right behind.

The children ran to Jessie and Mrs. James.

"Do they have a spaceship to take us away? We want to go to Mars! Like the book." They were hopping up and down and giggling.

"No, not to Mars this trip. Maybe if they come back another time. How about we hide you from them over at Cathy's house tomorrow? Wouldn't that be fun?" Mrs. James played along. Cathy would love this. She had been reading to them recently. One of the stories was about an alien. Detective Shot helped himself to some coffee. Jessie asked him how he could find out anything about her sister if their friend wasn't around to ask. She also wanted him to go with her and Mrs. James to the FBI office.

"These two cases have to be related. That much I agree with the FBI about. I'm not sure how much information they'll be willing to share though. I'm going back to the office to talk to my captain.

Maybe she can get them to open up a little. I'll call you later." With that, he left.

Jessie, Mrs. James, and Detective Shot were waiting to see Agent in Charge Ike at precisely one o'clock as arranged. Jessie was so nervous she was shaking. She had to get some answers soon or go completely bonkers. Shot had not gotten anywhere with the captain. She wasn't there or answering her phone.

A.C. Ike showed them into a conference room where two other agents were waiting.

"Mrs. Stevens, I want to extend my condolences for you husband."

Jessie just smiled expectantly.

"His murder may be connected to your brother-in-law's current difficulties, however. What do you know about what happened to your husband?"

"All he said was he had seen something he wasn't supposed to, and we were all in danger. He was going to tell me more when we were somewhere safe. Then he sent me and Irving to wait for him while he met with some mysterious person who was to give him money and a new identity. I thought it was all very weird, like some Mafia movie."

"And he never gave any indication as to who he was meeting with?" A.C. Ike wanted to know.

"No, not a clue. But he was very scared. I've never seen him like that before. We had very ordinary, boring lives. This makes no sense." Jessie started to get a lump in her throat trying not to cry. "Agent Ike, what is going on with Dorothy and Rinnae? What kind of trouble could they possibly be in? Let alone be connected to Matt's murder."

Detective Shot spoke up. "One of the men we arrested in connection with a related break-in said he thought Stevens had some pictures that belonged to the suspect, Carla Shultz. She does not appear to have a record. At least not one we can find. Her father was a person of interest in two homicide cases a few years ago. It was rumored that her father had been some kind of freelance hit man, but nothing anyone could put a handle on. No investigations ever turned up anything, anywhere. He disappeared about a year ago. May or may not be related."

"We read the reports from your department, Detective. They don't seem to go anywhere, a lot of possibles and dead ends. Other than the arrests of the two men, there are more questions than answers. What about that guy, Washington? How does he fit in?" the other agent asked.

Jessie answered him. "He was just a guy Irving and I met on the street. He had a really ugly dog that Irving liked. We only talked for about five minutes one day on a street downtown. We had never met him before that."

"Other than him coming by the houses twice." Mrs. James reminded her.

"It was all very innocent, I'm sure. He had been walking his dog a few days before we saw him downtown. He happened by when Irving was outside on the front porch. He let Irving pet the dog and then went on his way." Jessie told them.

"A few days after they met downtown, he showed up at the door asking for her. I sent him on his way, denying anything about them. He hasn't been back." Mrs. James offered.

"Detective Shot, your reports say this Washington shot one of your suspects as he was breaking into his house." the A.C. stated.

"Right, after the meeting on the street. One of the guys we arrested said an informant told him of the meeting, that she took the guy to Washington's. He passed that on to Shultz. They were going to get information on Mrs. Stevens' whereabouts. She was there a few days ago again, but she got away." Shot verified what was in the report.

"Washington is a non-starter, Agent Ike. Wrong place, wrong time. He's innocent of any real involvement. I couldn't find any connection."

"That's what I got from the reports. But now he is involved, and he needs looking after until we get this cleared up. We don't need any more bodies of those threatening him. Where's his father's weapon?" the agent inquired of the detective.

"It's still in evidence. Ballistics came up with nothing on it. I want him to have his permit secured befor I give it back. It's processing."

"Give it back. There's no reason to hold it. He might need it."

"Arming civilians? Is that what we're about now?" Shot was incredulous.

"Not my first choice, Detective. But we can't be everywhere, and this Shultz woman is still out there. She's obviously dangerous. Give him a chance to defend himself."

"You still haven't told me what is going on with my sister. And what does it all have to do with Matt? I want answers! Can I see Dorothy?" Jessie stood with impatience.

"Sorry, Mrs. Stevens, you won't be able to see your sister any time soon. They are in protective custody and it would be too dangerous for them and you. We haven't finished questioning them. The only connection we have is the name of Carla Shultz. She is the constant. When the house on Drake Street was searched we found a picture of Rinnae Rola. Mr. Rola worked for a company that does accounting work for some criminal elements, money laundering, offshore trades and creative accounting, Just for starters. Apparently, your brother-in-law has been borrowing money for years and not intending to pay it back. Someone finally caught on and a friend warned him.

That's when he contacted us and came in. Now he wants protection for himself and his family." Agent Ike finally explained.

"So, what does any of this have to do with Matt?" Jessie repeated.

"We really don't know yet. Until we talk to this Carla Shultz and hopefully she will shed some light on things."

"We dont't seem to be any further along than when arrived here." Mrs. James mused. "What do you want us to do now?"

After discussing various scenarios for Jessie and Irving's safety, it was decided to keep them at Mrs. James' home and beef up patrols for her and Valient Washington. Jessie and Mrs. James were escorted home by an agent posing as a taxi driver. Detective Shot went to talk to Washington.

# CHAPTER 29

CARLA WOKE UP WITH COTTON mouth and snakes in her belly. God, why did she think getting drunk was such a good idea? She got herself out of the bed and thought her head would explode. She made her way to the kitchen and blessed the gods. Mr. Craft had coffee already made. Coffee in hand, she went to find out if her father had called back yet.

Mr. Craft was in the study on the satellite phone when she walked in. "Yes, sir, I have the itinerary. I will be there with the car. Anything you need me to do in the meantime?" Her father made some reply. "All right, yes, sir. See you then, goodbye."

Carla stared at him hoping she didn't just hear what she thought she heard. "Dad is coming home?" she asked shakenly.

"Yes. And he is none too happy, as you may well imagine. My instructions are to keep you here and wait for his return. So don't even think of going anywhere. There are two of his associates due to arrive this afternoon. They will stay with you while we wait for him." Mr. Craft frowned at her.

"You look like hell. Take today and get yourself together. I suggest you don't repeat last night's activity. Your father is due back tomorrow evening. He wants to see you as soon as he arrives at the house. I know you won't disappoint him." Mr. Craft moved past her and left the room.

She was in as much trouble as she imagined, more actually. Dad was coming home. Two babysitters! House arrest. She slowly made her way back to her bedroom via the kitchen for more coffee and toast. At least she'd live until he got home. That had to mean something. But even that thought didn't calm her frayed nerves. He'd killed his own brother for not getting a job done she remembered. Carla went back to bed.

Her father returned just after dinnertime the next day. Apparently he had left his wife on the yacht. Carla gave a small thank you to that in her mind. She met him at the door as he came up the steps.

"Hello Dad." she said tentatively. "Good flight?"

Taking her hand, he led her to his office. He gave instructions for his bags to be taken to his room and for no one to disturb him and Carla. He pushed her before him inside and closed the door firmly.

"Now, would you tell me why you screwed up this very easy job?" he glared at her.

"Dad, it has gone wrong since the beginning. First being overheard. I didn't see the guy standing there until it was too late. I found him and took care of him right away. Problem was he sent his family away before I got there. The guys I hired to get them screwed up and got caught. Nothing has gone right." She was whining and knew it. None of her "reasons" were forgiveable.

"You did everthing wrong!" he bellowed. "No planning, no backup, just excuses! Nothing I taught you for the last ten years made it to your lame brain! Now you have a dead associate, two targets in the wind, two witnesses in jail, and some guy who had nothing to do with anything able to identify you because of your stupidity! Have I missed anything?"

She knew better than to answer him. So she didn't.

He strode to his desk and sat down. "I made some calls on my way home. I managed to get the client calmed down. I had to promise to get this done at my expense. You will repay me."

"What am I to do?" she asked quietly.

"Oh, don't think you are out of this. You will work with me. One mistake, just one, and you will pay. Understand?" he said coldly.

Carla took a step back. She understood alright. She'd heard that threat before and saw its fulfillment.

"Go to your room. In the morning we will make a plan. I have some more calls to find the target and get the current facts. We need current reports." He picked up the phone and turned his back on her.

She ran.

Once back in her room she allowed herself to breathe. As she changed for bed, she tried to figure out what her father would do. She knew he had contacts everywhere. Cops, agents, and gang members were on his payroll. She was such an idiot not to use his people. But she had wanted to be independent, make her own way. How'd that turn out for ya? She asked herself sarcastically.

Mr. Shultz called his inside man at the FBI. The whereabouts of the Rola family was still unknown. The agent in charge had them stashed away good. Since Shultz's man was not part of that investigation. He was having trouble getting any information. It wasn't even in the database like it was supposed to be. He was trying to be assigned but the A.C. wasn't looking for any more help. The three agents working with him were by-the-book straight arrows and not giving anything away. He'd keep looking and let him know the minute he found out anything.

Next, he checked with the police department. Pay dirt! The Stevens woman and kid were staying with an ex-cop, according to the woman he had there. She gave him the address and let him know his old "friend" Detective Shot was in charge of the investigation targeting his daughter. She also had the address of the man who identified Carla. Detective Shot was nothing if not meticulous about his reports to his boss, the captain told Shultz. After promising her a big deposit in her offshore account, he hung up.

Now isn't that interesting, thought Mr. Shultz. That idiot daughter of his may just have handed him a way to get rid of his nemesis. This may not be a waste after all.

It was decided they would hit Washington first and then go after the Stevens woman. The Rola family was still in the wind.

Washington lived alone and had no protection other than intermittent drive-bys. Carla knew the layout of the house. One of the associates would take care of him tonight.

Stevens was a bit more of a challenge. There were children involved. No children could be harmed at any cost. Shultz did not kill kids. Period. The woman she was with was an ex-cop but retired. Not much of a threat. Carla and her father would take care of that job. Somehow, they needed to get Stevens separated, if not away from the house. They would go tonight to look at the property. Tomorrow two of his associates would watch the house and occupants. Everyone would report to Mr. Shultz the day after and from there a plan would be made.

# CHAPTER 30

V ALIENT WAS WORKING ON THE last of the library when Detective Shot rang the bell. Buddy was jumping and barking. She was showing Valient pictures of Jessie, Irving, and the woman they now knew was named Carla. Buddy wanted answers as much as he did.

The detective came through the door holding out a plastic evidence bag. "Present for you from the FBI." he said.

Valient realized it was his father's Glock. "I thought I had to have a permit before you'd give it back."

"The agent in charge, a guy named Ike, wanted you to have it back for protection. He's not sure Shultz is finished with you. The drive-bys may not be enough, and the captain can't spare any more men to watch you." Shot didn't look happy.

"Tell him thanks for me. Have you had dinner yet? I was about to make a quick supper. Spaghetti and a jar of Ragu, salad, and a beer. Care to join me?" Valient was starving and Detective Shot didn't look like he wanted to leave just yet.

"Sure. I was looking at fast food and heartburn all alone. Even your company is more welcome than that. What's wrong with that dog? Too much cleaning fluid? Shot reached down to pet Buddy, who had been pacing around him and staring.

They walked to the kitchen with the dog racing ahead and then sitting next to the table. She looked at the men expectantly.

"She wants to know what you have been up to the past couple of days. She wants to go see the kid and if this Shultz woman is still after us."

Detective Shot just laughed. "And you know this how?"

"Because it's the same questions I was going to ask. Now that I have, how about some answers?" Valient started the water for the pasta. "If you want to be useful, how about getting us a beer."

Going to the refrigerator, Shot asked, "Want me to get the salad fixings while I'm here? Which beer do you want?"

"I'll take an Adams. The Yuengling is Micco's but you can help yourself if you want one. The salad is in a bag in the drawer. I like easy. Dressings are on the door. I like them all so just pick one."

Shot put it all on the table. He opened the beer, handing one to Valient. They sat in silence for a minute while Valient continued to prepare dinner. When had they become friends? Or was Shot just being cautious?

"Why is the FBI involved now? You haven't mentioned them before." Valient asked, sipping his beer.

"Jessie's sister and family are in protective custody. Her husband embezzled money from the company he worked for. Turns out they are laundering money for some very nasty people. The sister asked them to get in touch with Jessie and let her know. The feds think this is all connected. Right now, no one seems to know how. Those two we arrested still think Stevens has some pictures this Shultz woman wants."

"What do you think? Isn't it a long shot?" Valient was confused. He didn't see any connection. He was an expert at puzzles, but he wasn't a cop. Aren't they trained to figure this stuff out?

"I think they're right. I just don't have the picture yet. Whatever is going on revolves around the Shultz woman. She's the constant. I investigated her father in connection with a murder for hire when I first made detective ten years ago. His name came up a couple years later in another one. I have a feeling about him, but no evidence in either case. Both are unsolved. His daughter showing up in these circumstances is just too much deja vu for me." Shot was in space for a minute. When he came back, he just shook his head and took a long draft of his beer.

The spaghetti was done. They set up a dining area on the coffee table and ate in front of the TV watching a baseball game. Turns out they both liked the Braves. As they ate, they talked about the players they like or hated, and armchair managed the team's plays.

Shot stood to go home when the game ended. Buddy was in the yard to do her business before bed. Suddenly she raced into the living room giving Valient a picture of a man in bushes. It had a red aurora that Valient had come to associate with her sensing danger. "Where girl?" he said out loud. She showed him the back porch and bushes. The only bushes were just beyond the back fence in his yard. "Are you sure?" he asked the dog.

"What are you talking about?" Shot was watching the interaction.

"I know you'll think I am completely nuts. But there is a guy in the bushes out back. She thinks he is here for me." Valient said without looking at the detective.

"You are nuts. But the way things have been lately, I should indulge you. Stay here and I'll check it out." Shot went to the kitchen and turned off the lights. He opened the door a crack and stood to the side, listening for any unusual movements. At first all he heard was his own heart racing. Then the gate squeaked faintly, leaves rustling. He waited. A few seconds later, he heard soft footsteps on the porch stairs. Someone was definitely there! Before he could react,

Buddy came sailing out of the living room. Growling like a tiger! Just before she hit it, Shot managed to swing the door open wide. The dog was on the man before Shot could move.

Buddy had the guy by the gun arm. His gun fired wildly as he tried to loosen her grip. She didn't let go. Shot tackled the man and dog knocking all of them off the porch to the ground. The guy dropped the gun and screamed to get the dog off him! Buddy was not letting go.

Valient came running behind with his gun in his hand. Shot screamed "FREEZE" and everyone, including Buddy, did!

Shot got the screaming man in a choke hold. "Okay, girl, you can let go now." he said to the snarling dog. Buddy let go but didn't move. Shot sat on the guy to put handcuffs on him. Valient was on the phone calling 9-1-1.

The guy had no I.D. on him. Of course, when asked who he was and who he worked for they got "Up yours and call my lawyer." as their answer. It didn't take a rocket scientist to figure this out. Carla Shultz was not giving up.

Valient got a picture of Jessie and Irving. "Detective Shot, since he's here. Don't you think we should check on Jessie? Shultz may have sent someone there, too."

"I don't know how anyone would find them. The only ones who know where she is are my captain and the FBI. I'm pretty sure they're okay. I'll call Mrs. James as soon as the patrols get here just to be sure."

No sooner had he said that his phone rang. It was Mrs. James. "Someone is in the yard. The camera on the back patio picked up two shapes. I think one is male and the other female. They are sneaking around the house. They just went out of camera range. I have Jessie and the kids upstairs. How soon can you get here?" She sounded excited, not scared.

Back in the saddle Shot thought to himself. "Five minutes. Stay inside, whatever you do." he said out loud.

He was going to call in to his captain for backup, but he called the FBI agent in charge instead. He gave him the particulars as he headed to his car. The patrols had just pulled up and he shouted to them that the guy was inside, and Washington would give them any information they needed. He would fill in the blanks later.

Detective Shop raced the three blocks to the James' house. As he pulled up, he saw two figures in his headlights. They bolted in opposite directions as soon as the light hit them, so he didn't get a good look. He took off after the larger of them but lost him in the shadows of the trees behind the property. He needed to get back to the house and make sure everything was okay. He didn't want Mrs. James shooting anyone in all the excitement.

He called out to her as he approached the back porch. He used her husband's code for 'all clear' so she knew it was really him. Without the light on she opened the door. She was standing behind it watching through the opening between the door and the wall as he came through.

"Always the cop." he laughed, kissing her cheek. "Everything okay in here?"

"Yes. I need to let Jessie know it's okay to come down. I'll be right back." With that she put her gun back in the holster in the small of her back and pulled down the shirt over it. You could hardly tell it was there Shot mused admiringly. She went to get Jessie.

Three dark sedans pulled up outside. So much for secrets now. Six agents fanned out along the property and the A.C. came up the front steps. Shot opened the door.

"They took off out the back in the trees. When I pulled up, I got a quick look at two people. One man sized, one female, I think.

They split up and ran. I followed the bigger one but lost him in the dark. Everyone is fine inside." Shot reported.

A few minutes later the other agents radioed that it was too dark to see anything. Nothing obvious could be found. Agent Ike told them to stand down.

Shot told A.C. Ike what had happened at Washington's place. He had an agent go with Shot back to finish up there. Agent Ike did not like coincidences.

Mrs. James, Jessie and Agent Ike were in the front room discussing the situation. Mrs. James had shown him the CCTV footage of the intruders from the back patio. You really couldn't see anything clearly. They were dressed in black and either a mask or face paint on. All that was discernable was the sizes of the bodies. Not much use otherwise. Agent Ike was hoping face recognition would be able to distinguish some features for matching.

He was curious as to why she had such sophisticated equipment. She explained about her past involvement with keeping battered women in hiding from violent spouses. Self-defense she claimed proudly.

Detective Shot had the would-be shooter taken to the station house for booking. He didn't want to leave Washington on his own, Glock or not. So he took him and Buddy back to Mrs. James' house. The agent had called ahead to let Agent Ike know they were coming. They had barely hung up before they walked in the door.

"You insist on bringing that mutt in here." Mrs. James complained with a smile on her face. Buddy looked up into her eyes. Mrs. James shook her head. She didn't look away from the dog. "What's she doing?" she said, shaking her head again.

"If you are seeing things like pictures in your head, it is probably Buddy. She's been doing that to me since she came into my life." Valient confessed.

"How does she do that?" Mrs. James was still staring into Buddy's eyes. "I'm seeing a picture of a man in some bushes. Is that what happened at your house?"

"Yeah, Buddy saw him." Valient explained. "I don't know how it works, but she can make me see these pictures, and I can feel what she is trying to say about them. It's scary but true."

"Okay, if you two are done with Physic Network, can we sit down?" Detective Shot was tired. "Agent Ike, any ideas? We can't leave these people here if Shultz knows about it. And it's pretty clear she does.

They discussed various places to stash everyone. Best case was a safe house the FBI had in the next town. It had enough room for all of them.

Detective Shot went to the station to interview the prisoner. He didn't hold out much help from him though. He had found out from Agent Ike that the elder Shultz was back home. Shot hoped it wasn't true.

# CHAPTER 31

R
UNNING FROM THE JAMES HOUSE, Carla and her father had circled back around to the car they had parked between some houses near Washington's place. The operative who was to take out Washington had parked a block behind them. His car was still there. Damn!

They had all met in the alley behind Washington's when they got there to confirm their plan. The operative was to take care of the man, go to the airport, and fly to the Atlanta house. The Shultz's would spend the next few hours watching the James' house. When they were sure all the occupants were asleep, Carla was to go in and get the layout of the interior. Nothing had gone according to plan! Damn!

Carla and her father had heard the sirens earlier. Hopefully his man had killed Washington because the alternative was that the operative was either arrested or dead. The fact his car was still parked did not bode well for the operative. Mr. Shultz would have to call Captain Kate to find out where he was.

They got as close to the Washington house as they could without being seen. There were cops everywhere. They watched Detective Shot walk through the alley behind the house and look in the area around the bushes. He called to someone inside to come out and look at something there. The person came out dressed like a space-man all in blue paper. The person radioed to someone else, and they brought out a box. Shot left them to do whatever they were doing and went back inside. They couldn't see any more from their vantage point, so they hugged the shadows to the street in front of the house. They had to stay on the corner of the alleyway because of all the commotion out in front of Washington's house.

Washington and his dog came on the porch. Damn! The dog started barking, looking in their direction. They ran back down the alley and went to their car. No one had followed.

With Carla driving Mr. Shultz phoned Captain Kate to see what she knew.

"I just got the report. Shot is on his way back here to question your man. He was at Washington's when your man tried to sneak in. The dog attacked and Shot took him down. No one got seriously hurt. Your man is in a cell as we speak. How do you want me to handle this?" The captain knew better than to let Shultz hear her frustration in her voice. She sat back and rubbed her eyes. God she was tired. She thought Shultz had retired and she was free of him. If anyone ever found out about their relationship, she could kiss her life good-bye. Literally.

"Make sure Shot doesn't talk to him. I'll get the lawyer there immediately. I don't care how! Just keep them apart until I get him out of there." Shultz told her.

She hung up wondering how the hell she was going to make that happen. Maybe she could just go home, and hope Shot thought it was too late an hour to interview a prisoner she thought hope-lessly. She called Detective Shot. "I just received a report of another attempted break-in at Valient Washington's residence. You were there. Why?"

"There have been some developments I haven't had a chance to get a report written up on yet. I had stopped by Washington's to check on him and we ended up watching a ball game since I was off duty. Is there a problem?" Shot wasn't sure why she was interested in the details.

"What kind of developments? Something I should have been told?" Captain Kate was not happy being kept in the dark about anything.

"In a nutshell, the FBI is now involved with the Stevens' case, and since the Washington case is related, they may want that one too." Shot told her.

"How are they involved with Stevens? It's a local murder case. Feds have no jurisdiction." Now she was worried. Did they know about Shultz?

"There is Mrs. Stevens' sister. Her husband embezzled money from his company. The company is suspected of laundering money for drug cartels and other criminal types. The agent-in-charge, a guy named Ike, thinks the Stevens' murder is related. They are trying to figure that out. And since Washington's situation is directly linked to Mrs. Stevens, Agent Ike thinks we should work them together. He's going to the Chief tomorrow to arrange the particulars. I'll have a full report for you by close of business tomorrow." Shot was waiting for her wrath. He should have phoned her before Agent Ike. She liked her subordinates to keep her fully informed.

"Other than being family how do they think a local murder and an embezzler are related?"

"They think a woman named Carla Shultz is the link. It's still not clear. The agent-in-charge is interviewing the family members." Shot informed her.

"Our information says gang hit. It's just a coincidence. I'm not handing it over to the Feds. Where are Stevens and Washington now?" Captain Kate was thinking furiously about how to keep this from blowing up in her face.

"The FBI is taking them to a safe house in Cherryville. There was an intruder at Mrs. James' place about the same time as the break-in at Washington's, so they got them out of sight." Shot informed her.

"Do you know where this safe house is?" she asked hopefully. She could give that information to Shultz and get rid of all the players at once she reasoned.

"No, for security they wouldn't tell me the address. I can reach them through Agent Ike if need be."

Shultz was not going to like this at all Captain Kate thought. She not only lost tabs on his prey, but she would also lose the payday that information would get her. Out loud she said, "What time is the agent meeting with the chief, do you know?"

"No, he's supposed to call the chief for a meeting." Shot understood her wanting to know. Whatever the Chief decided directly affected her and her department.

"I would hope you keep me better infored in the future, Detective Shot. And I expect that report as soon as possible." She hung up, forgetting about keeping Shot from talking to the prisoner.

Her next call was to the chief of police. "Dan, I have a situation here. The Feds have become involved with one of my homicides. They are coming to you to arrange to take over my investigation. Don't give it to them." she said after the preliminary hellos and about the time they were getting together. "We'll talk about it more later." She should call Shultz. He was not going to like his daughter being in the middle of this mess. Tomorrow was time enough. There was nothing more she would learn until she talked to the Chief anyway.

Trying to get anything from that operative was a total waste of time. His lawyer had shown up before Detective Shot pulled into the station. In the interrogation room the attorney did all the talking.

All the client did was glare at Shot. Somehow an arraignment had been bypassed, and the guy had been let out R.O.R. This was not right. Less than four hours from arrest to release. The lawyer and client left together. Shot called Agent Ike.

# CHAPTER 32

"The intruder from Washington's house is already in the wind." Shot said without preamble.

"When?" Agent Ike wanted to know. He was sensing something not quite kosher here.

"Ten minutes ago. He already had the lawyer there and ordered the released by the time I got to the jail. I attempted an interview but got double-lawyer-talk and nothing from the suspect. Something feels real fishy here."

"I'll make some calls and see if I can find out how this happened. Who signed the release order?"

"Judge Coles. He's a liberal judge, but this is weird, even for him. As far as I could tell no one even did a background on this guy before he walked. From what I can see by this non-existent file he wasn't even properly booked, just put in a holding cell. Judge Coles ordered him released to his attorney." Detective Shot was furious! How could something like this happen?!

"Okay, we can be pretty sure Shultz allies are at work here. We need to find out how deep this goes. Meet me at my office at nine." Agent Ike hung up and immediately dialed his protection team leader.

"We have a plant, or probably more than one. How secure is your team?" he asked the agent.

"I hand-picked all of them and have used them before. What's going on?" He was immediately wary and thinking of worst-case scenarios.

"The suspect from the Washington house has been released without processing. Double check all your security measures and stay alert. We don't know who is involved or how close our plant is. We may have to move quickly to another location. I'll keep you apprised of what we find from here."

Agent Ike rubbed his temples trying to let go of some of the tension building there. Instead of going home he just sacked out on the office couch. He kept a blanket and pillow in the sideboard cabinet for just such occasions. Lately he had too many opportunities to use them.

Detective Shot, Agent-in-Charge Ike, and the heads of the protection teams for the Rolo family and Stevens/Washington party met at 9:00 am at the government building in Charlotte. They were deep in discussion about how best to find the plants giving information to the Shultz's. They listed who had access to the cases. Their names and their teams were on top of the list and individually discussed and discarded.

That left:

| **Police Department** | **FBI Personnel** |
|---|---|
| Captain Kate, Homicide | Agent Suzzy, Dispatch |
| Sgt. Baker, Booking | Agent Wilson, Forensics |
| Officer Kirker, Records | Agent Kurtz, Computer |
| Judge Cole | |

"From here there are just too many possibilities. D.A.'s office personnel, judges, court clerks, patrolmen...it goes on and on. Where do we start?" Shot was getting overwhelmed with information.

"We start at the top and work our way down. Bank and phone records. Talk to spouses, friends, co-workers. Someone has to know or suspect something. Check out any gossip going around about each of them. Keep it civil, but don't worry about stepping on toes. We need answers. We do the job within the unit. No outsider without my say so. Understood?" Agent Ike dismissed everyone to do their parts.

Agent Ike and Detective Shot left to keep the appointment with the Chief of Police. After a heated and less-than-friendly discussion with the reluctant Chief they got permission to have Detective Shot work with the FBI for the duration of this investigation. The Chief, while agreeing to the possibility, did not want to concede that any of his people were involved in double dealing with the suspects. He wanted iron-clad proof of guilt before any charges were brought against his officers. Detective Shot was to report directly to him with updates on the cases. The Chief would inform Captain Kate. He didn't bother to mention it would be pillow talk.

The team met again three days later. Everyone had some part of their reports completed.

Sgt. Baker was too easy. His bank accounts showed way too much money for a man of his rank. He drove a Lexus and owned a condo in Charlotte. How stupid could he be? When questioned he had a reason for it all. The car had belonged to his uncle, who recently passed away. He had won a substantial amount in the lottery. The condo was bought with some of the winnings. Unfortunately for the investigation it all proved true. Dead end number one!

Officer Kirker was dead end number two. Nothing suspicious could be found in any of his records. Everyone loved him and his work record was exemplary.

Agent Suzzy had some issues...divorced, alcoholic, and skirt chaser extraordinaire! He didn't keep any of it a secret. The women in the office all knew him (some in the Biblical sense), and all steered clear for the most part. Other than being inappropriate with some of the females, his bad habits didn't carry over to his job that anyone could tell. He never heard of the sexual harassment policy; he was the poster boy for why there was one! Another dead end.

Agent Wilson was a science nerd. Unless it was a test tube or microscope slide it didn't exist in his world. He lived his work. General consensus was he was the best lab rat ever. The go-to guy and otherwise clean as the proverbial whistle.

Then there was the rest: Captain Kate, Judge Cole, and Agent Kurtz had bank account balances that were unaccounted for. The amount varied. The dates of deposits coincided with investigations either ongoing or grown cold. All unsolved. The origins of the monies were still being traced but preliminary information pointed to companies and accounts held by Shultz either directly or indirectly. They were assigned for further investigation.

The FBI unit took their own computer technician and Judge Cole. Detective Shot went to the Chief of Police for permission to access personnel records for Captain Kate. To his surprise the Chief denied his request.

"May I ask why you don't want us looking at her records? With what I just presented, Chief, it would be the logical next step." Shop tried again.

"Unless you can prove to me absolutely that she's involved, the answer is no. She is a decorated member of the police department, not some criminal. Do not invade her privacy any further. This is the end of your inquiries. Go in another direction. I was not in agreement with this collaboration. The mayor ordered it. But it doesn't mean I have to let it run over my best people. You are dismissed, Detective." The Chief had promised his lover he'd protect her as best he could. That was before he even *thought* she could be involved in any wrongdoing. With what he'd just been given by Detective Shot he knew it was a mistake.

As Detective Shot left the Chief's office, he was absolutely convinced of Captain Kate's guilt. Now all he had to do was figure out a way to prove it to the Chief without losing his job.

Agent Ike's team had better luck with Judge Cole, turns out he was a cocaine addict. He was caught by his clerk doing lines on his desk when he went to tell him the FBI was there. The agents were right behind the clerk so there was no hiding it. The judge was being held at the A.C.'s office at the moment awaiting his attorney. It shouldn't be very difficult to get his cooperation.

The computer tech was gone. He didn't go to work yesterday or today, and no one seemed to know anything about where he was. His computers at home were erased and his bank accounts were empty. They had watches at all the ways out of town, but he hasn't shown up on any cameras. Someone had hacked into the systems and looped a video for the last twelve hours. Guess who? This guy was good. Now all they had to do was find someone better to find him. Good luck with that Agent Ike had said.

# CHAPTER 33

Aᶠᵗᵉʳ AFTER EVERYONE SPENT A NIGHT with very little sleep at Mrs. James' place an agent had accompanied Valient back to his house to get some clothes and Buddy's supplies. They locked up and set the alarm system when they left. One of his neighbors was outside doing yard work when they walked out to the car.

"Hey, Valient! Going on vacation?" She wanted to know.

"Yes, Mrs. Yates, just for a few days. Look after things for me, okay?" Valient smiled back.

"Have a good time. Don't upset too many pretty ladies." She laughed at her own comic wit.

"Neighborhood busybody?" the agent asked.

"Pretty much." Valient verified. "She's harmless. Been looking out for me since forever. Nice lady."

They went back to Mrs. James' house. They were packed and ready. The kids were lugging a big suitcase down the stairs. "We packed all our stuff." they said proudly.

"What about clothes, toothbrushes, and shoes?" she asked.

"His mommy already did that silly. We got the stuff we really need." Sarah looked like she was going to challenge anyone who would take the 'important stuff' away from them.

"Good thinking. It's always better to be prepared." Agent Ike smiled at the children and took the suitcase. "Let's get going."

While two agents watched the street, the group was led to the waiting cars, the women and kids in one car, Valient and Buddy in the other. Agents in cars ahead and behind.

It took about an hour to reach the safe house in Cherryville. It was in the middle of nowhere, an old farmhouse, barn, and storage building. The kids were excited. "Are there animals in the barn?" they asked. The agent driving wasn't sure. She had never been here either.

A man came out of the farmhouse and waited on the porch for the party to disembark. He didn't look like an agent, dressed in jeans and tee shirt.

The women had to hold tight to the children to keep them from running to the barn. "Stay quiet! Both of you! We will tell you when you can go. Now behave!" Mrs. James was not taking any nonsense.

The man introduced himself as they walked into the house, his name was Jack. He was the caretaker of the property. He had been alerted of their arrival that morning and had put in provisions and freshened up the house for guests. There was one other staff, a cook. A couple farm hands took care of the horses and chickens in the barn. All the staff were armed federal agents.

Horses! The kids were ecstatic! Could they ride them? When could they see them? Jack told the children it would be up to the women, and he couldn't give them an answer until they gave permission. That got frowns from the kids. They didn't look too sure permission would be forthcoming.

"We need to get settled and unpack. If you would show us to our rooms, please Jack. Then we will all go to the barn to see the animals. Think you two can wait that long?" Mrs. James was already taking charge and organizing things.

"Lunch will be ready in about an hour. Mr. Pete is in the kitchen putting the provisions away. You'll meet him then." Jack said as he led the way upstairs.

He showed each of them a room off a long hallway. Mrs. James and Sarah, Jessie and Irving, and the Valient and Buddy took rooms in succession with a communal bathroom at the end of the corridor. There were agents assigned to a room at the beginning and end of the hall. The permanent staff had rooms downstairs in the back of the house. A.C. Ike and most of the transport team would stay for lunch and make sure everything was secure before they left.

Mr. Pete had sandwiches and homemade vegetable soup laid out on a long dining room table. It smelled wonderful. Even the children ate with gusto. But the second the bowls were empty they were begging to get to the barn. The farm hands, Joe and Leon, had joined them for lunch, and the whole party left Mr. Pete to clean up and went to the barn. A.C. Ike and the other agents left to back to Charlotte.

There were six horses and too many chickens for the kids to count. They kept moving around so the count kept getting mixed up. They giggled as they kept losing count. Joe and Leon showed them where the chickens laid their eggs and how to collect them. The kids promised to help in the mornings to get breakfast eggs. The horses scared the little ones because they were so big. The men picked them up to sit on the beasts. Their little legs barley draped over the sides. It was decided a ride would be organized in a day or so with an adult doubling with the kids. Joe and Leon kept the children to help with chores while the other went back to the house.

Buddy watched the goings on from the barn door. Horses were beasts she wanted no part of. They were big and threatening. Outside by the door was as close as she had intention of getting. She seemed to smile at the children's enthusiasm for them though. The men would take care that they didn't get hurt. She was worried about being out in the open though. Valient and Mrs. James kept seeing pictures of Carla and meadows. Valient tried to tell Buddy this was a safe place. Being there surrounded by all these people was as good thing. Mrs. James petted her on the way past. The dog did not seem consoled. They kept getting and uneasy feeling from her. Leon kept staring at the dog and shaking his head. Valient wondered if he was getting Buddy's message too. He didn't ask though.

The dog walked back to the house but did not go in with everyone else. She took off across the front yard toward the trees. Valient watched her as she patrolled the tree line from north side, around to the back pasture, and back to the house. As she came up the porch stairs Valient saw various animals and birds. "So, convinced all is well, girl?" he said as he knelt to pet the dog. She lay down and went to sleep.

# CHAPTER 34

The judge was brought to Agent Ike's office early the next morning after spending the night in a holding cell. His attorney, being incommunicado the evening before, met them but he was none too happy about it. In his opinion the judge should quietly resign and disappear. Cooperating with this investigation was not in his best interest. Agent Ike disagreed strongly. With the drugs and money hanging over his head cooperating was his only way of possible avoiding jail time Judge Cole needed to tell what he knew and now.

They started with how long he had been working for Shultz. He had been on the payroll for the past ten years. He did his best to get the cases connected with either Shultz or his people assigned to his court. The deal was he saw they had modest, if any, bail. And if a trial ensued the sentences were suspended or minimal. Since it didn't come up too often no one noticed the discrepancies. He was paid very well. If anything came up in the courthouse rumor mill, he reported that to Shultz too. Monies were deposited in and account in the Caymans. Communication was on prepaid cell phones. A new one each month. He had just received the last one a week ago. One number was programmed into the phone. It was different each month. Simple and sweet.

Did he know who else had been approached by Shultz? The judge named a few names in the D.A.'s office. Clerks mostly. And a few ranking police personnel and he suspected there were other in other agencies including the FBI and possibly some international agencies. Shultz operated all over the world and so it stood to reason.

For all the names and information, the D.A. made a deal with the judge. Full immunity but he had to give up the money obtained illegally and resign. The attorney worked out the details and all papers were signed, money exchanged. What the FBI didn't know was that the judge had over the past few years already moved a great deal of the money elsewhere. He was still set for life. He left smiling. Within a day he and his wife were sitting on a balcony overlooking the ocean in the French Rivera.

Now they had the "who" and "how" but not any concrete way to connect the dots. The two suspects Detective Shot had in jail had connected Cala to the Stevens' murder but there was no physical evidence connecting her. And absolutely nothing on her father other than the information network.

All Agent Ike could do at the moment was to get eyes on the Shultz farm. Without proof Carla was in residence there was too much fire power in there to just raid the place. Now it was a waiting game.

In the meantime, they would cut off his local information pipeline. With the names Judge Cole had given him they could move forward and shut him down. They rounded up as many people named by the judge as they could quickly find. All were interrogated but none could give more than the telephone number they currently had to contact Shultz. A few of them weren't even sure it was Shultz. A few of them weren't even sure it was Shultz they were talking to. They thought it may be one of his associates being a go-between. A few others hadn't had any contact for over a year. They thought he had retired.

Captain Kate hung up from the chief. He had informed her they were no longer involved. He told her of the meeting with Detective Shot and what she was being accused of. He gave her one day to resign and leave town before he called Detective Shot back. She always knew it would eventually come to this, but still, she wasn't ready. She never expected it would come from him.

She left her office and went home to pack. One parting shot, she called Shultz. "If you want Stevens and Washington they are at a farmhouse in Cherryville, on Route 24, about a mile from the town. I have been compromised and am leaving now. Good luck." She threw the phone out the car window.

When she reached her house, the FBI was there waiting for her. She never got out of the car. They found her brains all over the window.

# CHAPTER 35

Detective Shot was going over all the evidence he had to work with. He realized in all the excitement he never contacted Kenny Stevens. He wasn't sure if the brother would have any real evidence to contribute but he should at least cut that loose string.

He called Agent Ike. They met at a diner near the office. After ordering the blue plate special and coffee they tried to get a sense of where things were going.

"We know Carla Shultz did the Matt Stevens' murder, but we have no physical evidence. No reason either. If he had pictures, why kill him before he gave them up? Doesn't add up. As far as we know there is no connection with Rolo and, other than a chance meeting with Mrs. Stevens, nothing to do with Washington. Washington became a target only to get to the Stevens woman after that meeting. Shultz is trying to tie up loose ends, but ends to what? This is going nowhere unless we get something concrete." Detective Shot looked at the agent for some kind of answer.

"That about sums it up, but it's not quite as hopeless as all that. We have the informants. And the picture of Rolo in her house. She never moved on him though. He thought someone was spying on him the day before he came to us. But her wasn't sure. Somehow all this connected. We just have to get the link. It will come. We just have to be patient."

"Have you heard from your chief of police?" The agent didn't look directly at Shot.

"No, why? I had nothing to report since the roundup of Shultz's informants. He and I spoke just before dinner time that day."

"You don't know about Captain Kate then?"

"No. Has something happened?" Shot sat up and leaned in.

"She's dead. Blew her brains all over her car. According to the chief they had been having affair. He had called it off after talking to you. As you know the judge had named her as one of Shultz's informants and we were at her home waiting for her. She pulled up but never got out of the car." Agent Ike looked sympathetic. "I'm sorry, Shot. I thought you knew and were just not talking about it."

"I had reported to her up until teaming up with you guys. She knew about Jessie and that she and Washington had been moved to the safe house. Do you know if she passed that on to Shultz?" This was not good Shot thought to himself.

"How much did she know? We never gave you the address if I remember correctly." Agent Ike was reaching for his phone.

"I really don't know. I told her it was in Cherryville. She may have gotten the address from someone else. Or Shultz could have gotten it from his FBI informant. Either way I would say it's been compromised. What do you think?" Shot didn't need to ask. Agent Ike was already talking to Jack.

"Is everything okay out there?" Ike asked before Shot finished speaking. "Quiet as a church mouse. What's up?" Jack didn't seem to have any concerns at the moment.

"We think Shultz may know where you are. The homicide captain was one of his informants. Now she's dead by her own hand.

Keep your head up and double the guard. I'll send backup agents your way within the hour."

Detective Shot was already at the counter paying the bill. Both men raced out to their cars and headed for Cherryville. Agent Ike called his backup team leader to meet them there.

Jack had radioed the barn to get Leon and Joe to get back to the house. The two agents with Mrs. James and Jessie were also alerted. When everyone was armed and positioned, they settled down to wait for any action. The guests were left to sleep since there was no immediate danger. Jack had taken all procedural precautions but saw no need for all the alarm. This was secure house. It had never been breached in the six years Jack had been there.

It was fort-five minutes later when the back-up team arrived. They met Jack on the front porch and then spread out to create a perimeter. They had just reached their assigned positions when Agent-in-Charge Ike roared up to the gate. Detective Shot arrived just behind him.

Buddy heard strange voices carrying through the windows. The door to their room was open just a crack. She pushed it enough for her to get through and went downstairs. She found Leon and tried to see what he knew. She saw dark figures and guns. Leon was star-ing out the back window when he felt something weird in his mind. Like a shadow moving through a dream. He turned to see Buddy staring at him. He smiled at her. He knew it was the dog invading his thoughts, but it didn't scare or concern him. There were a few things he had seen growing up that had made him a believer in things he couldn't always explain. He made himself think of danger, bad guys coming. The dog took off back up to the room She jumped on the bed to wake Valient. She showed him what Leon showed her.

He was immediately awake. Rolling out of bed he pulled on his shoes and grabbed the Glock from the closet where he had stashed it in his backpack "Where are the women and kids?" He asked Buddy. She showed him beds. "Okay, let's see what's happening here."

They went downstairs looking for Jack. They found him with Agent Ike and Detective Shot in the kitchen. "Care to share?" Valient joined them for coffee. "What's all the excitement?"

Agent Ike spied the Glock in the pocket of Valient's pants. "I see you didn't come unprepared. I suppose we should find you a holster for that thing before you shoot off something important. You do know how to use that thing properly, I hope. Wouldn't want you shooting the good guys by accident'"

"No problem. I have a bit of experience that may not be advertised." Valient answered mysteriously.

"Read some interesting things about you in a classified file. We have to have a talk sometime soon. Right now we have a possible situation. Carla Shultz and her father may know where you are. Shot's captain was one of the informants Shultz had in his pocket. She shot her brains out yesterday. We have reason to believe she may have told Shultz where you all were before she took herself out."

Nothing happened the rest of that night. Nothing happened the next day or that next night. Jack suggested maybe nothing was going to happen and that they should all get on with investigating and he and his team would handle protection. Do the jobs they were all supposed to do. It was finally decided to leave the additional team for security and Agent Ike and Detective Shot would go back to the office.

The highlight of the next day happened when Joe and Leon went to care for the animals. Jack allowed Sarah and Irving, along with Buddy, to go with them. An additional agent went just as a precaution. As Irving reached for an egg in one of the nests a snake reared up hissing! Irving screamed! Sarah threw the egg she was holding at the agents, and all took off fleeing the coup!

Joe and Leon came running, gunsdrawn. "What happened?" they shouted at the three quaking figures in front of them. "SNAKE!" they all screamed at once!

Leon went into the coup to find it. He returned a few minutes later with a three-foot black rat snake wrapped around his arm. It had a bulge in the middle where it had swallowed a couple eggs.

"What are you going to do with it?" the kids wanted to know.

"How can you hold that thing?" the agent wanted to know, backing away and pulling the kids with her.

Leon petted the snake's head. "It's harmless, unless you're an egg or a bird. They keep the mice and other bad stuff away. I'll take him out by the woods and let him go. He can find other eggs to eat and leave these for us humans." He started out toward the woods with Buddy hot on his heels.

Suddenly Buddy stopped! She sent a picture of a bear near the edge of the woods. Leon dropped the snake and ran back to the barn. Snakes he would deal with, bears not so much!

"Since the horses are taken care of and we have all the eggs, maybe we should head back to the house before we get any more company. Ay objections?"

They closed up the barn after giving the horses each an apple. Then made sure the chicken coup had no more visitors. Making their way back to the farmhouse, the group marveled at Leon handling the snake. He was officially a hero to agents and children alike!

# CHAPTER 36

Mr. Shultz listened to his messages from the prepaid phones, deleting each in turn—until the one from Captain Kate. He replayed it three times, making sure he had the address correct. The message was almost a week old. He had read in the newspaper of her death, reportedly in the line of duty. No real details other than she had been shot. He would miss her. She had supplied good intel over the years. Not to mention pleasant distraction from time to time. He would have to close her bank account. Getting that money back at this time was fortuitous. The latest wife spent faster than the accountant could pay the bills. He made a note to call the accountant to put her on an allowance.

Unbeknownst to his informant he kept access to every account for just such an eventuality. Usually he took back from informants he terminated himself. Refunds he called them. Most of his operatives here were compromised and didn't know him anyway. All were hired by associates who were blackmailing them. The FBI had questioned them and had confiscated the prepaid phones but got no real information from them. He wasn't worried about traces on the phones either. His call back number was routed through so many servers it would take them months to trace it, especially with their best computer nerd in the wind. The number would have changed today anyway.

The one piece of information he still desperately needed was the location of the Rolo family. With the FBI computer whiz gone he had no one left who could get that information quickly and without being traced. Recruiting a replacement would take more time than he had. His current employers were getting very impatient with the way their problem was being handled. First his daughter's incompetence and then the seeming delay in his own handling of the situation. If *their* client got wind of the situation no one would be safe. The only option left was a direct assault on the Cherryville house, with the capture and interrogation of the agents there. He had an idea of who he wanted to help carry out that assault. After dinner he would start contacting them and devise a plan.

It would take at least three more days to get his team together. Everyone he had contacted, with one exception, was available and ready to help. He made arrangements for them at various hotels and airlines. A meeting was set for late in the afternoon at his farm three days from now. They would arrive separately or in small groups. It would be a guise of a dinner party, and they would dress accordingly. Shultz invited a few neighbors and local guest just to keep up appearances.

Carla was busy setting up the actual dinner menu and service. She hadn't arranged anything like this in years. It only became her task when her father was between wives. This time it was because her newest stepmother was floating around the Riviera in her father's yacht, thank the stars. The cook looked over the menu, made a few suggestions, and between them they finalized the food, wine, and serving crew. Everyone who would be there that night had worked there at some time in the past and was trusted.

It looked like everything was set. There were seven men and women due to arrive by 5:00 P.M. two days from now. After the party they would staying at the farm. There would be three teams of three. Carla and her father would lead two of them and oversee the operation. They had an expert to interrogate the agents they captured.

Everyone arrived on schedule. The property had a party atmosphere. It did not fool the agents watching. Pictures were taken of every car and every person by a valet with camera hidden in a lapel pin. The valet company was only too happy to assist the Agency but did not inform the workers of why they had new company pins to wear. Cameras had been hidden in the dining room and parlor as well as the study by agent posing as delivery people during the preparations. Computer technicians tapped into the property's security cameras and were recording everything.

Some of the cars were rentals and the credit cards used to procure them were registered to non-existent names. Preliminary face recognition software was coming up with several unsavory individuals. All were associated with mercenary backgrounds or criminal elements. Most were wanted by one country or another but none in the U.S. Many were just neighbors and local dignitaries.

Agent–in-Charge Ike was monitoring the situation from his office. Now he knew why there was no action at the safe house yet. When nothing had happened in Cherryville, he had ordered stepped up surveillance of the Shultz compound. It paid off big time when agents monitoring the security cameras and audio tapes heard the plans for at the dinner party.

They had hit the jackpot. The biggest question was when to move on them. They had no cause to crash the dinner party. Detective Shot was beside himself. Years of chasing Shultz may be coming to a head! He could close at least three cold cases if this panned out. However, there were no warrants outstanding on any member of the party here in the States and it would take a few days to get through the international red tape to get any. Carla Shultz was under suspicion, but the D.A. wouldn't move without real evidence.

So, for now, they wait and watch. Getting to the Shultz's was the priority, but there were some pretty big fish swimming in this pond If they could get the paperwork right. Agent Ike called the director's office to set up a meeting to get started. It was set up for the next morning by video conference.

His next call was to Jack. He gave him a rundown of the evening's events. They went over his strategy to handle and assault if it came to that. Jack seemed to think he had everything under control. His own people, the extra team, the ex-cop, and Washington were all fully armed. He had plans to move the party to another house in the next day or so anyway. There had been a kitchen fire at the new house, so it was not readily available. He didn't want to split up the group, so he's wait until the repairs were completed in the next few days. "So don't sweat it, I got this" was his parting comment. Agent Ike hoped his abilities matched his confidence.

The Shultz party broke up about eleven. From the valet's surveillance video it looked like everyone left except the bad guys. The team waited to hear what was happening and when they would begin planning their assault on the safe house. What they heard was everyone saying their good nights and going off to bed. They waited about ten minutes and still saw and heard only the staff cleaning up after the party. This made no sense. Why would they go through all the trouble of getting these people here and then do nothing? Did Shultz think he had time to procrastinate? They checked and double checked their equipment. Nothing. They had no equipment in the upper level so all they could do was wait. At abut 3:00 AM it went totally silent when the last of the cleaning crew was finished.

Mr. Shultz was smiling at his team. They were in the meeting room under the barns. After the dinner party broke up, they had gone to their rooms to change and then took the back stairs to the tunnel entrance in the T.V. room. It was hidden behind the television console and ran not only to the barn but the garage as well. In the tunnels was a room big enough for meetings. A gun range, an arsenal, two bedrooms that could be used as holding cells when needed and a fully stocked galley kitchen. All were furnished quite comfortably. Now they all sat looking expectantly at Mr. Shultz.

"I thank you all for coming to our party." he began with a smirk. "As I explained in our phone conversations, I need your expertise in eliminating several witnesses and other loose ends in an operation that has gotten out of hand. We need also to find and eliminate a second target that is under the protection of the FBI. We have lost our informants in an FBI sweep. One of them was caught with drugs in a very compromising situation and he turned on us to save his own ass." he said by way of explanation.

"That will be dealt with another time. We know where the loose ends are being kept. We will hit there first. The objective of the raid is twofold: to eliminate the witnesses and to detain as many of the FBI agents as possible for interrogation. The information I need about the second target is the objective of our friend here in the interrogations." He smiled at the operative. "One thing there are children involved here. They will be left alone at all costs. No children have ever been hurt in my operations and we will not start now. That must be understood."

He looked around the room at each face individually and saw agreement in each one. "Okay then, moving on. We need a layout of the farm they are being held at. That will be the job of your team, Mr. White (Each operative was given the name of a color for expediency and anonymity, corny but effective.) Once we have that, we will finalize our strategy. I expect to have you all on your way home day after tomorrow. When the job is complete your agreed upon fees will be deposited into your accounts. We will meet again tomorrow afternoon and hit the farm tomorrow late night. Any questions?"

There were a few questions and a bit more discussion of the specifics and then the meeting broke up for the night. Everyone returned to the house the same way they left it.

The next thing the FBI agents watching saw was Carla going to the kitchen for some juice at about 5:00 AM. Then nothing until about 7:00 when the cook came in to begin breakfast preparations. There seemed to be a few guests missing from breakfast.

# CHAPTER 37

Mrs. James, Jessie, Valient, and Jack were lounging on the front porch finishing the coffee from breakfast. The kids were in the front room playing with the contents of their 'treasure suitcase' as they called it. An agent was near them watching TV. It had been quiet the past couple of days and they were hard pressed to keep focused. The air was fresh, the days lazy, and they were bored. It was both a blessing and a curse.

Jack's radio buzzed. It was the agent in the office who was monitoring the CCTV system. At the same time, Buddy alerted. Valient and Mrs. James got pictures of figures in the woods near the barn. It was the same information the agent was telling Jack. Everyone was awake now! Valient held on to Buddy's collar preventing her from dashing away. "Stay girl. Just keep watching for now." He told her. She just sat up and stared at the wood line.

"Jessie, Mrs. James, go inside with the kids. Go to the panic room and don't come out until one of us comes for you." Jack said.

The women left as the others checked their weapons. Mrs. James and Washington had previously been given the option of being with the team or staying in the panic room protecting Jessie and the kids. Each of them reasoned the panic room would not be breached unless the protectors were all dead so it would be better to have Mrs. James in the panic room as she was less agile than she used to be and her gun might prove useful as a last resort.

Washington chose to stay and lend his abilities to protecting them from the outside. He didn't tell Jack he was claustrophobic.

Joe and Leon had two of the other agents in the barn helping with the animals this morning. They were radioed and were watching the woods with telescopes from their vantage points in the hayloft. They could see three figures with cameras and binoculars. One was close to the front gate, one on the right nearest the barn, and one moving left flanking the house. They lost sight of the one on the left as it moved toward the house.

They watched the figures for another fifteen minutes while the backup team went out to intercept the intruders. They managed to get the one on the right. The other two managed to elude their pursuers and make it back to their car making their getaway.

Jack called A.C. Ike to send a transport for the intruder. They had her in the barn trying to get some information from her. She had no identification on her and the camera showed pictures of the house and everyone on the porch as well as the barn and paddock areas. She wasn't talking. The only thing she would tell them was her name was Mrs. Grey. She thought that was very funny.

Leon went to get Buddy and Valient. He had an idea. If Buddy could get into the woman's head, they would save a lot of time and effort. All he had to do was convince Jack he wasn't suffering from brain damage from breathing too much horse crap fumes.

Buddy sat in front of the woman and stared into her eyes. Valient and Leon knew it was working because they could see what Buddy was thinking. She was showing them pictures of Carla and Mr. Shultz, a room with lots of people, a TV with a door behind it, and a long corridor with doors leading off it. The woman was squirming trying to get away from the dog's presence. She closed her eyes to avoid looking at it, but Buddy already had her thoughts. She tried to think of meadows and flowers, but Buddy somehow got them erased and back to the picture of Carla. The woman seemed to give up. She thought of the bedroom she had slept in last night and not much else. The only thing Buddy could see was a picture of Mr. Shultz. It seemed the woman had a thing for him. They stopped when she started picturing him naked. Leon had been telling the agents with them what they were seeing.

Jack was dubious. They already figured she was working for Shultz. The room and corridor were intriguing, but not conclusive. He didn't think they learned anything they could use. He wasn't too sure they didn't make it all up either. Telepathy wasn't something he could understand. Wasn't it science fiction? He had no time for fantasy when he was trying to keep people alive. He didn't mention any of it to the agents who came to pick up the prisoner.

Agent Ike had just finished the teleconference with his director. The information was going to be forwarded to the State Department for further processing. They probably wouldn't get an answer anytime soon. Washington worked slower than the proverbial turtle. In the meantime, they were to keep surveillance on the Shultz compound and the witnesses under protection. The director reminded him there was a lot of manpower and resources going into this operation with very little return as far as he could determine. He needed to get some resolution soon or he'd have to pull the plug on it. No timeline was discussed, but the threat was there.

Detective Shot and another agent were in the interrogation room with the woman from the farm. She said as much to them as she had to the agents at the farm. Nothing but her fake name. They were running her prints and facial recognition while they wasted time trying to talk to her. She was one of the guests from Shultz's party, that was least something. They needed her to *say* something. And fast.

A.C. Ike waked into the room smiling wide. "Hello. Remember me?"

The prisoner's eyes widened just slightly but enough that the agent noticed. "San Francisco, wasn't it?" she smiled back. It wasn't a pretty smile. She looked sick.

He had known her name was familiar when they were going through the pictures last night. It finally hit him on his way down to the interrogation room. Five years ago, they had met during and international murder investigation that went cold. She disappeared before they could arrest her. There was no US warrant because the murder actually took place in Spain. The FBI became involved when she kidnapped the victim's husband living in San Francisco. Agents freed him before she could kill him. The guy couldn't identify her, but she remained a person of interest.

"You had not proof then, and you can't prove anything now." she glowered at him.

"You're right. But I do have that warrant from Spain, and now that I have you here you will stay our guest until Spain is notified, and extradition is arranged. So you might as well get comfortable, *Mrs. Grey.* Name's a nice touch, by the way." Agent Ike leaned in to emphasize his point. "What do you have to do with Luke Shultz?" The agent came straight to the point.

"He's fun and great in bed." She gave him an *up yours* smile.

"Must have been a crowded bed with the other guests at the party." he said snidely. "What were you doing taking pictures at the farm?"

"I like picturesque places. The old farm building caught my eye."

"And your friends? Who left you hanging if you recall."

"Those people had guns. They must have gotten scared."

"How would you have gotten back to the Shultz compound? We know that is where you are staying. Wouldn't Luke have missed you?"

"I was hoping that some Good Samaritan would give me a ride. I'm very resourceful if I have to be." She looked Agent Ike in the eye mockingly.

"When is Shultz set to raid the farm?" Agent Ike was done playing games. He needed answers. He had turned off the video feed. She didn't notice.

"I have no idea what you are taking about." she said tiredly, studying her nails.

"Why is he after the people at the farm?"

She continued to study her nails, not looking at the man. "I have to use the bathroom."

"Not until I get some answers. I'd guess I can wait longer than you to get what I need." he said expectantly. She drank two cups of coffee while sitting there. And as far as he knew, she hadn't used a bathroom since being captured at the farm. He sat back and waited.

"You can't do that. I have rights." Sheilla was incredulous. He wouldn't! She glared at him. Agent Ike just smiled. She turned to Detective Shot and the female agent in the room and said, "You just gonna stand there? I need to go to the bathroom! Now!" They didn't even look at her, just stood there smiling.

"This is illegal! You can't withhold the necessities! I know my rights!" she all but screamed at them. She stared at each in turn, waiting for one to react. They just waited, smiling. "You're serious! REALLY?" She waited. "I'll report you! Nothing I would say would be admissible! You *do* know that!"

She tried a different tact. "I want my lawyer. NOW!" She sat back and glared at them.

"You're not under arrest. As of this moment we consider you a material witness. You don't get a lawyer." Agent Ike glared back.

"If I'm not under arrest that means I can leave." She stood and started to turn toward the door.

"No, you can't. We are detaining you awaiting the warrant from a foreign country. Once their officials are notified and give us guidance as to their wishes concerning their outstanding warrant you may or may not be released. In the meantime, sit down." Agent Ike was losing patience. "The faster you answer my question the faster you get what you want. Do we understand each other?"

She sat back down. She looked at each one in turn. They weren't playing fair or by the rules. Deciding she was defeated, she sighed. "Alright, you win. What do you want?

Agent Ike smiled. He knew she was too much of a lady to pee on the floor. "Good girl. I knew eventually you'd see this my way. Now, why is Shultz after these people?"

"All we were told is his daughter was hired to take down an accountant and was overheard in a restaurant setting it up. The nosy guy was eliminated, but his wife and kid got away. While she was still looking for them the accountant got away. Luke wants his whereabouts to finish the job before the client comes after him and his kid. There are some extenuating circumstances involved in the original job. He didn't say what exactly. The other guy is collateral damage. We were hired to take out the people at the farm and make you agents tell us where the accountant is. Happy?" She was shaking her leg and had wrapped her arms around herself. "Can I go now?"

"When is all this to go down? And how may operatives?"

"God, you are rotten. Tonight, after midnight with three teams of three, minus me now obviously, okay? Will you *PLEASE* Let me go the damn bathroom?" She was about to embarrass herself.

Agent Ike motioned to the female agent and Detective Shot. "Don't let her out of your sight. And bring her right back here."

When they came back, she was a bit calmer. "You're a peach." she said sarcastically. "You know I'm dead now. Don't you?"

"Then it's a good thing you're stuck in here. No one can get to you. You'll be on your way to Spain in no time flat. Consider this protective custody." Agent Ike smiled at her. "Get her comfortable in our *guest suite* he told the female agent.

"We'll talk later. Rest well." he said to her as he left the room.

She gave him the bird.

# CHAPTER 38

Agent-in-Charge Ike and Detective Shot were on a speaker phone with the detail at the Shultz compound. There seemed to be no movement, other than the usual servants in residence. The guests all had meals together in the dining room but weren't seen or heard other than that. There were no other noises picked up on the microphones from any other part of the house. The watchers had no idea where they spent their time.

Jack was alerted to the impending raid. The alternate safe house still wasn't ready so that was not an option. He would make sure everyone was rested and ready.

Valient and Leon were discussing whether to tell Jack what else Buddy had seen in the woman's mind. They knew how the operative had eluded the surveillance team at the Shultz compound. Jack thought they were nuts, liars, or worse, colluding with the enemy. How would they convince him?

They decided to give it a try anyway. They went to find him. He was in the CCTV room making sure everything was working properly.

"Jack, we know you don't want to hear this, but we do have some information from that woman that could prove useful. Just hear us out, okay?" Valient looked at him hopefully.

"I don't need fairy tales right now, Washington. We have real information from real sources to worry about. I'm sure nothing Buddy could say would be of any use to me." He walked past them into the living room.

"Even if we told you there were tunnels under the compound that had a range and a fully stocked arsenal? Or what kinds of weapons are in that arsenal?" Leaon tried.

"And the only way you could know that is if you'd been there. I'm beginning to think you both should be locked up as spies. I have to be able to trust everyone. I thought I could trust you, Leon. I need to call Agent Ike back. Excuse me." With that he pulled out his cell and walked to the porch.

"Agent Ike, I have a problem here. Your buddy Valient and my Agent Leon may be plants here." he told his boss.

"Why do you say that? There's nothing to indicate that in their records or in their movements." Agent Ike waited.

"They have information they say came from the prisoner yesterday pertaining to how the operative are eluding the detail at the Shultz compound. Things they wouldn't know unless they had been there." Jack informed him.

"How do they claim they got this info?"

"That's just it. They claim it came from the dog. That she's telepathic or something. How stupid are they? Couldn't they come up with something more believable? I need them out of here before the fireworks start. I'll lock them in the basement cell until you can get someone out here to pick them up."

"Hold on." It was Detective Shot. "Was the dog in the area when the woman was being questioned?"

"Yeah, so?" Jack asked.

"They may be right. I know it sounds totally nuts, but Mrs. James can apparently communicate with the animal, too. I've seen the interactions, and they've proved on the level. We should hear what they have to say." Detective Shot knew what it sounded like, but he was willing to concede the point.

Agent Ike was staring at the Detective. "You sure about this? Lord, I can see how this will look in a report. We'll all get straitjackets." he moaned. His aunt claimed to be clairvoyant and had helped with some law enforcement cases where she lived. He wasn't totally convinced, but he knew she knew things no one else did. It was spooky but he couldn't discount it.

"I can't afford to put faith in a bunch of hocus pocus when there's a firefight on the way." Jack was incredulous! How could his agent-in-charge be buying this crap? "Just please get someone out here and get me some replacements, sir."

"We will be there within the hour. Don't let them out of your sight. We can all talk to them when Detective Shot and I get there. I'll bring a couple extra agents, just to be on the safe side." With that the agents hung up. Shot and Ike left for the parking lot.

"I can't believe this!" Jack mumbled to himself. He went back inside to confront Valient and Leon.

"You two, stay in this room. Do not move. Agents Ruiz and Carp will stay with you. Agent Ike and Detective Shot seem to think this is legit. I think you're both plants. Move from here and I will have you shot, understand?" He glared at the men. He went to find Mrs. James and Jessie in the kitchen with Pete.

"We are having company tonight. The woman we captured says her boss is attacking after midnight. I want you and the children to sleep in the panic room. Tell them it's a picnic or camping trip. Whatever you tell them you need to keep them calm and yourselves, too. Mrs. James, make sure your weapon is fully loaded and you have at least one extra clip. That will give you at least a fighting chance if it came to that. We can't go to the alternate house yet, not ready so we're stuck with what we have."

"I'll set it up." Jessie said. "I'll get the kids to help. They can make a blanket fort and bring some of their treasures. It'll be fine. Pete, would you get a picnic basket ready for us, please?"

"Yes ma'am, I'd be happy to. Peanut butter sandwiches, cookies and some chocolate milk cartons sound good? I'll fix a couple thermoses of coffee and snacks for you ladies as well. Fix you right up." Pete said with a smile.

"Thank you." she said, leaving to get started.

"You seem unduly upset, Jack. What else is happening? We heard you with Valient and Leon, and you sounded angry even though we couldn't hear the words too clear. Anything we may need to know?" Mrs. James waited quietly.

"Nothing to concern you. A difference of opinion is all." Jack hedged.

"I did hear you mention the dog. The boys told me what happened in the barn. I can hear the dog too. I know how it sounds" she said as she held up her hand to silence him, "but it's real. Buddy told me of the tunnels too. Sometimes there are thing going on in this world we can't explain. It doesn't mean it doesn't happen. I didn't believe it at first either. But now I do. She's proven herself."

"Mrs. James, with all due respect, it's nuts. Science fiction. No one, save the fictional Dr, Doolittle, can talk to animals. How do you expect me to believe such crap?" Jack just shook his head.

"I don't know how to explain it in rational terms. I just know it's real. We could conduct a test if you like." Mrs. James offered.

"What do you mean a test? How? How do you prove something that can't be proven? Besides I don't really have time for parlor games. I have a fight to get ready for, saving your lives, in case you've forgotten." Jack challenged.

"How about this: you keep Buddy with you for the next hour. When you come back, we will tell you everything you did. To make it better, hide something with her watching, and we'll tell you where and what it was. Fair enough?"

"You could have a camera planted on her somewhere." He was hedging again. She seemed too sure of herself.

"Take off her collar and leave it with us. And pat her down before you take her. She's a dog, not too many places to hide things." Mrs. James was smiling now. She had Jack's attention, and she knew it.

"All right, just to make you happy. Anything to get an end to this psycho stuff. I have work to do. Where's the dog now?" Jack was already getting a headache, and it was barely noon.

"I'll get her." Mrs. James left to talk to Valient and Leon and get the dog.

"I made a proposition to Jack to prove Buddy's telepathy. She's to spend the next hour with Jack. When they return Buddy is to tell us what they did. He agreed to the test." she told the men.

"You got that, Buddy?" Valient asked the dog.

She showed him a picture of Jack and was wagging her tail for all she was worth.

"I'd say she understands." Leon said. Then maybe we can get back to work and hopefully save some lives tonight he thought to himself.

Jack and Buddy went to the arsenal to make sure the agents there were cleaning and loading the weapons they would use later. They were deep in concentration on their tasks. The weapons were already cleaned, and they were filling the extra clips. Jack pocketed two of the clips as he left them to their work.

Next, he walked to the barn to make sure the animals had been secured. Joe thought the horses should be left outside in the far paddock in case their visitors set fire to the barn. If they were set free from the paddock, they were trained to go back to the barn. There were no worries about them running away. The chickens would be locked in the coup. That's all that could be done with them. Jack agreed and radioed for and additional agent to lend a hand. From the barn, they went to the storage building to see how much gasoline for the tractors and lawn mowers was available. Jack didn't want their own supplies to be used against them. All he found was one two-gallon jug that was half full. He took that back to the house, but not before hiding one of the clips in the torn seat of the lawn mower. He didn't let Buddy see him do it. He had made her stay outside the building. That way he could prove all this talk was nonsense and prove his point.

He put the gas can under the back porch as far out of sight as he could reach. Then he walked the primeter of the house, checking for entrance points and vulnerable places. Satisfied he'd done what was necessary he went back inside. After he put an end to all the nonsense, he'd have lunch and call a meeting when A.C. Ike got there.

Show time. "All right let's get this over with. First, Agent Ruiz, did anyone leave or enter this room?"

"No, sir. Not even to use the head." She replied.

"Okay, so now what?" He looked at Leon and Valient.

"Buddy, what did he do?" Valient addressed the dog.

Buddy showed him, Leon and Mrs. James the sequence of events.

Mrs. James smiled. "You started in the arms room, where you put two clips in the left pocket of your trousers. From there you went to the barn. Joe and your other agent put the horses in the paddock near the woods and closed the chicken coup. Then to the storage building, where you hid one of the clips in the seat of the lawn mower and took a small gas can. That gas can is now under the back porch pushed pretty far in. Oh, the second clip is on the chair on the back porch under a cushion. Did I miss anything?" She looked at Buddy for minute. "Oh, the clip in the tractor is empty. The one on the chair is full."

Jack just stared at her in disbelief. Not possible! "How did you do that? Who was watching me? It's not possible! I didn't let her see me hide the first clip! How could she know?" he stammered.

Buddy was jumping on Valient and wagging her tail off. She looked so happy! She had won!

"It's not only possible, but you know it's all true. It's obvious she read your thoughts. Now, will you release these two and let them tell you what they need to say?" Mrs. James felt like slapping the fool.

"We are going to have a meeting with Agent Ike and everyone after lunch. We'll get to it then. Right now, I need some coffee." Jack's headache was roaring now. He wished he could have a drink.

Buddy came to him and put up her paw. "She wants to shake on being friends." Valient explained. Jack took her paw and gave it a quick shake. He was dumbfounded! She stared at him for a minute and then went back to Valient.

"Why can't I see what she can see too?" Jack wanted to know.

"Not sure." Valient replied. "I don't know why some people can communicate with her and others can't. Apparently, she can see into almost everyone's mind, but only a few people can read her messages. It was kinda scary at first, but then it got easier over time. So far, myself, Mrs. James and Leon are the only ones. That woman seemed to realize what was happening, but I can't be sure hers was real communication. Neither child has said anything about it. So, I don't think she affects either of them."

"Fine. It's time for lunch Let's get everyone rounded up and go eat. A.C. Ike and Detective Shot should be here with additional agents in a few minutes. We'll have a strategy meeting after that." Jack said tiredly. He was hoping to get an hour or so of rest after that. He looked at the dog and shook his head. He was getting as crazy as the rest of them. What he had just witnessed was not possible.

Mrs. James went to the kitchen to help Pete serve. Jessie and the kids were washing up in the half bath. Jack radioed the rest of the inhabitants of the house as Agent Ike and his party pulled up the drive. Lunch was served with lot of conversation and laughter. The kids were in heaven because they got to have a sleep over party in the *special room*. They told any adult who would listen about their plans to watch movies on 'Mr. Jack's private computer' to eat popcorn and to have soda all night! They didn't even have to go to sleep all night if they didn't want to! How cool was that? At least someone was looking forward to nightfall the adults were thinking.

# CHAPTER 39

J ESSIE TOOK THE KIDS INTO the panic room shortly after dinner. The FBI agents took up positions in a close perimeter about fifty yards from the house. By 10:00 PM they were as set as they were going to be. They settled down to wait. Mrs. James was sitting by the opening of the panic room waiting for the signal from Jack to go in and close the door.

A.C. Ike was with Valient on the back porch steps. "So, do you want to tell me why you have a classified file with the military? I thought you were a mechanic." He smiled knowingly.

"You read the file, so you already know. Why, by the way?" Valient asked.

"Why what?"

"Why did you even have that file? It should have been above your pay grade." Valient wondered.

"You may be surprised what my pay grade is Washington. As the saying goes, 'We served together at different times.' You joined the unit the month after I was reassigned. Major Crike was the C.O."

Valient nodded at him in understanding.

"I called him to check on you. He said you were one of his best until you had a mission go wrong. Sends his best, by the way. How did you end up unemployed and so messed up?" Agent Ike was curious about Valient in more ways than this one.

"When my last assignment went bad. I was wounded and spent almost a year recovering. It messed me up mentally, as well as physically. I lost my nerve. Then while I was home on leave, I found my dad dead in his store. He had and unexpected heart attack. I'm still trying to get straight after all this time. I have a great therapist, an ex like us, but I've had a hard time readjusting to having a normal life."

"Can I trust you here, with a firefight?" Now Ike was really concerned. Some of this was in the file, but not all. It mentioned his expertise but not that he had been wounded. There was a lot of the black marker in the file he had read.

"I believe you can. I get better every day. I'll stay close to the house, so you aren't worried about my interfering with your agents." Valient assured him with a smile. "No one else needs to know any of this, right?"

Agent Ike just smiled. "I'll keep your secret if you keep mine. That's what the unit's all about right?"

Valient smiled back. Bond made, secret filed.

"How are you going to use the information Leon and I gave you about the woman?" Valient changed the subject.

"We've got agents watching the place. But we don't know where the back entrance is for the underground tunnels. The woods and surrounding area are being watched, but it could be anywhere. What you learned explained why there has been no activity in the house. As you are aware, knowing what weapons we're up against helps the defense. Knowing the exact layout of the house and tunnels is invaluable, if we ever get the go-ahead to get in there." They had been talking quietly, but Agent Ike suddenly sent silent. Valient heard it too.

There was a very faint click. Close. Agent Ike slipped to his belly next to the steps as Valient did the same on the porch, near the rail. They saw a flashlight flicker twice about ten feet from them. They looked up and saw red pinprick lights near the barn. Valient counted five. They were here.

From their vantage point they could see the red lights moving around to the storage building. They stayed there for about a minute and then moved back to the barn, disappearing inside. The agent monitoring the CCTV saw seven bodies huddled together. They were all in black, but the infrared picked up the body heat. They heard the report in the earwigs.

Agent Ike tapped his mike three times. The agent nearest the front door of the barn moved to it and threw in a stun grenade. Before it could detonate five of the bodies had run out the other side. Two down, five to go. Another agent joined the first and tied up and taped the mouth of the two downed men. They were dragged and secured in one of the stalls as per the plan. The agents resumed their posts on the perimeter. The red light had disappeared.

Valient heard four clicks on his radio. He watched as three agents converged behind the storage building. Noise of a scuffle was heard for about a minute. Three red dot lights took off toward the side of the house. The agents did not reappear.

Two clicks on the radio. Valient got up to his feet and moved to the side of the house, hugging the wall. As he slid around the corner, he was shot in the chest. It knocked him back and hurt like hell. He freaked! His heart went nuts. He started to shake violently. After a minute or two of panic he took a few deep breaths and managed to gather himself enough to move back to the corner, where he dropped to a knee and lead with his gun as he looked around. The flak jacket had done its job, but he was going to have a bruise. I'm back, he thought with a self-satisfied smile. There were two more agents down and now only two red dots. He couldn't tell if the bad guy was down or gone. He fell to his belly and low crawled forward. He saw two more agents converging with him. They open fired on the men with the red lights. One more went down and then another one took off around the front of the house from the shadows. Where'd he come from? There was one more coming from the opposite direction. Agents converged from the sides of the house. They used tasers on the last two bad guys.

They heard five clicks from the radio. Lights went on everywhere. Two of the agents had one dark clad figure by the arms. Two more came around to the front with another one. The two from the barn were brought to the house to join the others. Two were dead. Two were missing. They looked as far as they could. They couldn't find the last missing dark figures anywhere, but they did hear a vehicle start up and screech away. Three agents were missing, one was dead. Joe was among the missing, as was the female agent who had been with Mrs. James. The last one of the agents who had come with Agent Ike and Detective Shot, the dead agent was on the backup team that had come out last week.

The medical emergency personnel had been standing by just down the road from the farm. They were called to take the wounded to the hospital. Once that was done, the FBI agents transported the prisoners to the government building in Charlotte. Detective Shot stayed at the farm to lend a hand with the search and cleanup.

After matching the prisoner's faces with the pictures from the Shultz party Agent Ike called the director in Washington. The two dead bad guys were on Interpol's wanted list, along with four of the others. The last had no warrants they could find. It was Carla Shultz!

A.C. Ike took Valient and Buddy with him to sit in on the questionings. He was beyond caring, regardless of how unconventional or how unbelievable. He needed answers and didn't care how he got them.

"Good morning, Carla. We finally get to meet. I'm Agent-in-Charge Ike." he began.

"Why is he here?" she pointed to Washington and the dog.

"He's just here to identify you and sit in on our chat."

"I don't want him here." she said defiantly.

"Where are my agents, Carla?" Agent Ike ignored her.

"How am I supposed to know?" She looked him in the eye.

"Are they at the compound?"

"What compound? If you mean our farm, why would they go there? I assure you we don't invite strangers to our home." She sat back and folded her hands in front of her.

"Washington?" Agent Ike turned to look at him.

"Of course she's lying. The agents are being taken to the cells in the tunnel. She doesn't know if they are there yet." Valient told him while looking at Buddy.

Carla glared at Washington and then at Agent Ike. "Bull, he's fantasizing about mystical places."

"Look, Carla, we know about the tunnels. And that they contain an arsenal and shooting range, a couple cells, and a self-contained kitchen. I need to know where the escape route is and how many more people are working with you. One-way or another I will get the information I need." Agent Ike wasn't in the mood for games.

"Not from me. I have no idea what you're talking about. I want my lawyer now please." She leaned back and closed her eyes. "

Agent Ike stood and took a long, cleansing breath. He looked at Valient and Buddy. Valient was smiling. "I know where the back entrance is." he said. Carla's eyes shot open, but she said nothing. Just stared at him.

# CHAPTER 40

OUTSIDE THE ROOM VALIENT TOLD Agent Ike what Buddy had seen. "There are three more operatives at the Shultz compound; Mr. Shultz, a woman, and another man. The tunnel has one exit near the road that runs next to the first stand of trees. It's in the roots of the biggest tree. The root system hides the door. As soon as you brought it up, she pictured it. There's another exit but she didn't show the location. The woman from the other day showed us an exit in the big garage."

They went quickly to Agent Ike's office. He had to get more personnel to raid the Shultz place. He called the team watching there. "Any movement out there?" he asked.

"Not at the moment. Shultz and two new guests just finished coffee in the dining area. They are out of camera range now." his agent informed him.

"You keep your eyes peeled. Three of our agents were taken at the Cherryville farm a little while ago. They are headed your way. Backup is on its way to your location in fifteen. E.T.A.: forty-five. Get a couple of your team around to where the stand of trees on the southwest side of the compound meets the road. There's an exit point there from the tunnels. We think that's how they'll take their captives in. Observe, do not engage. We'll be there with help shortly."

Agent Ike hung up then dialed the on-call team leader. He explained his need and told her to meet at the stake out van. They were just leaving the Cherryville farm. He called to Valient to meet him at the car in five minutes and then went to use the facilities and get coffee for the road.

It had been more than two hours since the raiding party had left the Cherryville farm. Agent Ike was absolutely sure they had already been at the Shultz compound for at least half of that time. He was praying they hadn't gotten around to killing any more of his agents. As he pulled up to the van he noticed there didn't seem to be enough lights on in the house for all the activity that surely must be going on in there. That meant they were in the tunnels.

The surveillance leader had sent a text to the two agents in the woods to look for the hidden door they were told about. They found it in less than ten minutes. It had recently been opened while the agents were watching in another area about a mile away. There were six set of footprints and an abandoned Jeep near the road.

Agent Ike left the communication tech in the van to monitor their radios. He had instructions to contact local authorities only as a last resort. Agent Ike knew of at least eight of the local sheriff's deputies who were on the Shultz payroll. They would be dealt with by the State Bureau of Investigation when this was over. NC State Police were on the way, but Agent Ike had wasted enough time. He wasn't waiting.

"Washington is that dog under your complete control?" he asked as they were donning the flak jackets.

"She understands what's going on here. I told her we were going to get Joe and she could go but must stay beside me. She'll be no problem." Valient crossed his fingers and looked into Buddy's eyes.

"You'll do what I say, right girl?" She wagged her tail and showed him a picture of Joe. He wasn't completely sure she could be trusted.

They piled into the cars to take the short drive to the woods entrance. Once there they split up into two teams. Buddy would be with Washington and Agent Ike in the first team along with two additional agents. The other team was four agents who had also been at the farm. Once their people were found and secured, they would split up to search the house. They locked and loaded the weapons and stepped into the tunnel.

Someone was talking deep in the tunnel. The teams could hear them but not quite make out the words. Within a few minutes it became very clear what was going on. One of the prisoners was screaming from being interrogated violently. Buddy started growling and pulling on her leash. Valient got a picture of Joe. He whispered 'hush' and pulled her back. He got a scowl from Agent Ike. Buddy settled down but wasn't happy as she kept pulling on the leash.

The teams hurried as fast as they could and still be comparatively quiet. Team One came upon a room where two men and a woman were surrounding the female FBI agent. Her blouse was torn down the front and one of the men had his hand on her breast and holding a knife. From her screams and the blood welts it was obvious what he was doing to her. The woman was asking her where the Rolo family was as the man cut into their victim's flesh.

The team kicked in the door. Shultz turned with a revolver in his hand. The woman pulled a gun and pointed it at the prisoner's head. The man torturing her tried to run past them to the door. The agent at the door knocked him out with the butt of this rifle.

"Well, if it isn't Mr. Washington bringing in the cavalry. Going to save the day, are we?" Shultz said with a smirk pointing the gun at the growling Buddy.

"If no one moves we will all be able to get out of here. I am going to walk out that door and Mr. Washington here is going with me." He motioned with the gun for Washington to move toward the door.

Agent Ike just looked at him incredulously. Was he nuts? You've been watching too much television. No one is going anywhere. Put the gun down, both of you. You," he addressed the woman holding his agent," step away from her. You have a gun pointed at your head over there."

She turned to see the agent standing not two feet from her pointing his weapon at her head. How had he gotten around her without her seeing him? She looked to Shultz but he was staring at Agent Ike. For a moment they all just stared at each other.

Buddy broke the spell from her place by the door. Valient saw two figures in his mind coming toward them down the tunnel. "Agent Ike!" he yelled as he swung around.

Shultz broke for the door as he shot the agent blocking his way knocking Buddy over. He was out the door as Agent Ike went for him. The woman jumped toward the agent beside her and got shot for her troubles. The men were out the door, guns blazing. Shultz was running up the tunnel zig zagging past the operatives and attacking the federal agents to avoid getting shot. He was running toward the main house. He was hit once in the side but he wasn't looking back.

Agent Ike and Washington were on his tail with Buddy streaking past and gaining on the fleeing man. She grabbed him just before he made to the TV room. He tried to get a shot off at her, but she had him by the back of his shirt, and he couldn't shoot her without shooting himself. Agent Ike shot him in the shoulder causing him to drop the gun. Shultz went down cursing at Buddy let go of him. Washington pressed a dressing to the wounds after Agent Ike had put handcuffs on him.

The rest of the team members had found their fellow agents bound to chairs in the other bedroom/cell. Joe had been wounded at the farm and was still seeping blood from a gunshot wound in the hip. The other agent had bruises beginning to color from being pummeled while they subdued him. Both of men were in shock.

Of the Shultz operatives, three from the tunnel were dead. One was still unconscious and four more were sleeping up in the house.

Agent Ike asked Washington if Buddy was getting anything from Shultz. "She's seeing beds and people with guns. I think its's the operatives from the farm. He's wondering where Carla is." Valient told him. "He is thinking of a few ways to kill you too." he continued, chuckling. "Buddy wants to bite him."

The agents waiting outside were radioed. The State Police Captain had the S.W.A.T. unit surrounding the house. Agent Ike opened the front door to let them in to help. The teams went upstairs to secure the people sleeping there. There was gun shots exchanged but it was over fairly quickly. One guy tried to escape through a bedroom window and broke his back when he fell on a short retaining wall. He as dead. Two tried to shoot their way out and were killed by the agents. Three more were in handcuffs and were now sitting in the SUVs waiting to go to Charlotte. There were more operatives than they had anticipated. They must have come through the tunnel unseen by the surveillance team. The only other people in the house were servants. They were rounded up and taken to the dining room.

The operatives were all taken to Charlotte. The servants were questioned by the FBI agents and then turned over to Sate Police for further questions and processing. Most of the servants were fairly new. The Shultz's weren't there very much anymore so they didn't need a full staff.

The overseer had been with Shultz for over ten years according to some of the servants. He did all the hiring and firing and went traveling with Mr. Shultz sometimes. He knew everything about anything going on here. Unfortunately, he wasn't there but was someone the agents really wanted to talk to. The cook thought he had gone to the movies. Yeah, right, the agent thought.

The Shultz house was searched from top to bottom, stem to stern. They took computers, tablets, and cell phones. Four safes were found and emptied. The conference room in the tunnel had file cabinets that were full on information on Shultz's life and jobs. It would take months to go through it all.

# CHAPTER 41

When they got the 'all clear' Mrs. James left the children sleeping in the panic room with Jessie with the admonishment not to come out until she came back. The house was a mess. There were a couple windows broken, the glass was all over the floors. There was blood on some of the furniture. A small side table was broken.

The woman went to find Jack and Detective Shot. She found the detective on the porch talking to the agent left in charge of the scene. Jack was at the hospital with his wounded agents. The men gave her a rundown on the night's events. She and Jessie had watched some of it on the CCTV feed in the panic room. Fortunately, only the cameras nearest house were fed into that room.

Jessie and kids were having breakfast in the panic room. Everyone else was meeting in the dining room. Thery broke out into three groups. They decided not to wait for the forensics people to get started. The first team worked the outside and grounds. They did not move any of the bodies. They just covered them with tarps. They photographed every inch of the outside. Yellow numbered markers were put out to show where shells were found from the various weapons used last night. There were so many of them that one agent commented it looked like a field of dandelions. The brass was picked up, marked, and bagged for the evidence people. Footprints were marked with blue and covered so the forensics people could cast them.

Meanwhile inside the house the second team took pictures and collected evidence. Mrs. James was concerned for the children. She wanted to get the mess cleaned up so they wouldn't see it when they came out of the panic room. After everything was documented, taped, and bagged they set to work cleaning.

They couldn't get the blood stains out of the furniture, so Mrs. James found blankets to throw over them. By the time they were finished the only telltale signs of the firefight in the house were the broken windows. The team who had gone to take care of the animals would bring back plywood to cover them once they were finished.

Leon and the third team were in the barn looking for anything the intruders may have left when they heard a noise from the tack room. They drew their weapons and cautiously approached the door.

"Federal Agents! Come out of there!" Leon shouted. There was no response, but they could hear labored breathing.

Leon tried the door. It was unlocked. He opened it slowly and jumped back when the person inside fired at them. The round landed in the door jamb where it splintered the wood hitting one of the agents. He screamed and fell back holding his arm. The remaining agents let loose with a barrage of fire. There was a scream and then nothing. Everyone stopped firing and Leon stepped into the room. The man was sitting on the far side of the room. He was unconscious and bleeding but not dead. Leon radioed for the emergency people to return and pick him up along with the injured agent. As the EMS pulled up the coroner's van pulled up behind them.

The rest of the search turned up plastic disks with small, red, cellophane holes in the middle that fit onto the lens of a flashlight they found. That was what the red pin lights were. They also found pictures of Jessie and Irving near the tack room. In the stall where they had secured the captured operative, they found a picture of Valient. It must have fallen out of the prisoner's pocket while he was struggling with the agents. They searched the hayloft and stalls and found nothing more of interest. Leon noted that the stalls were in bad need of cleaning.

They fed the animals and opened the chicken coup before returning to the house. The horses were left in the paddock near the barn. Leon's team forgot the plywood. Two agents were sent back to get it.

Mr. Pete made a quick lunch of sandwiches and chips with the "best iced tea this side of heaven".

That was his own description but everyone at the table concurred. It was like a party the kids decided because there were so many people, but no one was smiling today. The Crime Scene Unit and coroner's people had been invited to join them before they started processing the scene. They reasoned they had to eat sometime and since it was all prepared, they could take a few minutes to eat. The drivers took theirs with them to get the bodies back to the morgue.

On his way back to Charlotte to question the prisoners Agent Ike called Jack for an update on the wounded agents. He called three times before Jack picked up.

"Sorry, sir. I was being stitched up. The doctor saw blood dripping from my shirt. I was hit in the side and didn't even know it. They have me fixed up now."

"What about your agents? Status report please." A.C. Ike was impatient to get back to the interrogations.

"We have four treated for relatively minor wounds. They were stitched up and given tetanus shots. All refused to be held overnight for observation. They are hanging out here waiting to find out about

Sandy Gates. He was the only one critical. He's in surgery. I'll let you know when we have any update." Jack sounded relieved and anxious at the same time. "What about your end? If I may ask sir."

"The captured agents are alive but all at CMC Main. We lost one more in the tunnel." Agent Ike told him. "The rest of the team is fine. Just a few minor injuries. We have Shultz in custody. He's been wounded but is going to live. We have three dead suspects and have four more in custody. We're on our way to interview them now."

Jack would call again when Agent Gates was out of surgery. A.C. Ike told him to relay to the other wounded agents his concern and to thank them for a job well done.

# CHAPTER 42

As the FBI forensics team was processing the farm Detective Shot reported in to the Chief of Police on his way home to get some much needed sleep. He updated him on the raid at the FBI safe house and subsequent rescue at the Shultz compound. The Chief sent A.C. Ike his condolences on the loss of his agents.

"Which of the informants told Shultz the location?" The Chief wasn't sure he wanted to know.

"Sorry, sir, we're pretty sure it was Captain Kate."

"I was afraid of that." was all the Chief said.

"Has a court date been set for Yats and Attics, sir?" Detective Shot didn't want them to get lost in the mix between the local and federal cases.

"You weren't notified?" the Chief asked.

"Notified of what sir?"

"Yats is dead. He fell, or was pushed, over a third-floor railing on his way back to his cell from chow two days ago. Broke his neck. The jail is still investigating."

"How could that happen? He was supposed to be isolated! How was he in the general population?" Shot was devasted. "And what about Attics?"

"The order for him to be released from isolation was requested by you according to the records. Seems you changed your mind. He put up a big stink about it, but they wouldn't let him call you. He was waiting to see his P.D. the next day. Attics is out. A new private attorney showed up to take over his case and managed to get the charges dropped. Cited his lack of criminal record and no involvement in the actual crimes. He now denies everything he told you. Says he was visiting Shultz when you arrested him. He's been out for four days now."

"Sir, I never gave any such order. Somebody forged the record." Shot was really mad now.

"I'll check with the warden to get that cleared up. Doesn't really matter now does it?"

There went his case against Carla Shultz. It was weak to begin with but with both accomplices gone there was no case at all. He didn't think Attics was going to show up again. The chief didn't mention it, but Shot was thinking he was now on borrowed time with the FBI. His case was dead in the water. It was all federal now.

He was in his office at the police station the next afternoon when the call came in about and explosion at the James' address. I thought everyone was still at the farm he thought to himself on the way out the door.

A.C. Ike was having a bit better luck. With the help of Buddy and Washington he had obtained valuable information on the people from the Shultz house. Each one had a past that Buddy ferretted out in their thoughts. The questions posed by Agent Ike brought memories to their minds they could not control. Each one was read by Buddy and transferred to Valient to write in the notebook Agent Ike had given him. The suspects didn't know what they were doing. The suspects were told he was a recorder for the FBI because the video feed wasn't working. It amused them no measure the unorthodox way they were obtaining so much information. Knowing full well not only would they not be believed but they would be committed to the nearest looney bin! Not to mention fired.

Luke and Carla Shultz, as well as all the others, were charged with numerous counts of murder of a federal officer, conspiracy to commit murder, and attempted murder of a federal officer. That was just the beginning. Their attorney was definitely going to earn that huge retainer they paid her every year. And then some! Buddy saw the pictures of the victims Detective Shot had cold cases on when Agent Ike mentioned their names. When they passed on that information to Shot. He was thrilled at first but when Shultz didn't cave, he was afraid he was back to square one. It seemed to be enough for him that the other charges were so much easier to prove. Shultz was looking at the death penalty with the federal charges. He could only die once unfortunately. You take what you can get sometimes. Luke Shultz stayed arrogant and uncooperative.

Carla, on the other hand, was singing like the proverbial canary! She told about the local murders to which she had accompanied her father. She was looking to make a big deal with the District Attorney. She thought if she told all she knew she'd get immunity and witness protection. They let her think that for as long as it took to finish her story. The deal she received was far less lucrative. Life without a possibility of parole was the best her layer could get the federal prosecutor to consider. And she would have to testify against her father. Carla was devasted! She had signed her own death warrant, and no one could help her. Just telling the police what she had told them was more than her father would tolerate.

For the next weeks Agent Ike and his team would take the information supplied by Buddy and research the dates and countries. When the corresponding cases were found, they re-interviewed the prisoners. When confronted with the truth of her crimes some of them confessed readily. Those with foreign warrants were threatened with extradition. Only one called the bluff and got disappointed. With deaths of federal officers, no one was going anywhere. They were looking at the death penalty and Agent Ike and his people would do everything in their power to see they got it.

The guests at the Cherryville farm were very grateful and grieving for all the scarifices the people guarding them had suffered. Jessie was inconsolable. All the events of the last few months were more than she could comprehend. How had things gotten this far? Her husband was dead, her sister was sequestered God knows where for her embezzling husband's crime and Valient, the children, and Mrs. James were put in harm's way because of her. And now people were dying to protect them! How could anyone cope with all this?! She ended up in her room under sedation. Irving stayed with Sarah in the front room playing with their treasures. Neither one of them were talking much after the adults met when lunch was done.

The party the children envisioned was very subdued. Lunch was eaten quickly so the adults could go about their business. When Jessie left the dining room with Mrs. James and a female agent holding on to her, Irving got scared. Mr. Peter gave the kids a forbidden treat of pie and chocolate milk. That got a least a small smile from both of them.

The 'space people' -the name the children had given the forensic people-left to start on the outside as soon as they finished up their sandwiches and fruit. They left a 'space suit' for each of the children, along with a couple balloons hands made from the rubber gloves. The kids were distracted for the rest of the day.

It took the rest of the day and part of the night to finish processing the farm. On top of the pictures the agents had taken the forensics people had taken many more of their own. The amount of spent ammo and blood specimens was intimidating to the uniniti- ated. Everything as finally completed in the wee hours as the vans were loaded and evidence stashed to be processed at the lab.

# CHAPTER 43

MRS. JAMES SUGGESTED ARRANGEMENTS BE made for her, Jessie, and the children to go back to her home now that the threat had been neutralized. She saw no reason to stay beyond the next morning. The agent left in charge contacted Jack. A detail would be assigned to take them back some time the next day. Jack seemed relieved to get that part of his responsibilities taken off his plate.

After breakfast the next morning Mrs. James helped the children pack up their treasures. They searched the whole house making sure they didn't leave anything behind. The children had mixed feelings about leaving. They would miss the horses and chickens. Mr. Peter feigned his feelings being hurt when he wasn't named in that group. The kids tried to redeem themselves by running to him and giving him their version of a bear hug. To show his forgiveness he gave the each a bag of goodies and told them not to tell. Mrs. James pretended not to notice.

Jessie still was not well. All the stress and emotions had taken their toll. She was barely aware of the world around her. Mrs. James was worried. What would happen to her and Irving? Jack had returned to the farm to see them off. He and Mrs. James discussed possible solutions to the problem. Finally, it was decided Jessie and

Irving could stay with Mrs. James for as long as needed. She had seen this kind of thing before in her work with battered women. Jessie had a form of P.T.S.D. or Post Traumatic Stress Disorder usually associated with military combat veterans. It was arranged to have a psychologist friend of Mrs. James come to the house to see Jessie when they got home.

Valient had returned just as Mrs. James and the children were packing up the SUV. He decided to join them in leaving. He too was anxious to sleep in his own bed. Buddy liked the idea too. She looked at Jessie and whined. Valient and Mrs. James saw Jessie's picture in their head. "She's just sad, girl. She'll be alright in a while." Valient told the dog.

Buddy didn't seem convinced. She kept showing them pictures of Matt and a woman and looking at them expectantly. Then she showed dead bodies. The dog was rubbing against Jessie, trying to get her to acknowledge her. Jessie just looked down and stared.

Buddy finally lay down near Jessie and watched her. When it was time to leave the dog jumped in the van between Irving and Jessie. Valient tried to get the dog into the third-row seats, but she wouldn't budge. Sarah's car seat had to be moved to accommodate the dog.

The trip back to Parkville was a quiet one. The children slept most of the way. Jessie just stared out the window. Mrs. James and Valient tried to keep up a conversation with the driver, but it was difficult from the back seat and the children sleeping. They abandoned it quickly and rode in silence.

They reached Mrs. James' house first. The driver and Mrs. James started to the door to check out the house. Valient and the other agent started taking suitcases out of the back.

"Put them back!" the agent hollered from the front porch.

"What now?" Valient shouted back.

"Mr. Washington, stay there. Mrs. James, I need you to stay outside." the agent named Carol said.

"What's wrong?" Mrs. James dropped the bag she was holding as she tried to look around the agent.

"The house has been broken into. Looks like the first floor is a mess. You need to see if there's anything missing after I check it out." Carol said quietly so Jessie couldn't hear her.

The other agent was calling Jack on his cell phone.

The kids were waking up and calling for someone to get them out of the seats. Jessie was just watching what was going on around her without really seeing anything.

Buddy had run into the house. She met the agents just inside the door. They were dragging a box. "What's that girl?" Mrs. James asked her from the door. She next saw a picture of smoke and flames. Buddy jumped on her practically knocking her over.

"GET OUT OF HERE NOW!" Mrs. James shouted. They all ran down the stairs and into the car. Just as they closed the doors the front door erupted! It wasn't a huge explosion, but the front of the house was in flames. The blast wasn't powerful enough to reach the car, but it would have killed anyone in the house.

They called 9-1-1 and pulled the car up the street to get it out of the way. Jessie was hysterical, trying to get her seatbelt unfastened in a panic. Thankfully she was so clumsy she couldn't get it off. Valient grabbed her hand and rocked her in his arms until she calmed to quiet sobs. The children were crying by this time too. Mrs. James was trying to calm them as well. Carol had stayed while the other agent ran back to the house to meet the fire department and EMS.

Valient looked over Jessie's head at Mrs. James and started to laugh! "What the hell is so funny?" As she got it and started laughing too. Carol was looking at them as if they had suddenly grown two heads. Then she understood. They were hysterical as an emotional response to absurdly intense situation. She had read about this. She did study psychology but wondered if she'd ever be a witness to it. In a few minutes they calmed and wiped their eyes.

"Sorry, Carol. This is so ridiculous! We couldn't help ourselves." Mrs. James said trying to catch her breath. She smiled at Valient. "Where do we go now?"

"We could try my house. I have the room and it's close to here for the cleanup detail. We are assuming this was planted before last night's escapades?" Valient volunteered.

Carol spoke up. "First thing we are going to do is call A.C. Ike. He'll tell us where we are to go now. You are still under my care you know."

Mrs. James and Valient just looked at each other. "A bit up tight, isn't she?" Valient said just loud enough for Mrs. James to hear. She bowed her head and smiled at him. The children had calmed while the adults had their laughing fit and ended up laughing with, them not knowing why. At the moment they were staring at the adults. Buddy was showing pictures of the farm and Valient's house. She was trying to ask where they were going to.

Jessie looked like she had fainted. Mrs. James asked Carol to call the EMS to get her to a hospital. When they got there and put Jessie on a stretcher, she screamed for Irving. Mrs. James tried to tell her he was fine, but she kept screaming. They finally gave her some kind of shot to calm her.

Valient stayed with the children while Mrs. James went to the hospital with Jessie and Carol. The other agent had returned to the car to be with them. Agent Ike sent two more agents to check the house and talk to the emergency personnel there. Detective Shot pulled up as the ambulance left.

"You all right?" he asked Valient.

"We're fine, but Jessie is totally freaked. They had to give her something to calm her. Mrs. James went with her to the hospital. He friend the psychologist is meeting them there." Valient looked at the kids. "We should find someplace to keep these kids. I'm sure the street is no such a good place."

"Since it's close how about your place? Agent Ike can meet us there." Shot suggested.

"Good idea. We thought the same thing. Let's hope no one left any presents there." Valient crossed his fingers.

The FBI agent drove them to Valient's house with Detective Shot following them in his own car. Shot phoned Agent Ike from the car on the way. He had already spoken to his agent on scene and knew most of what Shot told him. He agreed they should stay at Washington's at least for now. He was still knee deep in interrogations so he wouldn't be meeting them. He would get updates from his people. He did say he'd have agents stay a Washington's and at the hospital just in case anything else happened. They were all praying this would be over and done with soon.

When they reached Washington's house the agent and Detective Shot checked it out thoroughly before letting Valient and kids in. Buddy had been locked in the car while it was being checked. They wanted to be the ones to find any more presents that may have been left. Fortunately all was well.

They got the kids and all their gear in with no more problems. Valient ordered pizza and an agent went to pick it up. No one wanted any more unexpected visitors. They were all paranoid. The kids took their treasure suitcase into the corner and got settled playing with Buddy. The men settled in front of the TV.

Mrs. James and Carol showed up a couple hours later. Jessie had been given a strong sedative and wouldn't awaken until morning. The doctor sent Mrs. James and Carol to get some much needed rest themselves. Another agent was parked outside of Jessie's room. The kids were already sacked out in one of the empty rooms upstairs with Buddy guarding the door.

The adults sat around having a much needed beer and discussing the events of the past few days. All were wondering why the bomb at Mrs. James' place. If the Shultz's knew where they were, and they obviously did, why blow up the house? Did they expect Jessie to return there before the raid? Again, it made no sense. When was the bomb put there? From past cases where Shultz was suspected any kids were gotten out of harm's way before any violence occurred. The bomb would have killed them all. Again, it made no sense if Shultz or his people had put it there. They weren't any closer to an answer an hour later. They decided tomorrow would be a clearer day and went to bed.

Valient had two more bedrooms upstairs and Detective Shot thought the couch would be comfortable enough. They checked the doors and windows, set the alarm and said good night.

# CHAPTER 44

Agent-in-Charge Ike finally finished the initial interrogations. There was enough information to keep the courts busy for the next twenty years. He was savoring a much needed cup of strong coffee, relaxing with his feet propped up on his desk. That is where Jack found him the following Monday.

Jack had come from the hospital where he checked on Agent Sandy Gates. Gates was still in the I.C.U. but was being moved to a regular room later that day. He and Joe were the only agents still in the hospital. Joe's hip bone had been broken by the bullet. He was looking at a stint in the physical rehab unit before going home. Both would be okay.

Funerals for the agents killed at the farm and Shultz's compound were to be held in the next few days. It was a part of the job no one looked forward to.

Jack gave A.C. Ike an update to the repairs to the farm. "The furniture came in yesterday. The windows were repaired late the day after the raid." her reported. "They broke through the storage shed back wall, so it needed to be replaced, the interior was trashed. For whatever meanness, they put sugar in the tanks of the mower and tractor. That had to be cleaned out. We lost two horses before we realized the water troughs were poisoned. Who does that? Leon wants to be on the firing squad for those bozos."

"I'll pass that on." Agent Ike said with a chuckle. "So, the rest of your team is doing okay? Have you all finished or at least made appointments for your after action interviews?" A.C. Ike hadn't read the reports yet. He was going to catch up this afternoon.

"Yeah, we're done. Everyone has been declared fit for duty. I don't think Leon told them about the magic dog, though. They let him come back to duty. For the record, I didn't mention it either. I like my job. It's still something I can't get my head around. It's got to be some kind of trick. Why did you buy into it?" Jack looked at him with a challenge in his eye.

"I know you think it's all smoke and mirrors even if Buddy gave you a firsthand show and tell. But I found out very young that you have to keep an open mind with things you can't explain. My Aunt Dee has some spooky way of knowing things. It drove the family nuts, but everyone called her when they needed to find stuff. I don't pretend to understand it."

"Well, I'm not even going to try, seeing that I'm done with them now. I'm not even gonna think about that animal. How is Mrs. Stevens doing? Any word?"

"She's still in the hospital psych ward. They've got her on some heavy meds and are trying to get her back to earth. Mrs. James is keeping the boy for now. Washington and she take turns going to see her. The doctor says she's taking a mental vacation. It's a pretty good description."

"Has Detective Shot got anywhere with the bombing at the James' house?"

"Not that I know of. We have an agent assigned to work with him, but so far nothing's popped. I'm convinced it was put there shortly after the attempted break-in as a backup plan. It was rigged with a timer attached to the front door. When the door was opened, it was to go off a minute later. Thet would give whoever came in time to get all the way inside. It was supposed to be escape proof. It's a good thing the dog found it. Otherwise, Mrs. James and Agent Cree would be dead too."

"The dog again! We should give her a medal." Jack said sarcastically. "Do you have anything for us? If not, we'll be on stand-by and getting our house in order. Are you going to replace Joe or just wait until he's fit for duty again?"

"For now, we'll just hold off and see how long the doctor intends for him to be out. There's no rush. I'll keep you posted. Anything else I can do for you?" Agent Ike was ready to be back to his paperwork.

"No, we'll wait to hear from you. Oh, are we going to replace the horses we lost?"

"I'll ask the director. My budget is a disaster after this last operation. Probably not too soon."

"All right. You know where to find me. Goodbye, sir." Jack left and headed back to the homestead, as he called it.

Agent Ike pulled off the folder from the top of the pile. Looking at the pile, he thought he was going to be here awhile. With a sigh, he got to work.

Three hours later, he was halfway through. He called it a night and left for home. On the way he stopped at the hospital to see his agents and check on the Steven's woman.

Jessie looked pretty good considering. She was in the dayroom looking out the window. When he called her name as he approached, she stiffened.

"Agent Ike, right?" she asked quietly.

"That's right. How are you?" He noticed she was shaking slightly.

"I don't' really know. I can't stop shaking. I cry a lot. How is all this happening to our family? We never hurt anyone. Matt didn't deserve to die. He was a wonderful husband and father. Why is he dead? Do you know?" she started to cry softly.

"I didn't mean to upset you, Mrs. Stevens. I wish I had answers for you. But sometimes there aren't any good ones. Bad people do bad things to good people. They don't always need a reason." Agent Ike tried to console her in some way. "Is there anything I can get you? Anything you need?"

"No, Mrs. James and Valient have been very kind. They are taking care of Irving. Did you know that?" She looked so sad. He wanted to do something, but he knew there was no one who could help her but herself right now.

"Yes, I know. Things will be okay, Mrs. Stevens. You're grieving finally. Take the time you need. Let it run its course. You can work through it. Please let me know if there is anything I can do." He left her as she turned back to the window, effectively dismissing him.

He received a friendlier reception from his agents. Agent Gate's family was visiting when he arrived. They were having a belated birthday celebration for his ten-year-old daughter. She was mad because her daddy got shot on the birthday and ruined her stay-over party. But she was prepared to forgive him because he promised to take her on a date when he got better. Agent Ike asked her where they would go but she wouldn't tell him because Mom might get jealous. Mom rolled her eyes at that and laughed. He declined a piece of cake and left them to celebrate.

Joe was ready to be gone. He hated hospitals and wanted out. Knowing he couldn't walk yet didn't do much to stem his impatience. He was worried about his job, the animals, and his family. Agent Ike assured him all was well. His job now was to heal. He asked when they were going to move him to the rehab unit. Joe wasn't sure but thought it would happen in a few more days. "And they better hurry up about it." he insisted.

When Agent Ike told him about the horses he asked if they still used firing squads and how could he be on it. "Leon said the same thing." Agent Ike told him, laughing. He felt the birthday cake Agent Gates sent to Joe and told him he'd be back to check his progress soon.

On his way home he called Detective Shot to see if he had time to meet with him. They decided to meet at the diner. Both were single and had no one waiting for them and neither one had eaten. Something was bugging Agent Ike about the bomb at the James' house. Maybe Detective Shot could help him make some sense of it.

They had finished eating and were relaxing with the coffee. Agent Ike was telling the detective about his nagging uneasiness concerning the event at the James' place.

"I've been wondering about the kids, too. Everything I know about Shultz leads me to wonder if he had anything to do with it. I know he denied it when he was questions but then that's what we expected him to say. He was adamant he would never harm a child or put a kid in harm's way. Every case he had been a suspect in, those involved kids they have been isolated out of harm's way before any kind of violence happened. It doesn't sound like his M.O. Why would he change now?" Shot was saying.

"I agree with the idea he wouldn't change without a very good reason. But who else could be at work here? We have all the players in custody. The only one not accounted for is the houseman. Think he might be behind this?" Agent Ike didn't sound like he believed it was a possibility.

"He's been with Shultz for a good many years. I suppose it's possible. A motive being revenge for the raid going to hell?"

"I haven't had a chance to sift through all the files on this yet. There might be something on my desk that will have some answers. Where are Mrs. James and Washington staying now?"

"They're still at Washington's place. Mrs. James' house won't be totally repaired for another month. I think Washington is enjoying having her there doing the cooking. I'd swear he's gaining some weight. The kids love the crazy dog." Shot reported.

"What's the deal with Washington anyway? I get the feeling there's more to him than just a pretty face." Shot watched the agent's face blanch just for a second.

"All I can say is you're right. There is more to him than meets the eye. I can assure you he's legit. He'll take care of business when it's necessary. You can trust him with your life. I do. I can't and won't say more than that." Agent Ike gave him a *don't push it* look.

"Okay, I will take your word for it." He dropped the subject.

It was getting late as they finished the last of their coffee. "I'll call you if I find anything on the houseman. Otherwise, we'll talk again after the funeral on Friday." Agent Ike took his leave and headed home finally.

# CHAPTER 45

Valient and Mrs. James were watching TV with the kids after supper when Micco called. "Nice to know you're still among the living." he greeted Valient. "When you gonna come see us? There's been no excitement since you left town."

"How about tomorrow? I'm getting a case of cabin fever here. We have a lot to talk about. I could come around two when you take your break." Valient suggested.

They were sipping cups of Micco's special coffee in the apartment front room. Valient had filled him on the last couple of weeks. Micco couldn't believe Valient took part in a firefight!

"I knew you were a nut case but that's extreme, even for you. Why? You develop a death wish you failed to mention?" Micco looked at his friend, sure he'd become certifiable.

"Sometimes things happen. Self-preservation is one hell of a motivator. When faced with the fact that someone wants to kill you, choices become limited. Remember when we were in school and that jerk, Coolie, was picking on Angie? We didn't walk away then and I'm not smart enough to walk away now."

Valient became pensive. He couldn't tell Micco the whole truth and felt bad about that. His reasoning was sound though. It always came down to kill or be killed.

"So what now?" Micco was asking.

Valient came back from his private world to answer him. "For now, they stay with me at the house. Mrs. James's place won't be habitable for another month. Jessie Stevens, that's her last name I know now, is still in the hospital recuperating so the kid needs to be looked after. So, for now we have to look to each other to keep it together."

"I thought the killers were all locked up. So you can get back to normal, right?"

"The ones we know about, yeah. We are not out of danger. I guess I'm just a little gun shy still. I can't help looking over my shoulder. I'm told it gets better though, just gotta keep living. The kids are cool to have around. They came through this whole ordeal better than the adults, I think. Irving, that's Jessie kid, misses his mom, but other than that he's just a normal five-year-old. I'm gonna miss them when the house is done."

"I guess that's a good thing. But you need to get your life back, buddy. You start looking for that job yet?" Micco thought Valient needed to get moving.

"Not yet. I'm thinking law enforcement. I already know how to shoot people." Valient joked.

On the way back to his house, Valient got a feeling of being watched. He literally kept looking over his shoulder. Of course, he didn't see anything out of the ordinary, but he couldn't shake the feeling. He didn't bring Buddy with him and felt vulnerable.

When he got home, he called Detective Shot. "I know I'm probably letting my imagination run away but I'd swear I was followed when I was out today. You're sure this mess is finished, right? We're safe now?"

"The Shultz's are locked up tight. The operatives were all hired guns and are out of circulation. It's over. Relax. It may take some time to put this behind you. If it continues maybe you should call the therapist I told you about. You've been through a lot too. It's no wonder you're feeling like you do." the detective assured him hoping he was telling the truth.

"Thanks. I guess I am just being overly sensitive. I don't think I gave you my personal thanks for all you've done these past weeks. I know it's your job but I'm alive and appreciate it. Hopefully we won't be seeing so much of each other professionally from now on. No offense. You're always welcome to come share a beer anytime though." Valeint felt a bit better but couldn't totally shake his uneasy feeling.

"I'll take you up on that. Take care of yourself. Call if you need to." Detective Shot hung up and turned to the FBI agent sitting across from him.

"Washington thought he was followed today. Was that any of your people?"

"Not that I've been told. I'll check with the A. C. and let you know." He left to get back to his office. He was tasked to use the federal resources to research the bomb from the James house, including the material used and the timer set-up. See if there were any cases with similar scenarios.

It was late the next day when Detective Shot received a call from the new captain. A body has been found in Lake Norman. I want you to handle it. Someone thinks it may be related to the Shultz situation. They are processing the scene now. You should get out there."

"I'll leave immediately. Sir, why do they think it's related to my case?" Shot thought he should have at least an idea of what was going on.

"He's been identified tentatively as the missing houseman, Craft. I'm not sure who made the connection, but you can get that from the scene."

"Thanks, sir. I'm leaving now." Shot gathered what he needed and left for the lake.

The coroner was just getting to the scene when Detective Shot pulled up. The body was laying on the boat ramp, wrapped in what looked like a bed sheet. The technicians were taking pictures and taking various samples of whatever they deemed important. Shot thought they sometimes took things just to have something to look at in the lab. It always seemed their idea of being thorough was overkill to him.

He stepped up near the body to look it over before the techies took it away. The guy was shot in the forehead. He also had cuts and bruises on the chest and face. Someone worked him over pretty good the detective thought. "Who identified the body?" he said to no one in particular. He looked around at the people milling about.

"I did, sir." A patrolman walked over to where Shot was standing.

"Why are you so sure of the identity?"

"I dated one of the maids who worked at the Shultz house for about a year in high school. He looks like the guy who was always kicking me off the property when I dropped her off after our dates. He even threatened me with castration if I touched the girl. He was very protective of the employes she had said. You remember someone like that." the kid said.

"Okay, thanks. Make sure that gets in your report. Good job, patrolman."

Shot walked over to where the coroner was working over the body. "Any idea when he was killed?"

"I'd say a couple days. I'll know more later when I've had a chance to work my magic." He smiled at Detective Shot. It was a running joke that the man was a corpse whisperer. That's how he got his answers from the corpses.

"I'll be waiting for your report with bated breath." Shot said sarcastically but with a smile.

He talked to the sheriffs who had fished the guy out of the lake and then with the fisherman who had discovered the body. When he had all the information he was going to get, he left to call Agent Ike.

"The Shultz's houseman, Craft, was just fished out of Lake Norman." Shot told him after the preliminary hellos.

"What have you got so far?" Agent Ike gave him his complete attention.

"The guy was identified by a patrolman. He had been shot once in the head after being beat up pretty bad. The coroner thinks he's been dead a couple days. Gave me the usual "I'll know more later' speech. From the pictures, I'm pretty sure it was him. We'll wait for fingerprints to verify though." Shot informed him.

"Any suspects?"

"Just the whole city. The Shultz crew has been in custody too long to be connected if the time of death is right. Something else is going on here. My instinct tells me it's all a part of the same case, but I can't get my head around it yet."

"I hate to sound like a cop cliche, but I don't believe in coincidences either. I'll call your captain to make sure you and Agent Kelly can keep working this together. Keep me informed."

Agent Ike hung up wondering what the hell was happening here. They would have to go back to the beginning to figure this out he thought depressingly.

Agent Ike called his task force in for a meeting. He included Detective Shot and added Valient Washington. Washington's inclusion raised a few eyebrows, but no one questioned the decision out loud.

"It looks like the Shultz case has a new wrinkle." he began. "Either his operatives were not all captured, or we have new players in the game. We need to review all the evidence and interviews. Look over everything." He went on to explain the new events. When he dismissed the agents to their assigned tasks he turned to Washington.

"You know what I want from you right?"

"Buddy and I will help any way we can. She didn't see anything from Shultz that would suggest he killed his houseman. Do you want to re-interview him?" Valient was hopeful.

"I'm not sure he's the doer here. But if we can get some kind of clue from him, even a suggestion of additional players, it would give us some place to start."

"What about the sister's situation? This all seemed to start with her husband's embezzlement. Didn't you say the company her husband worked for have some questionable clients?"

"I have thought about that. Anything's possible. Why would they kill an employee and not go after Shultz?" But Valient could tell Agent Ike had an idea forming here. "What are you thinking?"

"I need to make some calls. We'll meet again with Shultz this afternoon at three." With that Agent Ike picked up the phone.

Valient left to go see Jessie.

# CHAPTER 46

Jessie was just about comatose when Valient got there. Around four in the morning there was an attack on her roommate. A strange orderly had come to work that night. He said he was a new hire. No one questioned him because he seemed to have all the right paperwork. The charge nurse even helped him to fill out he employee information on the hospital computer system.

He had bed check duty for that side of the floor. At the four o'clock check he took a chucks pad from the bed and held it, plastic down, over the woman's face. Her thrashing woke Jessie, and she jumped on him, screaming bloody murder. The other nurses flew in to find the woman not breathing and did CPR. She survived the attack, but Jessie was more withdrawn than before. The orderly was nowhere to be found. He must have escaped by way of the staircase near the room.

"When were the police notified?" Valient wanted to know. He thought they may have come and gone by now. It was after noon.

"We haven't called them yet. We are short staffed and were busy taking care of our patients!" was the indignant reply. "We weren't totally sure Mrs. Stevens didn't do it for some reason."

Valient was incensed! How could no one think to call the cops? Didn't they care one of their patients had been attacked? Or where the orderly had got to right at that time? He called Agent-in-Charge Ike. "I am still at the hospital with Jessie. Her roommate was attacked early this morning. Someone, more than likely an orderly who had disappeared, tried to smother her in her sleep. I can't see any reason to kill her. She's a seventy-year-old with Alzheimer's. I'm thing it was a mistake. Maybe he was really after Jessie. She's about the same size and shape in the dark. Jessie's out of it. They have her drugged. Apparently, she became understandably hysterical when the guy was on the lady. No one called the police or even security!"

"No one even called security? How stupid are they? Any I.D. on the suspect? Can anyone describe him?" Agent Ike's mind was racing. He needed to get Mrs. Stavens out of there. But where?

"When I asked, they each described a white guy with black or brown hair and black, blue, or grey eyes. He's on camera. The nurses say he touched a lot of stuff buy always wore rubber gloves. He said he was germ phobic. He took off through the stairwell. I'm beginning to wonder who are the patients and who are the staff people here." Valent said, exasperated.

"Okay, stay there with Mrs. Stevens. We have to move her if I can find a place. Don't leave unless I say so."

"Gotcha. We could take her back to my place. Problem there is the kids. Do we want them to see her this way? Should we talk to Mrs. James?" Valent suggested.

"I'll call her doctor. Let's see what can be done." Agent Ike was seething inside. "I'm also calling the hospital director. Heads are going to roll here!"

"Good. I'll wait to hear from you." He hung up and sat down by Jessie's bed. She was sobbing softly in her sleep. He took her hand.

For the next few hours, he just held it while she seemed to cling to him with a death grip. She finally woke up near midnight.

"Welcome back." Was all Valient could think to say when he saw her eyes. "How are you feeling?"

Jessie frowned slightly. "That man. He tried to kill Sadie. I couldn't stop him. I tried, but he was too strong." She began to cry again.

"Shh, I know, the nurses told me. You are a hero. Sadie's alive. They put her in a room near the nurses' station. They thought I'd disturb her." Valient gave her a smile.

"I hope she doesn't remember. She is so sweet. Why did he want to kill her?" she whispered.

"No one is sure. Maybe her beneficiary wanted the life insurance faster." Valient tried for a lame joke.

"You are kidding, right?" Jessie said aghast!

"Yeah, I am. Go back to sleep. I'm staying right here until we can figure out a safe place for you." Valient put his hand over her eyes to make her close them. He leaned in to kiss her forehead. He'd wanted to do that for ages, among other things. Good thing for Jessie his father put the fear of God in him about disrespecting women. Maybe when things were normal again, he thought wistfully. All she did was give a small, sad smile.

The next morning Agent Ike found Valient sound asleep in the chair with his head leaning on the bed. Jessie was awake already, looking out the window.

"Good morning, Mrs. Stevens. Feel like a little trip?"

Valient woke up with a start when he heard a male voice in the room, grabbing the handle of the pistol at his side. Instead, he stretched and reached for the coffee Agent Ike was handing him. "So you found a safe house?"

"There's a small sanitarium near Ashville. We've talked to the director there and they have a room." he said as he turned to Jessie. "Mrs. Stevens, I spoke to your doctor. She agrees it would be better for you to be out of here. She is worried about lawsuits, I'm afraid. Your discharge is in the works now. How soon can you be ready?"

Jessie just looked at him. She wasn't quite sure what he was asking her to do.

Valient looked pleased at the prospect. "What made you decide on Ashville?"

"Expediency. Everything is in order. We've used it before." Agent Ike looked pensive. "I'll get a nurse to help her get ready." he said to Valient as he left the room.

While the nurse was working with Jessie, the men went to the lounge. "You have something on your mind. How about sharing?" Valient challenged him.

"I've been thinking of the interviews we did with Buddy present. From your notes, we got the impression this was finished. Did you see something you didn't record?"

"No. I recorded everything Buddy showed me." Valient was a bit put out at the accusation. "Maybe they aren't part of this new set of attacks."

"Don't take offense. I had to ask. But I think you're right. Someone else is at work here. It has to be coming from the sister's situation. That's where I'm going to start." Agent Ike had the good grace to look contrite.

They discussed various ideas over the next twenty minutes waiting for the nurse to fetch them. Finally, she let them know Jessie was ready. Agent Ike and a female agent left with Jessie while Valient headed home. He and Agent Ike would meet the next day to re-interview Luke Shultz.

Luke Shultz glared at the jail guard. "What do you mean my daughter's dead?" he roared at him. "How?"

"She hung herself in the cell. I don't know any more than that." The guard seemed to take a perverse joy in relaying the message. He walked away without saying anything more.

"I want to see my lawyer! You hear me? You get her in here!" Shultz screamed at the retreating guard.

Detective Shot was at his desk in the squad room when he got the news. What the hell was happening here? He was beginning to think Jessie was right, aliens had taken over the world! Carla Shultz was dead and then there waa the situation with Jessie Stevens. He really needed a day off he thought ruefully.

Agent Ike looked at the evidence photos and file of Carla Shultz's suicide. Something didn't look right. Then he saw it written on the body drawing. Her neck was broken, but it was a spiral break. Like what happens when the neck is twisted violently. She was murdered in her cell. Someone was preying on the people connected to the Rolo case.

He grabbed his coat and was out the door in minutes. He was headed for the safe house in Burnsville. One the way he called Washington to postpone their meeting one more time.

Dorothy Rolo was an angry woman. The agent sitting across from her in the front room of this shack could understand the source of her ire. Her husband was grateful for the protection of her family. She just wanted to go home and have her life back. Nothing short of that was going to bring back her peace. Agent Ike felt sorry for her. She was the true victim here.

Rinne Rolo was scared. If 'they' could get to someone in jail, couldn't 'they' get to his family here? Was his brother-in-law's death due to his crime? For the millionth time, he wondered why he was to stupid. How could he ever think he'd not get found out? His wife wouldn't even look at him. Whenever possible in this small space she wouldn't stay in the same room. She kept the kids away, too. The only time he was with them was at mealtime. Dorothy took her meals back to her room to eat. Forgiveness was something that would never be. He refocused his attention to what Agent Ike was asking him.

"Rinne, I know you've given us the financial information from your company. Now I need specific names of the criminal enterprises you kept books for. One, or some of them, are killing anyone connected to your sister-in-law. I am convinced it starts with your situation."

Dorothy left the room. She couldn't take any more of this. Rinne watched her go with tears in his eyes.

"I didn't have the names. Every company I worked with was known by a code. The only ones with actual names were the senior account managers. Accountants were specialized. Account payable to some, accounts receivable to others, and reports were handled by still others. We all sent out our finished part to the account manager to check and pass on to the next step. That way no one had all the information. I got away with the embezzlement because I did actual deposits, as well as receive payment to our company. We had discounts for various clients. Those are the one I could manipulate." Rinne was wondering when Dorothy was going to leave. That's what he was thinking while trying to explain to Agent Ike.

"But you do have files you took. I understand from Agent Clark that you spirited them away in the days before you came to us."

"I gave those to Clark. I don't know where they are now." Rinne felt hopeless.

"Fine, I'll get with him." Agent Ike could see the torture in Rolo's demeanor. "Dorothy asked me to get her out of here. I'm not sure what to tell her right now. You are set to be in Witness Protection next week. She doesn't want to go with you. But before that happens we need to make sure whoever is hunting here is stopped. We don't want anything to happen to you family after you're gone."

Rinne hung his head. "I don't care what happens to me. I've lost everything already. Take Dorothy and the kids where she wants to go. She deserves more than a thief."

"I'll see what we can do to make her comfortable for now. We'll do what we can." he assured the man.

Agent Clark was at his desk when A.C. Ike returned to the offices. "I've been to see your charges." he said without preamble.

"And you didn't tell me? Do you have something I should know?" the agent asked his boss.

"You are aware of the deaths involving the case with Luke Shultz?"

"Yeah, it's the sister-in-law you have in seclusion now, right?" Clark asked.

"Right. But it's become a great possibility that whoever hired Shultz has now hired someone else to get rid of the whole group. I'm not sure how long it will be until your people will be targets. I want these investigations combined. You take lead, but I will be involved. Please put the files from Rolo on my desk later, so I can read them over. We have to figure out who is committing the latest round of murder. I have a great deal of time invested in this. I need to see it through." Agent Ike thought of the dog and Washington. He couldn't let anyone know how he was using them. As Jack had said, he like his job.

Valient and Agent Ike were finally sitting across from Luke Shultz. Buddy sat next to the table studying the prisoner.

"Mr. Shultz, who is killing your people? First your man Craft and now your daughter. Any idea?" Agent Ike did not extend his condolences. He knew he would not be believed at any rate.

"I have many enemies. I don't know any that would attack my family. Most would come directly at me. Believe it or not, there is an honor code we live by. The new generation, however, have no scruples. Inflict as much fear and mayhem as possible is the new way of things. They're no more than common thugs." Shultz said sadly.

Buddy cocked her head. She was showing Valient a man dressed in business clothes. He felt fear surrounding the man. It seems Shultz was afraid. He made a note and showed it to A.C. Ike.

"Who is it you are most afraid of, Mr. Shultz?" Agent Ike asked. "What kind of business is he in?"

Shultz looked at him with narrowed eyes. "It seems you know more than you are letting on, Agent." He thought for a few moments and then replied, "You're not going to believe me. It's Kenneth Stevens."

"Really? What does he have to do with this?" Agent Ike wasn't buying it.

"I told you that you wouldn't believe it. He travels extensively, and if you check his itinerary, you'll see what I mean. He's so arrogant that he doesn't ever use aliases. He was asked to kill his brother first, but refused, of course. He warned the employer not to touch his family, or he'd get even. My daughter either didn't know or didn't care he was the mark's relative. She had only met Stevens once when she was young and probably didn't remember. By the time I got the word it was too late. She had already killed the brother. The Stevens woman contacted Kenneth that his brother was dead. That's how he had realized Carla took the job. I had tried to contact him, but he wasn't available or just not taking my calls. He's not going to stop until everyone is dead, unless by some miracle you can stop him"

"Knowing that why did you continue to come after Mrs. Stevens? Wasn't that teasing a tiger?

"Carla had already accepted payment. We had to finish the job." Shultz said as if it was the most natural of reasons.

Agent Ike really couldn't believe this. Now he may have Jessie's own family with a vendetta. He looked at Buddy and then Valient. Valient made a note that said Buddy believed Shultz. Man, this is a full-blown nightmare, Ike thought to himself.

"Who is still out there stalking Mrs. Stevens?" Agent Ike asked aloud.

"I didn't know anyone was. To the best of my knowledge, my people are all accounted for. Whoever it is isn't working for me."

Shultz was taken back to his isolation cell. Agent Ike wondered if he'd ever make it to trial. Between the assassin and the revengeful cops, his odds weren't good. He didn't feel much compassion for the killer.

# CHAPTER 47

Valient and Buddy were on their way home when Buddy sent Valient a feeling of fear. "What is it, girl?" She was sniffing the air and looking around them. He saw a faceless man with a red aura. "Where is he?" She continued to sniff and look around like she wasn't sure but was on alert.

Suddenly she stopped and began a low growl. Valient saw a man about ten feet away, staring at them. When he realized Valient was looking at him. He turned and bolted. Buddy pulled Valient and took up after him. He dashed up an alley and out of sight. "Who was that, girl?" Valient bent to pet the panting dog, catching his own breath. She showed him a picture of Shultz. "I don't think so. He said he doesn't have anyone after us anymore, remember?" She showed him the picture again with a red aura. "I agree he's dangerous, but Agent Ike believes these are new bad guys. Let's just get home, okay?" She just pulled him along as fast as she could walk.

Detective Shot was in the kitchen with Mrs. James when Valient and Buddy reached the house. "I'm taking you up on your offer of that beer." he said, raising his bottle in a salute. "I hear Jessie is in the mountains for a rest."

"Yup, lucky her." Valient said without too much enthusiasm. "Where are the kids?"

"Playing in the yard, why?" Mrs. James answered with a tilt of her chin.

"There is a new wrinkle going on here. Buddy and I were followed, or stalked, I'm not sure which is more accurate, on the way home. He took off when Buddy spotted him. Agent Ike now knows there is more going on here." He went on to explain what had gone on at Agent Ike's office.

"So now there are two factions at work here. The ones after Jessie and her family and the brother-in-law after the Shultz people. I guess that explains why I haven't been able to reach Ken Stevens. Does that mean the A.C. thinks you and Mrs. James are safe now?"

"I'm not so sure. They were followed again. Maybe the people after Jessie don't know where she is now. Which is exactly what we want, isn't it?" Mrs. James offered. "But will they try a go at us again to find her is the question. I'm thinking probably. At least that's what I would do if I were looking for someone."

"So far all they've done is follow and watch. We'll just have to continue to be vigilant until we know for sure." Valient said hopefully.

"When is your house going to be ready, Mrs. James?" Shot changed the subject.

"The new carpets are being laid Friday. I've been shopping for curtains and furniture. Somehow, I just can't make up my mind on the colors. The last time my house was decorated Sam was still alive. It was easy then. Brown everything in one shade or another. He didn't have much style sense." She smiled at the memory.

"With what's going on, I think we should stay together for a while longer anyway. It'll give you more time to make up your mind. Haven't you been preaching safety for the last month? Besides, how am I going to get along without you to cook for me?" Valient tried to look pitiful.

Mrs. James rolled her eyes and smiled at him. Detective Shot laughed.

Sarah and Irving shot through the door. "What's for supper? We could eat a whole cow!" they hollered.

"You two settle down. No need for all that noise. We can hear you just fine. How about hamburgers and salad? Should we ask Detective Shot to stay, too?" Mrs. James addressed the hooligans.

"Please, Detrecsive Shot?" They couldn't get the word right.

"Sure, and you can call me Mr. Shot, okay? It's an easier word."

"Okay, you like hamburgers?" They didn't wait for an answer before running back out the door.

"They're going to be unhappy when we all get back to our lives. They've become inseparable." Mrs. James said sadly. "We'll all just have to stay friends. That's all there is to it."

Dinner was over and the kids were upstairs getting ready for bed when Buddy started growling at the door. Detective Shot reached for his gun, as did Mrs. James. Valient called through the door asking who was there. He received no answer.

Shot looked out the front room window. There was a man wearing a basball cap pulled low over his eyes. Valient called again, "Who is it?"

This time the man replied, "Washington, I'm Jessie's brother-in-law. I know she's not here, but get Irving, he knows me."

Valient looked to Detective Shot for guidance. He nodded his head. Mrs. James went upstairs to get Irving. They opened the door but kept their weapons in their hands. Even if he was who he said he was, they had reason to believe he'd already killed two people and didn't trust him for a second.

"Uncle K!" Irving launched himself at the man. He caught the boy up in his arms and hugged him. Sarah was coming with Mrs. James, both looked wary.

"Hey little man, what's shakin'?" He kissed boy on the cheek and carried him to the living room. The other adults put the weapons back in the holsters and cautiously closed the door and followed.

Buddy was not pleased. She was showing the danger aura to both Valient and Mrs. James. Valient petted her and whispered for her to lie down. She did but wasn't happy about it. She studied the newcomer. Finally, she settled down. She was showing pictures of Jessie, but not with the danger aura.

Valient saw another man with the danger aura. He and Mrs. James looked at each other. Neither had seen that man before. Who was this now? Why was Stevens there?

"How have you been, little man? Ya miss me?" Stevens was talking to the boy but looking at Valient.

"We had lots of adventures, Uncle K. Then we got to see horses and chickens and even got the eggs to eat! But bad men came, and we had to leave that place. We were gonna go to Sarah's house again, but it blowed up. Mommy got sick and had to go to the hospital. That's why we're here. How did ya find me?" Irving couldn't talk fast enough.

"Wow! Sounds like a busy life, little man. You had some fun times! Horses, you say? Did you get to ride one?" Stevens asked the boy.

"No, we were gonna, but the bad men came before we could. But Agent Ike says maybe we could go back someday, just to visit."

"I see. Well, maybe you can. Who's your friend here?" Stevens leaned to the boy's ear and whispered, "She's cute. She your girl?"

Irving giggled. "That's just Sarah. Me and Mom went to live at her house for a while, and then we all been together stayin' away from the bad people. You gonna stay with us now, too?" He looked at his uncle hopefully.

Stevens looked at the adults. "I have a room already, but I will be around, okay?"

"Okay." Irving sounded disappointed. He didn't push the issue when he looked at Mrs. James' face.

"I need to talk to the big people for a little bit. How about you kids to back upstairs to play and I'll see you in a few minutes. That okay with you?" Stevens asked the children. They weren't too happy, but they did go.

"Where's Jessie?" Stevens asked when the kids were out of earshot.

"She's in a hospital. All the events proved too much, too soon. She's suffering from P.T.S.D. but is in good hands." Mrs. James offered.

"I know some of the *events,* as you call them. I'd appreciate it if you'd fill me in with some details. First, I obviously know my brother's been murdered. I did get to the funeral, but I didn't see Jessie there. Where was she? Second, I know a pro named Shultz was trying to kill her, but he and his idiot daughter were picked up attacking your safe house, along with his hired guns. Who turned out to be not so efficient, thank you for little favors, even though some of the agents were hurt or killed. The daughter is dead by suicide I understand." he said with not a hint of guilt. "Third, someone blew your house up." He looked at Mrs. James. "What have I missed?"

Detective Shot took the lead. "Jessie was in the back of the church. She was too frightened of the people who killed your brother to show her face. Before she contacted you, she was on the run, living on the streets or in shelter to keep away from the killers. I introduced her to Mrs. James here. She'd been there for a couple weeks before Shultz found her again. The FBI got involved and put all of them in a safe house that was compromised. The attack at the farm and then Mrs. James' house being destroyed was the last straw for her. She just shut down. Did you know about the sister's troubles?"

"Yeah, her egghead husband embezzled from his employer. I only met him a few times. Never cared for him really. I hear he's in FBI custody. What's she have to do with Matt being killed?"

"We know now that Matt ran into Carla Shultz at a restaurant where she was negotiating to kill Rolo". He overheard the conversation. Then she tracked him down while he and Irving were having ice cream. A waiter happened to knock into her. Her purse spilled with a picture of Rolo and a gun landing out in plain sight. Matt recognized it and realized who it was when she lied and told him it was her uncle's picture. He must have finally understood what he had overheard previously. She made a meeting with him, but he sent Jessie and Irving away, so she didn't get to them. The rest stems from all that. She claimed she didn't know Matt was related to Rolo. Detective Shot was wondering where all this was going. What is Stevens' agenda?

"So what is going to happen with Jessie and Irving? How long does her doctor think she's going to be in the hospital?"

"For now, Irving is staying with me by court order." She wanted him to know he wasn't walking out of there with the child. "With all that's happened to Jessie, it's going to be hard to say how long she's going to be an inpatient. We're all hoping she recovers soon. The hard part is for regular people to be thrown into these kinds of catastrophic events one after another and not be mentally derailed. Each event alone would be hard enough, but she's been hit with a sequence of events. Some of us are trained to deal with crime and its after effect, most regular people are not."

"To put your mind at ease, Mrs. James, I have no intention of taking Irving. I have no way to care for him, as much as I would love to. But I'll be making sure he is well cared for. I do hope we can come to some understanding." His smile did not look friendly. Mrs. James felt threatened by his demeanor, even if his words were not. Buddy growled low in her throat. Valent and Mrs. James were seeing a red aura. It was silently agreed he could not be trusted.

"She's rather protective, isn't she?" Stevens glared at the dog and got growled at for his trouble. Buddy wasn't intimidated. He laughed. "I like this ugly mutt. I think we understand each other."

"Why are you here, Stevens?" Valient had enough small talk. He wanted a real answer.

"To make sure you all stay alive. No offense to you, Detective Shot, but I'm the only one right now who can guarantee that happens. I don't have the restrictions that the police and like agencies are subject to. There are forces at work here you aren't prepared to deal with." He sat back and let that sink in.

"That sounds very dramatic. What the hell do you mean?" Shot sat forward to emphasize his point.

"That idiot daughter of Shultz opened up a Pandora's box of bad guys. When she failed to kill Rolo and killed Matt instead, she enlisted the help of a wannabe to go after Jessie. He reported her to the cartel for some brownie points. They found out about what Rolo had done, and the whole mess cascaded. Now they are looking for you all and are going to settle up with the accounting firm. They won't stop until they finish the body count or have a better reason to keep you alive. I intend to give them that reason."

"How? What can you possibly do that would make this go away?" Mrs. James's bad guy radar was screaming.

"Trust me, you don't want to know." Stevens smile that smile again. Buddy went ot him and stared into his eyes. "What's she doing?" He asked as he sat back away from her.

"Trying to read your mind." Valient told him with a straight face. "She knows you killed Carla Shultz. And Shultz's man Craft. You tortured him to find Luke before you shot him. You posed as a corrections officer to kill Carla. They aren't the only ones. I count fifteen...no, wait...nineteen from all over the world while you traveled for your equipment business. How am I doing?"

"You play a dangerous game, Washington. Without admitting to anything, there's no way in hell you can have any idea." Stevens squinted his eyes as he looked menacingly at him. Buddy growled and stood between the men.

"You can't use that knife with so many witnesses." Valietn said to him with a smile. Mrs. James chuckled.

Ken Stevens blanched but didn't reply. He looked at the dog. He could swear she smiled at him. He looked at Detective Shop. "He tells good stories, doesn't he? Naturally, I have no idea what he is talking about."

"Naturally." Shot agreed.

"Is it okay if I go upstairs and visit with my nephew for a while? I haven't seen him in forever." Stevens stood and started for the stairs. Buddy intercepted him in the hallway. She studied him for a minute and then moved out of his way, but she followed him to the children's room. "I guess I asked the wrong ones." he chuckled and shook his head as he made his way upstairs.

"What do we do with him?" Valient asked Detective Shot.

They spent the next hour discussing the evening's surprises. It was the general consensus they could only wait to see what happens now. Detective Shot would contact A.C. Ike on his way home.

By the time Stevens came back downstairs they were resigned to the idea they could use all the help they could get. Buddy let them know she didn't think he was going away. None of them had any experience with the kind of people he alluded to.

"I already tucked the buggers into bed. Cute kids. Too bad they have to grow up." he said wistfully. "I won't make a nuisance of myself. But I will be back to see the kid. You may see some strangers hanging around. I'll text you their pictures, so you know they're mine. I will have someone looking over Jessie by tomorrow night. Take this, Washington." He handed Valient a cell phone. "You really need to get one of these of your very own soon. Don't ask how, but I have both your numbers." he said to Detective Shot and Mrs. James. "I'll keep in touch." With that he was out the door.

# CHAPTER 48

VALIENT FELT AN UNEASY SENSE of Deja vu. He had seen Ken Stevens somewhere. He couldn't put a finger on it, but he was sure. Fortunately Mrs. James had thought to get a picture of him on her cell. Bless that lady!

Detective Shot called A.C. Ike from Valient's house. As he filled him in on the strange visit, Mrs. James forwarded the picture. Agent Ike would check him out and get back to them.

Shot left shortly after. He planned on coming back the next day.

Agent Ike called back an hour later to talk to Valient. "You have met with him before. He was part of the unit when you were. I called Major Crike, he confirmed. Look out for him, Washington. After leaving the unit, he started his own covert business. His tentacles reach into places we can't legally go. He's either a great ally or our worst nightmare. We'll have to wait and see. For now, be careful what you share with him."

"He pretty much has the whole picture already. From our conversation tonight, he actually knows more than we do. He knows who is after Jessie. By the way, he says he'll have some looking out for her by tomorrow. How will he find out where she is? I thought you put her under an alias."

"He has resources everywhere. I'll alert the director to let him in. The more people watching, the better. He won't hurt Jessie. I think he's in love with her." The agent tried to sound reassuring.

"He gave me a cell phone. There will be people here watching us too, he said. He'll text pictures to us. We'll make sure we forward them to you. What are you going to do about the murders? He did Cala Shultz and Craft, Buddy showed us."

"For now, nothing. I'll show his picture to the guards, but I doubt if they'll remember him. Our Major Crike says he can get in and out like a ghost. There are no forensics in either case." Agent Ike wasn't totally sure if that was a good or a bad thing. He just hated unsolved cases on his record.

Ken Stevens stood in the shadows near the Burnsville safe house. The operatives from the cartel were lurking not ten feet from where he stood. He could hear their voices in the dark. They had already killed one FBI agent and weren't too worried about any more apparently. Stevens used his owl call to alert his people. Each warble denoted one person. He noted seven around the house.

They started, bold as you please, to walk up to the house. Before they could get more than a few feet, they were attacked by Stevens' people. Very little noise came from them as their throats were cut. One man, who Stevens had deemed the leader, was spared. He was incapacitated and gagged. When they were all accounted for, Stevens called A.C. Ike.

"We just saved you a bit of further embarrassment, Ike. We're outside your not-so-safe house in Burnsville. Tell them to let us in, okay?"

"What the hell are you doing? Why should I tell them any such thing?" Agent-in-Charge Ike was incredulous! What the hell is happening now?"

"We've been watching the house for about a week now. You had visitors tonight. My people neutralized the threat. One of yours is dead. They got to him before we arrived. Sorry. Now, will you let us in? We have one we need to ask a few questions. When we're done you can have him. Fair?" Stevens couldn't help gloating a little. He wasn't a government flunky anymore.

"I have no number to call you back. Your caller ID is blocked. Hold on while I contact the house." Agent Ike put the phone down. He picked up the land line and called the house. "There are men outside. They're bringing in a prisoner. Give them what they need. But keep your people away from them, understand? They are to have no access to the guests. I'll be there in an hour."

He got back on his cell. "They should be opening the door. I'll be right there. Don't leave the premises before I arrive."

"I don't take orders from you, Agent-in-Charge Ike. But I'll be here waiting this time." Stevens growled.

"Major Crike says you do." Agent Ike growled back as he hung up.

Stevens stared at the phone. Now this was a development he didn't expect.

It turns out the dead operatives were only a scouting team. They were supposed to find out how many agents were guarding the Rolo family and what kind of fire power they had. A listening device was supposed to be planted at each window to transmit via satellite. Pretty sophisticated stuff for this kind of operation.

An hour later, they had all the information the prisoner was going to give them. He was having a hard time talking anymore. Agent Ike had arrived after they finished the inquisition. While grateful for the help, he didn't approve of the method.

Ken Stevens was on the back porch, drinking coffee. Agent Ike sat down next to him. So you're acquainted with Major Crike. When?" Stevens asked.

"We overlapped by a few days. I left; you joined. He sends his regards."

"Why don't I think so?" Stevens laughed.

"Well, he says you were good at your job but had a problem with authority. I think I can see that." Agent Ike looked around at the body bags waiting for the coroner.

Stevens followed his gaze. "They didn't want to leave peacefully."

"What happens now? I'll have your report filed by morning. But what is the plan for this family?" Stevens wanted to know.

"The wife wants out. She is hell bent on going back to her old life without him. He's set to join Witness Protection tomorrow. What are you informants telling you?" Agent Ike didn't want to but knew he had to use this guy. Stevens had resources the FBI didn't.

"Not much. We only knew of these losers because we happened to be here. It's quiet."

"What is your plan now?" Agent Ike was hoping they'd just go home. Like that was going to happen.

"We're going to augment your force here, at Washington's and the hospital. Now that I know the score, we work with you. I have a meeting in Venezuela in two days. Hopefully that will get the innocents out of the line of fire. Rinne Rolo and accounting firm are your problem. I'll pass on the intel I get. More than that, I don't know." Stevens finished his coffee and stood.

"Before you go, you should know Washington is one of us. You served at the same time, same place. I told him about you, too. He remembered you, but the missions never overlapped. He's capable."

Stevens acknowledged with a nod but didn't comment.

# CHAPTER 49

DETECTIVE SHOT WAS TRYING TO make some sense of his cases. Nothing was coming together. They knew who was killing who, but they didn't have one shred of evidence on anyone. The FBI side of it wasn't as complicated. The Shultz cases were pretty sure conclusions. Everyone who was there was guilty. End of story.

The building shook violently! What the hell? Was there an earthquake? People were picking themselves up and running to the doors. As Shot made it to the door he saw a building two blocks away crowned in thick smoke. He ran with the other officers toward it to help. People were running away covered with ash and debris.

It was the accounting building! The biggest occupant was the firm Rinne Rolo worked for. The blast shook buildings as far away as five blocks! Sirens were blaring everywhere. The first of the rescue people arrived and it became clear the extent of the damage. The building was a total loss. So were the buildings on either side. Glass from the windows was still flying everywhere. Smoke was billowing from all floors as the fires spread from floor to floor and building to building.

People were streaming from the wrecked doors of buildings up and down the block. Those who weren't badly injured were trying to help those that were. Some poor souls were trapped on upper floors screaming for help. It was total chaos.

Detective Shot grabbed as many patrolmen as he could find. He split them in teams to get some order while waiting for the fire department and EMS people. He wouldn't let any of them run into the buildings. There were already other officers doing that. As much as he wanted to save those still inside, the fire department was their best chance at any survival. They had to clear a path for the emergency vehicles to reach the scene.

Instead, he began corralling the waking wounded away from immediate danger to a makeshift triage area a block away. Those who couldn't walk were carried by Good Samaritans and any rescue personnel on scene. A few police people were wounded by debris but still functioning. Shot put them to work directing traffic away from the area.

The fire department roared on to the scene. Four trucks got to work either suiting up for rescues or pulling out hoses to lay down suppressing foam and water. The captain looked like a ballet dancer spinning around and getting everyone where they needed to be. Radios were blaring instructions a mile a minute. Each new arrival was seamlessly fit into the operation. Despite all the activity at once, it was soon an organized, well-oiled machine. Ambulances were directed to the hastily set up triage area. The EMS people jumped into action separating the minor from major injuries. Those hurt the worst were loaded into the ambulances and taken to the nearest hospital. The already dead were laid out behind a line of dumpsters.

Soon there were tents up with cots for the wounded waiting for transportation. There were so many dead. The area was overwhelmed within minutes. People were walking in circles not sure where to go for help. Blood was everywhere.

The Red Cross set up information tables to help family and loved ones find their missing people. Volunteers were getting names of everyone they could in the medical tents. Others were assisting the technicians from the coroner's office by going through the pockets of the dead for any kind of identification. Still others were assisting crime scene technicians using portable fingerprint scanners to identify those they were able. The lists were updated every fifteen minutes and emailed to the volunteers manning the information booths. Grief counselors stationed themselves at the scene and the hospitals to help the survivors and loved ones of the lost.

Somehow there didn't seem to be enough. Enough medical workers. Enough body bags. Enough ambulances. Enough time. Enough anything. The only thing there was more than enough of was victims. They kept coming and coming. Dead, dying, walking wounded, shell shocked---they were multiplying with no end in sight.

Three buildings were completely destroyed. Each was at least fifteen stories of business in full swing at eleven in the morning. The main blast took out the middle building on the seventh floor. It was powerful enough to blow the top floors to the sky. The floor below caught the back blast. The adjacent buildings suffered extensive structural damage. Windows were blown out for at least a block up and down one side of the street and in a V-shape area across the street. Debris was still falling like soft snow over an hour later.

Detective Shot stood looking at the scene in front of him. Who would be evil enough to cause this kind of devastation? This must be what 9/11 or Oklahoma City looked like. He couldn't process what his eyes were taking in. Was this all because of an embezzler? That couldn't be it. All this devastation had to have a deeper reason. Didn't it? He turned to see Agent-in-Charge Ike moving toward him. He looked shell shocked too.

They spoke for a few minutes. A.C. Ike agreed with Shot's assessment. This couldn't be all because of Rolo. They both hoped they were right. This was truly extreme for a relatively minor crime of embezzlement. But the epicenter was the floor where Rolo's employer's offices were located. It was too much of a coincidence.

It took the rest of the day, all night, and half and next day to clear the victims, living and dead, from the scene. There were still so many people missing. It would take weeks to sift through all the rubble. Only three people were known to have survived from what was thought to be the target accounting firm. Two were going to be okay. The third was in critical condition. The Red Cross kept the tables in the area for one more day and then moved the information desks back to their offices.

Agent Ike was exhausted. He hadn't slept more than an hour at a time for the past four days. His agents were no better off than he was. They had all refused to go home until every person was accounted for. Even they knew it was unrealistic, but it gave them something to reason with.

The director had shown up the evening of the blast with an army of agents. Everyone was getting in everyone else's way at the moment. A meeting of the senior agents was scheduled in an hour. Ike was trying to put together a working breakdown of tasks. He was failing miserably. His mind was so tired. He was on auto pilot. Giving up he took to the couch and was asleep in seconds.

The conference room was full to beyond capacity. All senior agents, representives from all local law enforcement, OSHA, ATF, and even the Secret Service were in attendance. ATF and the local fire marshal were still working on the bomb. Their preliminary findings figured C4 and a lot of it. Where and how it was placed was still complete speculation. No one else had much more of concrete information. Numbers of known dead and wounded were the easy part. More than that was going to take a lot of investigating. Each Department head had some kind of input. A few were even helpful, but most were not.

In the end, the director assigned teams and each team a task. He ordered all of them to go home, go to bed, and not report back until noon the next day. He needed them fresh in order to be effective. The meeting broke up near eleven that night.

Ken Stevens was holding his own meeting that evening. His operatives were also working on adrenalin and coffee. They had been chasing ghosts form Venezuela. So far all they could find was a low-level arms dealer who supplied some of the C4. Not enough to do the kind of damage it needed to take down three buildings, but his contacts were the real dealers. In questioning that would never hold up in a court of law, he shared all the names and locations he had in his rolodex. He didn't know the why of the attack. He was just a supplier. The dumped him at a small animal clinic in Tennessee.

When Rinne Rolo watched the news the day after the devastation he completely fell apart. So much and all because of him, the ripple effect. He went to his room with the bottle of rye from the bar and the bottle of valium the doctor had given his wife. He didn't bother to say goodbye.

# CHAPTER 50

Detective Shot got the call the next morning. Agent-in-Charge Ike wanted him to rejoin his team. It had already been cleared with all the powers needed They would meet for dinner that night after Shot had cleared his desk at the precinct.

"Do you have the number St4evens sent you?" Agent Ike asked as they started to eat.

Shot pulled it up on his cell and forwarded it to Ike. "What do you need him for?"

"I think he has information we desperately need. Rumor has it he's found an arms dealer we should be talking to." His phone rang.

His face blanched as he looked at Detective Shot. He ended the call and said, "Rolo is dead. When he didn't show up for breakfast, no one cared, but when he didn't go to lunch, one of the agents went to find him. He had pills and booze in his room."

"Guilt or what?" was all Shot could think to say. "Why did they wait util now to tell you?"

"I did get a call earlier, but I was in a meeting with the director and didn't answer. I got busy with other things and haven't taken the time to check my messages yet."

"What about the wife and kids? What happens to them now?" Shot looked pensive.

"They get to go home. It was the husband anyone was after. That's what she wanted all along anyway. My agents will be happy. Now they get to join us. According to Agent O'Neil, they are taking them back to her place tomorrow morning."

"She's not wasting any more time, is she?" Shot shook his head.

They had finished their meal. It was time to get going again.

"Report to my office at nine." Ike told Shot. "We'll go over what we have then with the other members of the team. I'm going to get Stevens to cooperate with the investigation to give us anything he has. If we get any real live bodies to interview, I'm going to bring in Washington to cut some corners. If we can"

The men parted ways about nine o'clock. Neither went straight home.

Agent Ike called Ken Stevens as soon as he got on the road. "What have you got for me?" the agent asked without preamble.

"Great timing. I was just calling you. The dealer we questioned was a lower level than we originally thought. We got what we could from hm and gave him to a vet in Tennessee to fix up. I thought it was a nice touch." He smiled to himself.

"Did he give you anything useable?" Agent Ike was not in the mood for humor.

"A few more names we're checking into. We think we have located two. My men are on it as we speak. It's going to take time to go up the food chain. I'll get you answers as quick as we can." Stevens abruptly ended the call.

Detective Shot stopped at Washington's on the way home. He wanted to see Mrs. James. She knew street people who may be able to ferret out rumors. Rumors can lead to real information. Information sometimes leads to actual evidence. It was a straw worth grasping at.

Mrs. James agreed to make some calls. She knew one person in particular who could find out almost anything. She was the first call. Mrs. James invited her to lunch at Micco's just to be somewhere she felt safe.

Valient called Micco to bring him up to speed on their plans. All was set for them to be watched. Buddy was going to accompany Mrs. James.

Micco set them up just outside the door where they could be watched by the staff without interference. Buddy was treated like royalty. Mrs. James smiled at the picture the dog was showing.

Her guest showed up a few minutes later. She didn't look like a street person. She was beautiful and dressed rather nicely. She was the clerk from the bookstore! She bent to pet Buddy. "I didn't know you knew Valent." she said as she leaned in to kiss Mrs. James' cheek.

"I didn't know you did, either. How do you know him?"

"I work for his father's friend. Valient is a cool person." Ceila said.

They ordered amid the small talk. Then Mrs. James got to the point. "I need a bit of information, Ceila. The explosion from the other day, we need any information we can get. Rumors, speculations, fantasy, we need to know what and who. As you can imagine, the people that count are hyperventilating waiting for any data out there."

"I'll see what's shaking out there. I have heard there's a group from South America who is very unhappy with their cash flow. I'll keep my ears open and keep in touch. Now, tell me how you know Valient." Ceila leaned back in her chair sipping her wine.

"Right now, we're roommates. My house is being remodeled. Sarah and I are keeping him company until it's done."

"Heard about your 'remodeling job'. You still haven't totally retired, have you?" Ceila smiled.

They finished their drinks and parted ways. Buddy didn't find anything more about the attack on downtown than what the woman said out loud. The dog was happy. She always liked Ceila. She did see other things she didn't understand.

"Don't give any of her secrets to Valient, girl. There are some things his parents never told him. Deal?" Buddy sent her a picture of sunshine which she chose to take as a 'yes'.

Dorothy Rolo was glad to be going home. She's had enough of Rinne, the FBI, and confinement. Now that the idiot was dead, she was free. When the funeral was over, she'd find a job and get on with life. The kids could get back to school.

She sat in her own kitchen sipping a much needed glass of wine. The kids were asleep in their own beds. There was a knock on the back door. Who the hell even knew she was home? She went to the window and pulled the curtain back just a crack. Her heart was beating like it would jump out of her chest. "Damn! What's she want?" she whispered to herself. It was her neighbor from next door.

Opening the door just a crack, she said "I'm really tired tonight, Mrs. Rederic. Thanks for checking on us. Can we talk tomorrow?"

"Dotty, (Dorothy cringed. She hated being called Dotty!) I just wanted to tell you I let the cleaners in this morning. They said you wanted the place done before you got home. Call me. Have a good night, dear." She turned and went down the back walk.

Dorothy closed the door. What cleaners? No one mentioned having someone come cleanup she thought to herself. Her cell phone was on the counter. Picking it up, she searched her purse to find the card the FBI agent had given her. She was shaking as she punched in the numbers. "Agent Gilliam, did you have someone come to clean my home this morning?"

"No, ma'am. Why?"

"My nosy neighbor just told me she let a cleaning crew in here this morning. I had actually forgotten she had a key. They told her I wanted it cleaned before I got home. You don't know anything about this?" Now she was nervous.

"No. I am sending someone right now. Get the kids and go with them. Call me when they get there, so you know for sure they are from me." the agent told her. "It may be nothing, but we need to be sure. Once we have you safe again, we'll have the house swept for listening devices or anything else. The agents will be there in a few minutes. Get ready to go."

Within ten minutes, Dorothy was packed and ready to go. She had let the kids sleep until the agents got there. Agent Gilliam verified the identity of the men, but she knew them from the safe house. They were all gone within a half an hour from the phone call.

"I thought we'd be out of danger when Rinne died. Who would want to do us any harm? I'm not a threat to anyone and the kids certainly aren't. I don't get it." she told the agents. "Where are we going?"

"For tonight we're to take you to the Westin. Feel free to have whatever room service you like. We're footing the bill." Agent Ted smiled at her. "I may join you for a glass of wine, if you like."

"Are you flirting with me, Agent Ted?" Dorothy was almost hoping maybe he was. Where did that come from? She wondered to herself. "Or are you just being nice.?"

"Not at all. I just thought you'd like a little company for a bit. I'm not that nice, according to my coworkers." He tried to look innocent and failed when he smiled.

Agent Ted and Dorothy were settled in on the sofa. The kids had gone directly back to bed and were asleep in no time at all. The adults had made good on the promise of a quiet glass of wine.

They were talking and sipping their drinks when Agent Ted's phone vibrated. "I know I should have turned the damn thing off." he growled.

"Gilliam." he answered. He sat up straight. "When? I'm with her now. Yeah, got it." He turned to Dorothy. "I'm afraid there's been another problem. Your house is gone. It blew up an hour ago."

"WHAT??" she screamed at him. "They blew my freaking house??? Who the hell would do that? Rinne is dead!! Can't they just leave us the hell alone?" Jumping off the sofa she almost ran around the room in a panic. She didn't know what to do. She started to cry. Heavy, heart-breaking sobs as she slid to the floor. Now she had nothing left. The agent just watched her not commenting. She wouldn't have herd him anyway. "What are we going to do now?" she whispered when she could talk again.

"We'll get to the bottom of this. One of our agents was injured when it blew. Fortunately, they were just getting ready to go so they didn't have anyone near the building." Agent Gilliam looked like he wanted to blow a gasket himself. These bastards didn't care who got in the line of fire. "I'll be staying with you for the duration. Until we know what's happening here, you're stuck with me." He picked up the wine bottle and refilled their glasses. Handing one to her he said, "Might as well finish this. It's too good to waste."

She looked at him like he had lost his mind for a minute and then clinked his glass with hers. "What the hell. Better order another." she said as she took a long drink.

# CHAPTER 51

VALIENT WASHINGTON, KEN STEVENS, AND Agent Fritz Ike were sitting across from Major Crike in a warehouse office. "Tell me what you think the unit can help you with. You do know you have broken a cardinal rule of this unit? Not only is this meeting irregular, but what you are asking is not unit business, as far as I can see. Where is the national security risk? Not one of our superiors has even hinted we would have an interest here."

"Sir, we know how this is a unit security breach. But we had no choice. Our intel says the people who blew up downtown Charlotte were from Venezuela. They masquerade as a drug cartel and do indeed sell some low-level drugs. But the informants have given us proof they are international arms dealers, military grade weapons. They are supplying all over the world, pirates, insurgents, militias, gangs, oriental triads, and even individuals if they have the price. They must be stopped as soon as possible. CIA and Homeland think it's Al-Qaeda because of the financial angle. It's not, and we can prove it if we get help from the unit. You know how splintered our law enforcement agencies are, even after 9/11. That why our unit was sanctioned. We need the unit to put these terrorists out of business." Valient Washington was taking the lead here. He had been briefed by the other two of the details. In the group, he was the ranking member.

"I see. The thief opened a big can when he chose that firm. I'll be meeting with our boss in about an hour. I'll meet you all here at nine tonight. Don't engage anyone or anything until we get the go ahead. Understand?" Major Crike looked at Valient. "Stay for a minute." He dismissed the other two.

"Are you fit for duty, Washington? I understand this is personal, but I need assurances you're not on a suicide ride."

"Yes, sir. You can check with Ceila, but I can tell you I'm okay. It took getting shot while in that fire fight at the FBI safe house to bring me totally back. Thank the stars for proper flak jackets." Valient smiled and rubbed his chest at the memory. "I freaked at first to be honest. But then my training kicked in, and I was back to my old self. I guess I just had to get back on the horse, as they say."

"Alright. But be warned, I am going to check. I can't have other lives endangered. You understand, I know. Dismissed." Both he and Valient rose to go their separate ways without another word.

By the end of the night, they had the go ahead to use the unit's resources and personnel. Now they could do some real damage to these creeps. Major Crike gave them six names to round out the team. Everyone was set to meet day after next.

They were meeting in the same warehouse two days later. Six men and four women with such specialized talents they only knew each other by reputation. They served in the same unit but had never met. This mission was unique in that sense. Usually, they were working alone with the only constant unit contact. The current person claiming the Major Crike moniker. There have been six of them—men and women—over the past thirty years of the unit's existence. The three new friends were the first group to personally know one another. It was only because they had been thrown together in the sequence of dangerous events that the current Major Crike deemed it necessary for them to be aware of each other.

"You all know what has happened in Charlotte. We are going to find and eliminate the terrorists who pulled that off." Major Crike started the meeting. "You all will be working together for the first time. Make it work. In this mission you are a team. Washington, Stevens, and Ike are the leads on this. They will be assigning your individual tasks. You report to them, they report to me."

He handed the meeting over to Fritz Ike. He brought everyone up to speed and handed the group over to Ken Stevens. Stevens gave each operative their assignments. They were to meet again in one week.

Valient had deliberately kept quiet this time. He really didn't have anything important to say anyway.

They needed to get Detective Shot on board. He couldn't know about the unit's activities, but he would benefit from the results. Valient called him to meet at his house for breakfast the next day.

The four men were finishing their coffee and discussing the cases. They listed what each was working on.

Agent Ike had the Rolo case to finish the paperwork on. It was closed as far as the husband was concerned. Now they had a new case with the attack on the family. His was on the downtown bombing as well. Every agent in the alphabet was getting in each other's way on than one. Only Agent Ike knew where to take it to find the bomber. It was tricky, but doable.

Detective Shot had a part in the downtown bombing case and the new attack on the Rolo family. He also still had no leads on the bombing at Mrs. James' place. The local police were working with the alphabets to help solve the downtown bombing. Shot was frustrated at the lack of cooperation. Each agent was stonewalling the others so they could solve it first.

Ken Stevens had the most to offer. His people were digging into the backgrounds of the few known members of the group they were after. They didn't have to work within the confines the other agencies did. With that they could find more associates and maybe figure out who was so hell bent on destroying everyone connected to these cases. Stevens was sure it was all actually one case. It was the general feeling of everyone at the table.

Valient's part in all this was compiling what everyone else gathered. His expertise was in seeing patterns to solve puzzles. The more information they gave him, the faster he could find the pattern.

Rinne Rolo had given the FBI a valuable list of his company's clients. He had smuggled the files of some and delivered them to Agent Clark, when he gave himself over to his custody. Ken Stevens' people had copies from Ike. They were working out the money trail. Copies were also given to Valient.

The operatives from the unit were travelling to South America. There they would put eyes on the bodies to go with the names Stevens' people were digging up.

# CHAPTER 52

Ceila and Mrs. James were siting once again, at the front table of Micco's patio. Buddy was under the table, savoring her favorite Shepard's pie very noisily. Celia ducked under to quiet her and received a foot full of gravy for her troubles. Mrs. James laughed at the picture of Celia in her head with a bowl of gravy dripping down her shirt.

"Any information I can pass on to our friends? They have been a little stranger than usual. I think they're working on something they can't or won't tell me about. What do you know?" Mrs. James sounded either intrigued or put out. Ceila wasn't sure which.

"What I can tell you is that it's being handled. The things they can't or won't tell you are being used to bring down the terrorists who blew up downtown Charlotte. Stay out of it and play with the kids. You're retired, remember." Ceila sipped a very hot cup of Micco's special coffee. She closed her eyes in delight.

"All right. I'm not sure how I feel about it, though. The cop in me still thinks it's on duty. The grandmother part of me is glad I don't have a part in it. I can't wait to get back in my own home. Valient's been so great to us, but my new bed beckons. Jessie's coming around. Hopefully she will be improved enough for a visit with

Irving soon. He misses her, and I'm sure he wants to be with her."
Mrs. James smiled as she downed the last of her special coffee.

They parted a few minutes later with hugs and air kisses. Mrs.
James and Buddy stopped at the grocery on the way back to the
house. When she came out, Buddy showed her a picture of a man,
the one she had shown her and Valient the night Ken Stevens showed
up. "Is he still here?" Mrs. James quietly asked the dog. She got the
picture again but with the red aura. She stood up and looked around
cautiously. "Let's go." She fished out the cell phone from her purse.
"Detective Shot, I'm being followed. I don't see anyone, but Buddy
knows. Do you have anyone cruising Main Street? Buddy and I are
walking toward Valient's house. Can anyone intercept us?"

"I have someone around the corner. Walk slowly. He'll be there
in a minute. Stay on the line." She heard Shot on the radio giving
instructions.

The car came around a minute or so later. As it slowed, Buddy
pulled on the leash to get Mrs. James going in the opposite direction. It was the guy Buddy kept showing her! "It's him!" she yelled
into the phone. "It's the guy Buddy showed me." She dropped the
groceries and ran.

Detective Shot jumped from his chair screaming into the phone.
"Sarah! Sarah! Answer me!" He stuck the phone in his pocket as
he got into the car. He screeched out of the lot and down to Main
Street looking for Mrs. James.

He finally spotted her just as she turned the corner to Valient's
street. She looked as though she would collapse at any second.
"Sarah! Are you all right?" Shot yelled as he pulled to the curb.
She stopped running and put her hands on her knees to catch her
breath. Buddy was pushing her toward the car. "Get in. I'll take you
the rest of the way."

They rode the last two blocks to Valient's house in silence as Mrs. James composed herself. The kids came barreling down the steps when they saw her pull up with the detective. "Mr. Shot! Wanna make more ice cream? Mr. Valient brought a new ice cream maker today! Wanna help?" they hollered to him.

"I think we need to get back inside right now." he said opening the car door for Mrs. James. "Grannie walked a longtime and needs to go inside to sit down. Would you help her?" They took her hands and walked up the front stairs.

"Why'd ya do that?" they wanted to know.

"I thought I'd get some exercise. I guess I went too far." She smiled at the kids. "How about you guys go play out back? Mr. Shot and I are going to have a cup of coffee. Then we'll talk about the ice cream. Okay?"

"Okay. Can we take Buddy with us?" Irving took the leash from Detective Shop.

Mrs. James looked at the dog, "You want to go with the kids, girl?" Buddy showed her a picture of her bed. "I think Buddy wants to rest now, too. Maybe later she'll play. Run along now." The children rushed up the porch stairs and through the back door before the adults made it to the kitchen. Cathy was there watching them.

"What happened to you, Mrs. J?" the girl came around the table to her a hug.

"Just a bit more exercise than I had planned." She smiled at the girl.

"Do you need me anymore? I have some homework to finish that I left at home. If I finish early enough, I could see Johnnie later." She looked at Mrs. James hopefully.

"No problem. Give your mom our best. Hopefully we'll be home soon. Tell her for me, okay?"

Mrs. James paid the girl, and she ran out the door to get home quickly. She would make it in less than five minutes and not even breath heavy, Mrs. James thought dejectedly.

Buddy went to her corner and collapsed on her bed. Detective Shot made Mrs. James sit down and then went under the sink to pull out the brandy Valient kept there. In no time, coffee was brewed and reinforced with the brandy.

Mrs. James gave the man a very big thank you smile. She had finally clamed enough to discuss this afternoon's adventure rationally. "So, who is that patrolman?" she began.

"It was supposed to be Patrolman Clark. It wasn't. Clark was found a few minutes ago. He had been unconscious in the parking lot. Someone hijacked the car. That was the call I received a minute ago. Whoever it was hid Clark behind some tires stacked out by the dumpsters. He came to and staggered into the parking lot, where someone saw him. He's on the way to the hospital to get checked out as we speak. Can you and Buddy describe him to a sketch artist? Clark can't. He was hit from behind and never saw the guy." Shop looked at her questioningly. "Who knew you were going out today?"

"As far as I know, only Valient. It wasn't a plan until this morning, And, yes, I believe we can describe him. What do you think, girl?" She quickly had a picture of the guy in her head. "That would be a yes, I'd say."

"Where's Washington this afternoon?" Shot didn't want to leave her there alone with the kids just yet.

"He's gone to meet with Ken Stevens. They had some computer work they couldn't do here. Apparently, Stevens has some kind of state-of-the-art equipment at his offices. He should be home soon." She looked at the clock to gauge his estimated time of arrival.

"I have to figure out what I'm going to make for dinner. I dropped the bag of groceries when I ran. I guess I better get to it."

She looked exasperated as she made her way to the pantry. "Maybe take out. I'm too flustered to think." she said, mostly to herself.

"Tell you what, you order what you want, and I'll get a real patrolman to go pick it up for you." the detective offered. "I'll even stay to help you eat it." he smiled at her.

"That's a deal." They went on to discuss possibilities. When they had finally agreed on something they made their calls and then sat down to another cup of spiked coffee.

Valient came in just a few minutes before the patrolman brought the food. He watched Detective Shot walk the guy back to his car. "What's that all about?" he asked Mrs. James.

"Come sit down and I'll tell you while we dish this out." He followed her into the kitchen. She explained what had happened that afternoon as Shot returned to the kitchen. Valient looked perplexed.

"Why would you be followed? Everyone seems convinced we're out of the line of fire. Why are we so important still?" Valient was trying to fit this latest inconsistency into his pattern. It didn't fit in he thought. What was the motivation?

"The patrolman is going to be driving by pretty frequently for the rest of the shift. I'll make sure someone is around after that too." Shot said as he sat at the table.

Mrs. James went to the back door to summon the kids for dinner. After telling them to go wash up, she set the table. All discussion of the day's adult adventures were tabled. The kids took over the conversation with their exploits with Cathy. They finished dinner with the kids begging for ice cream. Mrs. James promised them they oculd have some the next day. She was exhausted. They weren't happy but agreed. They didn't argue too much with Grannie.

After dinner Valient went to call Stevens. "Are any of your people watching Mrs. James? Someone stole a police car to follow her.

He could have had more in mind, but Buddy recognized him. She's really too old for this sort of thing."

"My people are only watching the house. You had a babysitter there today, the neighbor kid, Cathy. She left right after Shot and Mrs. James went in. One of my people tailed her home, just to be safe. But to answer your question, no, no one was on Mrs. James when she left the house." Stevens answered him. "What happened?"

Valient explained the afternoon's adventures. "Everyone's okay. No harm done. But what's going on?"

"I'm going to have someone come sweep the house for bugs or cameras. It'll be Stacks. You already know him. Watch what you say until he tells you otherwise. I'll assign someone to watch the house outside, just in case. Call me tomorrow." He hung up without a good-bye.

Valient just looked at his phone. "Why'd he do that?" he wondered out loud. "Mrs. James!" he called as he walked into the house. "Yes?" she came into the front room wiping her hands on a towel. She'd been doing the dishes. "What did he say?"

"Walk outside with me, please. It's beautiful out here tonight."

She looked at him questioningly but followed.

"Stevens is sending someone over th check the house. He said to watch what we say until the guy says we're all clear." Valient said keeping his voice low. "He's also going to have the house watched tonight."

"Between the patrolman and Stevens' guy we should sleep pretty well then." Mrs. Jamess smiled.

# CHAPTER 53

Finally, a break in the case, maybe. The operatives from the unit were meeting with an informant in Anaco, Venezuela. He reportedly had information on who had sanctioned the attack on the accounting firm. The meeting was set for later that day. Ken Stevens was hopeful but anxious for anything they could find out.

Around eleven that night, the satellite phone finally rang. It was more than anyone had hoped for! The attack was ordered by the head of the organization herself, Adalaid Ocho! And she was in the States visiting her daughter. Coud this get any better? The daughter was a naturalized U.S. citizen married to the head of the accounting firm they blew up! Mother was here consoling her newly widowed child. How hypocritical could a person get? Now all they had to do was get some proof of her involvement. The next great piece of information was the best. It was the name of the person who made the bomb. Juan Ricco was the best in the business and he worked for Adalaid Ocho. No one knew where he was at the moment, but the informant was sure he would be the one she goes to for something of this importance. She didn't trust easily but she trusted him. The only thing they couldn't find out was who actually placed the bomb in the building. But they were finally getting their feet wet here.

It wouldn't be easy to track Ms. Ocho. She had her own people watching for anyone intent on watching her. They would have to get creative here. The address for her daughter was public knowledge and in the file of the Rolo case. No problem. Not knowing how long she would be in the area meant they would really have to get something set up fast.

Stevens called a meeting of the team, minus the ones in Venezuela of course, for early the next day. After a few heated discussions, they finally agreed on a plan.

Since they had access to not only their own devices but the FBI's as well, it gave them carte blanche for what they could appropriate. Toney was a surveiliance wizard. He made a list of what he would want. He said he felt like a kid at Christmas with all the fancy toys he would get to play with. Powerful dish listening devices that could pick up a mouse running at over a half-mile away, computer recording equipment that could differenciate sound directionally and by source, cameras that could be attached to outsides of windows by being shot out of a modified grenade launcher without being damaged from a hundred yards. All of there could be interfaced wirelessly with his existing software.

Fritz Ike would go to interview the daughter in his capacity as FBI agent. He could easily find out how long the mother was going to be in the States. He would also do his best to plant a camera somewhere inside the house if the opportunity presented itself. He would take Washinton and Buddy along. The dog would be explain as a companion dog for the hearing impared Washington. Someone reminded them of a TV program with that idea a few years ago. "Where do you think the idea came from?" Ike chuckled. Not all the people around the table understood the significance of Buddy's presence at the meeting, but no one asked.

Buddy was giving Valient pictures of everyone at the table she didn't know with the red aura. He just petted her and whispered that all was well. She knew they were all dangerous but didn't understand why Valient wasn't concerned.

Sitaly was the premier computer hacker/programmer/interface expert on the planet. She would get into any computers in the daughter's house and find whatever there was to find. She had already gotten into the daughter's husband's computer in connection with the Rolo case. There really wasn't much there other than what was expected to do with his work. It didn't appear he had much direct personal interaction with clients. He mostly emailed his coworkers. The man took being a workaholic to a whole new level. Very little personal material was found other than a few emails with his wife. Those had to do with personal conversation but nothing of substance for the case. With the daughter's IP address already on her database the rest was child's play she reported with a self-satisfied smile. She couldn't find any record of any other computer the man had used and had no go ahead to get into any other family member's private computers before now. A.C. Ike made a mental note to talk to her about the computer guy, Kurtz, who had disappeared.

When the meeting broke up Stevens asked Valient and Agent Ike to stay a minute. After everyone had left to carry out their assigned tasks he motioned for them to sit back down. "I think we have an additional problem at your house, Washington. There were three microphones found when your house was swept, Walmart sourced. Any idea when or how they may have gotten in to place them? Definitely not in the league of the people we're dealing with."

"We did have an electrician and a security man come because a wire burned out while we were at the farm. I'll check with the company." Valient was understandably angry. He should have known better.

"My people guarding the house don't think the guy who followed Mrs. James the other day has anything to do with our situation.

"Who do they think he is? And why?" Agent Ike asked.

"The sketch Detective Shot gave them was run through the face recognition software. And I think I already told you not to ask how we got the access to things." he said as Agent Ike's face wrinkled, and he sat up straighter in his chair. "Anyway, he came up as some guy named Doug Shell. He's recently been discharged from a mental hospital, where he'd been for the last eleven years. They're still checking him out. There's not much more right now. I don't see him being a part of our current problem. Do you?"

"Why would he be in the face rec system?" Valient wanted to know.

"He applied for a driver's license when he got out of the hospital. His picture is on file now." Agent Ike answered with a sigh.

"Did Mrs. James say anything about knowing the guy?" Valient looked at Stevens.

"Not that she can remember. The name rang a bell, but she couldn't place it." Stevens told him.

"Thanks. Keep us up to speed on that, too. Whatever you find out we give to Detective Shot. We have enough on our plate to deal with without working local cases." Agent Ike was a bit dubious about the legal status of Stevens' activities but was in no position to question it. The others agreed that was best.

Agent Ike was at his desk the next morning on the phone with Mrs. Bakersmith. She would meet with him and Washington the next afternoon. Agent Ike explained he was bringing his associate with service dog. Did she have an objection to his attendance? Of course not, she assured him it would be just fine. Would her own dogs be a problem for them? He thanked her and called Washington.

"The meeting is set for three tomorrow. She's fine with my hearing-impaired friend and his dog. She has dogs of her own. That's not going to be a problem for Buddy, is it?" Agent Ike was crossing his fingers.

"No, she'll be fine. She knows what her job is now. I think she even thinks she's some kind of superhero. I probably should buy her a cape to wear for Halloween." Valient chuckled. "You can uncross your fingers now."

"How did you know I was doing that?" Ike laughed.

"Because I'm doing it too. See you tomorrow." Valient hung up and went to find Buddy who was playing with the kids in the yard.

He found her under the porch with Irving. "What on earth are you doing under there?" he asked the boy.

"Hiding."

"Why?"

"There was a man at the fence a little while ago. He scared me."

Valient looked at Buddy for some kind of picture. Buddy had nothing but a red aura it seemed. Was it possible Buddy couldn't read Irving? "Was Buddy out here with you when the man was here?"

"No, she was sleeping in the kitchen."

"Okay, come inside. I want to show you something." Valient took the boy's hand to help him out. The kid was shaking.

Mrs. James was in the kitchen having coffee. "Want some?" she asked indicating the pot.

"Yes, please. And do you have a copy of that sketch the police made?"

"Yes, why?" she looked at the boy who was way too quiet she thought.

"Irving says there was someone at the fence a little while ago who scared him. I want to see if it's the same guy." Valient just realized Sarah wasn't around. "Where's Sarah?"

"She wasn't feeling well so I told her to go lie down for a while. Is everything okay?" Mrs. James was concerned now too.

"Please, find that sketch for me. I'll pour my own coffee."

Mrs. James left the room and was back in just a minute. "Here it is." she said as she put it on the table by Irving.

"That's the man. He said he was a friend, and I should let him in. I ran under the porch to hide so he wouldn't get me." The boy started to cry. "Am I in trouble?"

"No, baby. But why didn't you come inside to get me?" Mrs. James asked the child pulling him into her arms.

"I didn't want you to get hurt like Daddy or go away lime Mommy." he sobbed.

Mrs. James looked over his head to Valient. "Get this creep. I don't care how or what you do with him but get him. Call these people you are involved with and get him."

He nodded that he understood. "We're working on it already." he said out loud.

Mrs. James sent Irving upstairs to play with Sarah. In minutes he came screaming back down. "Grannie! Grannie! Sarah is breathing funny, and her face looks weird! Hurry up! Come see!" The boy was almost hysterical.

Both adults race dup to check on the girl. Mrs. James got there first. "Call 9-1-1!" she yelled to Valient as she heard the child gasp for breath. Sarah's face was ghastly blue, and she was laboring for every ounce of air. Her grandmother pushed back the blankets and straightened her little body. Mrs. James took the small roll pillow from where it had fallen on the floor and put it under the child's neck to open the airway. It seemed to help some. The little body felt hot. What the hell happened to her? She was fine when she got up this morning.

The EMS workers were there within minutes, although it felt like hours to the people waiting and watching the child fight for her life. She was raced to the hospital with her grandmother by her side.

Valient and Irving watched the ambulance pull away. Valient was on the phone with Detective Shot giving him and update on the emergency. Irving was pulling on his pant leg. "Just a second, little guy." The man shushed him. Irving kept it up.

"What is it?" Valient said hanging up from Shot.

"Did the candy make Sarah sick?" the child asked in a small voice.

"What candy? Where did the candy come from?"

"We found it on the table out back. The one by the fence. I didn't eat any but Sarah did."

"Show me. When did she do that?" Valient asked him as he took the boy's hand and walked quickly out back.

"It was when we first went outside. Before Sarah got feeling sick."

"Did you tell Grannie about the candy?"

"No, Sarah said not to because Grannie doesn't like us to have junk. She said she would tell Grannie I had some too even though I didn't." The boy was upset at the thought.

They had reached the table with the candy. There were two pieces still on it. Valient took a tissue out of his pocket. He pulled out his borrowed cell phone and took a couple pictures. One to show the proximity to the fence and another to show the placement of the candy. It was a safe bet the candy had been thrown over the fence. He picked up the remaining candy and wrapped it in the tissue. He called Mrs. James to give her the information for the doctors of what the child had eaten. His next call was to Detective Shot. They needed to get the candy to the hospital for the doctors to check for poisons. Valient didn't have a car, and a taxi would be too long. A patrol car was at the curb in minutes, thanks to Detective Shot. Valient and Irving jumped in and were whisked away to meet the detective at the hospital.

"How is he doing?" the men asked Mrs. James.

"She's a little better. The oxygen levels are up slightly. They had to do a tracheotomy. She's on a respirator. I hope that candy will show what she was having a reaction to. I can't tell you how many times I have told that child about eating things she doesn't know where it came from! She has always been as pig headed as her father! He was a hellion as a kid. That's what killed him, you know. He never knew his limitations and was driving drunk. His stupidity finally killed him. I want so much more for his girl. When she pulls through from this I hope she's learned her lesson." She sat down hard on the nearest chair.

Detective Shot took her hand and sat with her. Valient took Irving out to the waiting area. For now, it was a waiting game.

# CHAPTER 54

DOROTHY AND AGENT GRASON WERE sitting in front of Agent-in-Charge Ike.

"What happens now?" Dorothy was asking.

"You are settled in the Witness Protection Program. There's nothing left for you here. Unless you consider your sister. She and Irving are your only living relatives. But I understand you have little or no contact with Jessie. Have you attempted to contact her at the hospital?"

"I didn't even know she was in a hospital. What's wrong with her?" Dorothy had the grace to look concerned.

"She's had a breakdown after a firefight at the safe house we had her in. Matt's death, being in hiding from killers, and your situation and people dying on her behalf put her into overload. They someone tried to kill her roommate at CMC. She shut down completely. I understand she's starting to get better, but its' going to be a long road according to her doctors."

"Where's Irving?" Now Dorothy was concerned.

"He's staying with a Mrs. James. She is a friend of the detective who was working Matt's death. Jessie and Irving were staying with her before they all went to the safe house. She has a granddaughter a year older than Irving. The kids have become close. At our urging the court gave permission to foster Irving to Mrs. Jamse to keep him from being any more traumatized."

"Where's Jessie? Can I see her?" Dorothy's sisterly love was at long last kicking in. "I'm not the best sister, but we are all we have now. I can't desert her. What can I do for her?"

"Right now, nothing. She isn't allowed visitors yet. But I'm sure cards, letters, or some flowers would be welcome." Agent Ike was relieved to see her want to help. He had had his doubts from what Jssie had said about Dorothy.

He hoped it lasted. He really liked Jessie and Irving. Dorothy was too self-centered for his taste.

"So, if I don't go into the program, what will happen?" You could almost see the wheels turning in Dorothy's head.

"I can keep you in another safe house. Keep the status quo until we figure out who's after you and the kids now. Grason here stays with you or we can assign someone else. It's up to you."

"All right. How long will that be do you think? The kids need to be in school or have tutors. I am not patient enough to home school. Can something be arranged? How am I going to support myself? Does the government still pick up the bill now that Rinne is gone?" Dorothy needed some assurances life might become some kind of normal eventually.

"I think I have just the agent to help out with the kids' education. Your friend here was a teacher before he became an FBI agent. The children already know and trust him. We will be taking care of things until we get someone in custody, and you are off the hit list. As for you and a job, if you want training we can arrange for you to do some computer classes. Under a different identity for your safety." Agent Ike offered.

"When would we move to a new safe house?" Dorothy sounded tired. She could understand why her sister shut down. For a second, she wished she could join her in that place.

"I could have it arranged by tonight. You could move this evening."

"And Grason stays?" Dorothy's eyes didn't look at either man. She blushed slightly, confirming what Agent Ike thought about the two.

"Just so you both understand, you will keep this on a professional basis. What your relationship may become after this is finished cannot be acted upon until it is no longer such a dangerous proposition. Are we clear?"

Now they both blushed slightly. "Yes, sir." Agent Grason said not very convincingly. Dorothy just nodded. A.C. Ike wasn't convinced but didn't push it. This is how he met his wife, but no one knew that at the office. God, he missed that woman. The cancer had taken her too soon. He did his best not to smile at the couple in front of him.

By late evening, Dorothy, the kids, and Grason were settled into the care of Jack and his team. Jack prayed their stay would be a lot less eventful than her sister's.

# CHAPTER 55

"Good afternoon, Mrs. Bakersmith. Thank you for seeing us." Agent Ike shook her hand as they came through the door. "Please accept our condolences on the death of your husband."

"Please come in." She stepped in front of him to lead them to the front room. "What can I do for you? I'm sorry, should I be looking at your associate so he and understand me?"

"Thank you for your concern, that would be helpful." Agent Ike looked at Washington and nodded to him.

Washington smiled at the woman. "Thank you." he said in a nasally voice.

"I know this is a trying time for you and your family. We won't take up too much of your time." Agent Ike started the conversation.

The woman just smiled at him. An older woman entered the room looking none too happy. "Who are these people? What are they doing here?" she addressed the men. "Don't you know this is a house of mourning?" she glared at her daughter.

"Mother, these are the agents from the FBI I told you were coming today. Why don't you join us?" Mrs. Bakersmith sddressed her mother.

"They don't need to be here. You didn't blow up the idiot's office!" She turned to the men. "Get out of here! Leave her alone. Jose, escort these men to the door." She stood with her hands on her hips, glaring at them as Jose, who had been standing near the door, started forward.

"Mother, please. I'm sure they are aware I had nothing to do with this. I want to talk to them. I may know something I don't realize. Please sit down with us." She looked at her pleadingly, her cheeks reddening.

"I'll do no such thing. If you insist on talking with them, it will be without me!" She turned on her heel and stalked off. Before she left, she said to Jose in Spanish (not knowing of course that the men were fluent) "Watch them Do not leave her alone."

"Si." was all he replied and took up his post by the door again.

"I'm sorry about that. She has been very protective since she's been here. I love her dearly, but she can be pretty overwhelming at times." She said looking directly at Washington. He couldn't help but smile. Buddy was staring at the door the woman had just stomped through. The dog was seeing a picture of a man with a gun and sending it to Valient. There was another picture of large packages, like paper boxes. That was all she got before the woman went out of the area.

"I'm sorry we upset her. How long is she going to be here with you? It must be comforting to have family around right now." Agent Ike looked contrite.

"I'm not really sure, actually. She is trying to get me to go back home with her. I can't seem to get her to realize this is my home now." She shook her head sadly. "What can I do for you Agent Ike? You didn't come here to referee for my mother's tantrums."

"We are just tying up loose ends. Do you have any idea who may have wanted to do this to your husband or his business?"

"Good God, no! He was totally dedicated to his business. This has to be one of those terrorists the goverment is alway trying to scare us with. What kind of monster kills like that?" She was shocked at such an idea.

What kind, indeed, the men thought but didn't say out loud. What was it going to do to her when she is faced with the fact her mother ordered this monstrous deed. Heaven help her then.

"So he had no enemies you know of?" Agent Ike continued.

"I'm sure he may have had business rivals, that sort of thing, but nothing that would precipitate this sort of action. All those people dead and wounded. Are you sure it was my husband's business that was the main target?" she asked hopefully.

"Unfortunately, it looks that way. Do you know who any of his clients were?"

"No, other than my mother and some other family members. I really didn't have anything to do with the business. Anyone who would know is dead now. Were all the computer servers destroyed? They are kept in the basement of the building I understand. That is the best I can do for you."

"You have been very helpful, actually. I hope we didn't cause you any issues with your mother by coming here. If there is anything we can do for you, please feel free to get in touch with me." he said handing her his card.

She turned to Washington and offered her hand. The men shook hands with her and took their leave.

Once in their car and looking back at the house they saw Mrs. Ocho in the upstairs witndow, scowling at them. Agent Ike waved to her. She didn't wave back.

"That was informative. We need to get to Sitaly about those servers as soon as possible. Do you have her contact number? I don't want to wait until I get back to the office to get her." Agent Ike was driving and couldn't use the satellite phone in the car. He hadn't set up the Bluetooth.

"Hold on. I think I do." Valient pulled out the phone Stevens had given him.

"Sitaly, this is Valient Washington. We just found out the servers for AccuRecords were housed in the basement of the building. Do you think you could get to them and get any information that may still be on them?"

He waited a minute while she made her answer. "Will you have to physically get to them?" Again, he waited. "Great! I'll pass that on to Fritz. Keep us up to date." He hung up after her good-bye.

"She will see what she can do. She may not have to physically to the site to access the servers. If they are still powered up by some miracle, she can hack into them. Hopefully they have battery backup. She says every business does now since everything is kept in computers. She thought, like the rest of us, that each business kept their servers in their office area. And all the information was lost."

"I wonder if Adalaid Ocho knows about the servers." Agent Ike offered.

"If she didn't, she will soon. Her spy in the room will have told her by now, I'm sure. Sitaly was going to work on getting in right now. We just need to get whatever is there before Ocho's people interfere."

An hour later Sitaly called back. She had gotten into the servers. In the next ten to twelve hours, she will have all the information uploaded into her hard drive. The servers held the information for everyone in the building. It would a take a day or so to interpret the initial data, but she would get it done as fast as humanly possible. She also had her team working on getting into the personal cyber account of Adalaid Ocho.

Agent Ike called his counterpart in Homeland Security to flag Adalaid Ocho's passport. He then called the Director of the FBI to alert the transportation people to watch the private charter services. The woman could not leave the country. She would disappear into her protected world if that happened.

The listening devices were in placed inside the house. Agent Ike had managed to plant four of them. Every surface he touched; the front door, the underside of the hall banister as he leaned on it briefly, the door jamb, and in the sitting room under the table, behind the sofa where they sat. Within minutes of their departure Toney had his recording in full flow.

"What the hell are you thinking talking to those men?" Adalaid Ocho attacked her daughter. Toney heard a slap and the younger woman cry out. "Why did I not know of the computer servers? I am a client of that useless man you married! My business is not the business of the U.S. Government or any other!"

"Mama, I didn't know it was a problem! You haven't asked me about anything to do with the business. How can your books be something anyone could use to cause your business to have an issue? If it is an honest business, you have nothing to worry about!"

"You are the stupidest child!" Toney heard another slap and cry. "You dare to question me? No wonder Bakersmith kept you at home like a whore!" She stalked out of the room, leaving the younger woman crying.

Toney had played that exchange to Agent Ike a few minutes later. "Very interesting, don't you think?" Ike commented. "We now may have a chink in the armor. Something to use against Ocho. Good work, Toney, thanks."

# CHAPTER 56

THE ELDER SARAH JAMES WAS devastated. She sat holding the hand of her namesake. The machines set up a melody of life. The doctors still couldn't isolate the poison that was slowly taking her baby from her. Valient had delivered the candy to them over twelve hours ago. What is taking so long to figure this out? "Please, God help them to help her." she prayed over and over.

A nurse came in to check the readouts and take stock of how the child was doing. "You need to leave now Mrs. James. Our rules state you can only stay fifteen minutes every hour in the ICU. We need to do our jobs and family cannot interfere."

Mrs. James just looked up at the scowling woman. "Not on your life, dearie. You want me gone, you'll have to bodily take me." she said defiantly.

"I will call security. You have to leave. I need to take care of your child, and I can't do it while you are present."

"Really? Then get someone in here who can. I'm not going anywhere." Mrs. James stared at the nurse daring her to make good on the threat.

The nurse glared at her then turned and stamped out of the cubical. Mrs. James put her head down on the bed. She was exhausted, but if the staff thought she would leave, they were mistaken. She could hear the nurse complaining to her supervisor and requesting that security be called. Fortunately, the supervisor had a brain. She heard her tell the nurse to leave her alone and just do her job.

After a bit more whining, the nurse was told to switch patients with a coworker who had an elderly man no one ever visited. Mrs. James made a mental note to talk to the hospital administrator about the nurse. She needed to be working in a different unit elsewhere.

An hour later the doctor came in looking dire. "We now know she ingested hemlock. The candies she ate were homemade and very potent. But I must be honest with you. By the time we got Sarah in here, the poison had done quite a bit of damage to her kidneys. We are going to start dialysis in a few minutes to give them a rest. She'll be having it every day until we see improvement. All we can do now is wait for her body to do its job."

"Why did it take so long to get the results from the lab?" Mrs. James was reeling at the news.

"To be honest, Mrs. James, the sample was mislabeled from the E.R. It should have been a rush, but it wasn't. I can only apologize and get her on the correct protocols as quickly as possible now."

The doctor looked as devasted as Mrs. James felt as she started to cry softly.

"Is she going to make it?" She whispered.

"She's young and healthy otherwise. We have every hope she will. But it is in God's hands how she will react to the treatments. Stay with her and keep up hope. I heard what happened earlier. I assure you no one will bother you like that again." He tried to smile but coulndn't when he saw her face. "Hang in there. Can we get you anything? Coffee? Tea? Anything?"

She just shook her head no.

Detective Shot came in around lunch time. "Come on, we're going to get a bite to eat." He too her hand and tried to get her to stand.

"I can't leave her. I'm staying here." She pulled her hand away and wouldn't budge.

"No arguments. I brought reinforcements. Valient is going to sit with her while I feed you. We bought clean clothes and your personals so you can get a quick shower. Now, let's go." he insisted and put a hand under her elbow pulling her off the chair.

She wasn't happy about it but knew he was right. She allowed him to propel her toward the door of the ICU. Valient gave her a small smile and a hug as they passed at the opening of the cubical. "Call my cell at the slightest change. Promise me." She looked beseechingly at Valient.

"You know I will. Go. Breathe. Get cleaned up. I won't leave her, I promise." The nurse who had given Mrs. James a hard time passed as this exchange was going on. She gave them a dirty look and started to say something but thought better of it when she saw Mrs. James' face.

After eating a small salad and sandwich, Mrs. James felt a bit stronger. Detective Shot waited as she took a quick shower in the doctor's lounge. It's nice to have friends, he thought to himself when he thought of the doctor he was currently seeing. He hadn't told anyone about her yet. They both like it that way. It lent an air of intrigue to the relationship. He smiled at a recent memory.

Sarah was having her dialysis by the time they returned to the ICU. There had been a delay because of scheduling issues. The doctor had to intervene to get it started. Since she was going to be another half hour, the men stayed with Mrs. James in the waiting room finishing a cup of coffee. "Any more information on the guy who did this?" Mrs. James looked pensive. "I have had a lot of time to think about this. I think I know the person."

"We were going to ask but wanted to wait for the right moment. I wanted to see how you were first. What do you remember?" the detective asked.

"When I first started taking in domestic violence cases, there was a woman who went back to the husband and was killed. There were three kids. The youngest one was killed with the mother. The older two ere in school when it happened. It was the oldest, Doug Jr., who had walked into the carnage. The father had beaten the mother so badly, she was a bloody pulp, literally. The baby, a girl, was drowned int the kitchen sink, presumably in front of the mother. The father was waiting for the older two in the garage for them to get home from school. When he attacked, the older boy ran up the stairs to get away. The father followed, but when he lunged, he fell, breaking his neck in the fall back down the stairs. The boy always blamed the system for allowing the father to stay free when he was such a threat to the family. I was part of the system, as far as he was concerned. He ended up in the mental hospital after attacking the social worker and trying to set fire to my house. I don't know what happened to the middle kid, his name was Brian. He went to live with a relative, the last I heard. I believe it was the Shell family."

She sat back in the chair with a heavy sigh. "What is taking so long? Shouldn't she be done by now?"

A few minutes later, they saw the dialysis machine being wheeled back out from Sarah's cubical. The men said their good-byes and left Mrs. James to go back in with her, promising to return later in the day.

"We need to find this Shell character and fast." Detective Shot was angry for himself and his friends. "I need to get back to the office to get started. Where do you want me to drop you?"

Valient went home to check on Irving. The poor child had been neglected during the crisis with Sarah. Cathy had been taking care of him. Valient shouldn't have been so concerned. The child didn't even look up from where he and Cathy were playing because he was so engrossed in the game. "What's going on over there?" Valient called out.

"Mr. Valient! How is Sarah? Is she coning home yet? Can I go see her?" Irving ran to him and jumped up into his arms.

"Sarah is very sick, Irving. She won't be home for a while. As soon as the doctor says you can I will take you, okay?"

"Cathy, can you stay for a bit longer? I have some work to do and won't be able to be watching Irving. Do you have time?"

"Sure, Mr. Washington, my mom said to tell you not to worry. If I have to leave, she'll just bring Irving to our house whenever you need her to. She knows how much trouble it can be when someone is sick like this. My dad had cancer and if it weren't for Mrs. James, my mom would have gone completely crazy with me. So, she feels she owes Mrs. J." Cathy explained.

"Tell her thanks for me. It helps a lot. Sorry about your dad. I didn't know." Valient understood the relationship better now.

# CHAPTER 57

Valient had turned the library into his workroom. Ken Stevens had provided a state-of-the-art computer system and graphic software for him to use. He felt like a kid in a candy store. His task right now was for him and Buddy to figure out the picture of the boxes she had picked up from Adalaid Ocho. He started by showing the dog a picture of a box of computer paper. She picked up on it right away. They worked on it for most of the afternoon and evening. Valient's eyes were crossing, and he still hadn't eaten by nine o'clock. Buddy hadn't even asked to go do her business. Cathy had interrupted him around six to ask what he wanted her to do about Irving. When she offered to take him home with her Valient jumped at the offer. Could they keep him for a day or so?

They quit to eat and to take care of personal duties. The picture of the box was almost done. Buddy wasn't happy with the color and logo. Valient thought he had enough for a search, so he went ahead and started the computer working on it while he ate his dinner. By the time he had eaten and come back, the computer had a close match. Buddy was pleased with it, too. Valient called Agent Ike and went to bed.

The paper company was in Pageland, just over the South Carolina border. Agent Ike took Valient and Buddy with him to be sure Buddy had the right box logo. They used the hard-of-hearing ruse once again when the owner balked at having the dog in the shop. Valient couldn't help but smile at how easy it was to pass this off.

The owner couldn't find an order for AccuRecords. It seemed they didn't order from them. Had any of their boxes gone missing recently he was asked. He could find no record of that either. They took a walk back to his storage area to make sure. That's when they saw a body. Feet sticking out from under a toppled shelf unit full of boxes ready to be shipped. The weight was enough to crush someone in the direct path of the fall. When asked how long it have been since anyone had checked back there. The owner had no idea. A few days at least he guessed. There had been no shipment for about three days. The next one was due to go out the next day.

The local authorities were called as a courtesy, but it was a pretty sure bet this was an FBI case related to the bombing in Charlotte. They arrived about the same time as the FBI forensics people and a heated discussion of jurisdiction ensued between the responding deputy and the lead CSI.

Agent-in-Charge Ike pulled rank and ended the discussion quickly. He put the deputy and his people to interviewing the workers letting the forensic people to do their jobs. Hopefully they could work together as the local FBI agents were pulled pretty thin on the bombing and James cases. So far, they were ahead of the rest of the alphabet soup working on the bombing. Agent Ike wanted to keep it that way for now.

The dead man was a new hire (no surprise there). He'd been hired only a week before the Charlotte bombing (again, no surprise). His main duties were to construct the paper boxes and fill them for shipping. It was a very small outfit and didn't have machines for that task. The owner liked it that way. His concern was for putting people to work and could afford it. Most of his orders were less than twenty boxes at a time, so he didn't think it would be efficient to put in and automated system anyway. It would take a day to take an inventory of the area to check if anything was missing.

A.C. Ike left a forensic agent there to supervise the correct procedures and make sure they included the pertinent areas. A guard provided by the Sheriff's Department would be there day and night until the scene could be cleared.

The man was fingerprinted and identified as Rafael Sito, a small-time thief. In the list of items found on the body was a satellite phone. Why would a guy like that need a satellite phone? Sitaly took all of two seconds to identify the numbers stored in it. Two were very interesting. One was traced to a satellite phone currently traced to the Bakersmith residence. No name, just a location. The other was in Anaco, Venezuela. Bingo! A link! Not perfect, but a beginning.

The next afternoon A.C. Ike received a call from the print shop owner. "Agent Ike, I swear I didn't know about this. Someone has been selling our boxes. Empty ones, go figure! It makes absolutely no sense to me. Who would want empty paper boxes? There are about thirty missing. No one would have figured that out if you hadn't asked. There were two invoices torn out of the hard copy invoice ticket book. We use the book and give the duplicates to our bookkeeper to input into the QuickBooks program we use. A very faint trace of writing shows a sale to a Luis Gale for ten boxes for fifty dollars. I can only assume the other invoice would show the same thing. I gave the book to your agent."

"Does the book show when the sale was made?" Agent Ike aske the distraught man. "Was it during the time Sito was there?"

"I think so. We had just started using that particular book only a few days before I hired him. So it had to be. I'm so sorry I didn't catch that yesterday. I really didn't know, I swear." The man must have been feeling like he was responsible. Only the truly innocent get that nervous when confronted with a crime of this magnitude.

"It's okay, sir. No one is accusing you of anything. Thank you for all your help and cooperation. I'll let you know if we need anything else. Goodbye." Agent Ike hung up smiling. It was time for the team to get together again.

The team was once again meeting in the warehouse. "We have a link from the Charlotte bombing to the Ocho cartel. It's tenuous at best but it's a start. We know the bomb, or more likely bombs, were planted using paper supply boxes from a company in South Carolina. We still don't know how or by whom."

Sitaly chimed in and said, "The body found at the printing company had a satellite phone. I trace two of the numbers back to our friend, Adalaid Ocho. It strengthens our case by a bit." She looked over to Toney.

Toney played the tape of Adalaid Ocho abusing her daughter. "Maybe we have a chink in the armor. I say we use this to make the chink a rift."

One of the agents who had been to Venezuela spoke up. "Our informant tells us there was an email sent from Adalaid to her son-in-law, berating him for the breach. In it she purportedly threatened him. We need to get our hand on that. Sitaly, have your people found her computer yet?"

"Found it and have uploaded everything in it. They're still sorting it all out. It takes time to read the stuff. I just emailed them to look out for that one specifically. It shouldn't take long." She looked at her screen for a minute. "Got it. I've forwarded it to each of you.

It's in Spanish, so if you aren't fluent, the translation is below it. I'm sure you get the drift. She was pissed, I'd say."

"Does anyone have a contact with the forensic people working on the bomb debris? We need to know if there are pieces of the boxes left. That would solidify our only physical clue."

Ken Stevens looked around the table for a response. "Alright then, we have to go through the channels. Fitz, that's got to be you."

"Right. I'll make the calls." He made a note. "Shana, what are the chance you can make friends with Mrs. Bakersmith so we can turn her?"

"By the close of today, I will be a member of her health club. It shouldn't be too difficult to make friends. She reportedly talks to everyone. The problem is going to be getting her in a private moment. She has had a bodyguard since her mother has shown up. She's never alone." The already too cut Shana smiled.

"Heaven save us from the fit." one of the other agents mumbled causing a ripple of laughter.

It was agreed they still didn't have much. The government agencies weren't working on this angle. They were still running down bogus tips claiming a jihad radical did the deed. No one had anything else to offer right now so they adjourned. Valient liked the idea of not being in the limelight. He could contribute without being so visible.

Ken Stevens took him and Buddy home because he wanted to see the kid. He asked if he could take the boy to eat. Irving wanted Cathy to go too since they were going to her favorite place. No one had any objections so off they went. Valient ask him for a ride to the hospital so he could check on Mrs. James and Sarah. They all went in because Irving wanted to give Grannie a hug to give to Sarah. It was arranged that they bring an order back for Mrs. James and Valient. They would then take Valient with them back to the house.

"How did this get so complicated?" Stevens teased his nephew ruffling his hair. "All I wanted was a sandwich with the rug rat."

"Any more news?" Valient asked when he and Mrs. James were alone again.

"They said the dialysis is keeping her blood cleaned out. She was fussy earlier. They gave her something to calm her because she may be in pain. Other than that, there's been no change." she said sadly.

"How about some coffee?" Valient offered.

# CHAPTER 58

Detective Shot was sitting in the outer office of Doug Shell's psychiatrist. He knew he probably wouldn't get much from him. Confidentiality. Doctors and lawyers were the bane of his existence. He needed to find the man. The detective had spent most of the day sitting on the address from the driver's license. It was all there was. Shot had confirmed the address the psychiatric hospital, but guy the wasn't there and in the four hours Shot had waited, he never showed. He needed to find out if he had a place to hand out. That's why he was sitting here wasting what was left of the day.

Finally, the doctor came to greet him. "What can I do for you, Detective Shot?" he said as he read the name from the card the receptionist had given him.

"Thank you for seeing me, Doctor. I need some information, if you can. I'm looking for Doug Shell. I know he's a patient of yours. Anything you can give me will help."

"You know I can't divulge information on my patients, Detective. You must be desperate. Actually, I haven't seen Douglas Shell in a few weeks now. He's supposed to come every week, according to his recommended terms of release. I have reported his absence to the hospital, but since he's not under a court order for care, I can't compel his cooperation. So, technically, he is no longer a patient. I still can't give you any specifics however." The doctor seemed sorry for not being able to help.

"I understand. I just need to know if he has any where he may hang out. Or if you can tell me if he's made any new friends since he's been in town." Shot looked at the man hopefully.

"A young lady came in with him a couple of times. She wasn't part of our sessions, so I guess there would be no conflict in giving you her name. Shell introduced her to everyone in here whenever she came with him. Her name is Marta. Marta Gracelyn. I think he's still seeing her. Wait a minute, he had me take a picture of them on one occasion. Let me get my phone."

The doctor went to the inner office and returned a few second later fiddling with his phone. "There, I've sent it to the number on your card."

"This is a great help. Do you know where she lives, by any chance?" Shot was feeling a bit less hopeless.

"Somewhere near Shell is all I know. I hope this helps." He shook Detective Shot's hand as a new person came into the room. "Have a safe evening."

Detective Shot now had a point of contact. He had a start. Now all he had to do is find her. There was a diner on the next block from Shell's apartment. He'd go there and show the picture to see if anyone could point her out to him. It couldn't be this easy! She was his waitress.

"I'm looking for your boyfriend, Ms. Gracelyn. Any idea where he'd be?" he asked as she brought his coffee.

"Which one?" she asked with a smile.

"Doug Shell. I really need to talk to him, so don't play games with me. I'm not in the mood." he growled at her.

"Ain't seen Doug in about a week. We broke up." She didn't seem all that sorry about it.

"Does he have a favorite hangout?"

"There're a couple places he goes. He eats here most days. But he hasn't been in today that I know of. And the only other place I know is the bar on the next block that way." She indicated the opposite direction from the apartment.

Shot ordered a sandwich since he hadn't eaten since last night to take with him. He finished his coffee and went to the bar to hopefully find Shell. He didn't bother with the car since it was so close. It would take longer to drive and park than to walk. He was there before he finished the first half of his sandwich. He looked through the window to see if he could spot the guy while he swallowed the other half. He didn't see Shell, so he went inside. He wasn't there. Shot showed his badge to the bartender told him what he wanted and left his card. The detective didn't hold out much hope of help from that quarter.

He walked back to his car, deciding to hang around for a while longer, just in case the guy went home. It was two more days before he showed. The stakeout team spotted him drunk and disheveled, staggering down the street toward home. They waited until he got himself inside before approaching him.

Douglas Shell was sitting in the interrogation room, swirling coffee in a paper cup. Detective Shot was trying not to gag, as the man smelled so disgusting. He slammed his fist on the table to get his attention.

"Please! My head is killing me!" the man whined. "I'm going to be sick!" He started to gag. The other policeman near the door handed him a waste basket just as he made good on the threat.

"Feel better now?" Shot asked him sarcastically. "Officer, get him a paper towel, please." Shot was trying not to breathe to avoid getting sick himself. This was disgusting.

Shell just looked at him bleary-eyed.

Shot hit the table one more time. "I asked you a question." he shouted to torture the guy.

"Don't know what you're talking about. I ain't seen that bitch since she killed my family." Doug Shell looked like he might be sick again.

"She didn't kill anyone. Your father did. Why are you stalking her?" Shot continued to raise his voice.

"That bitch! She said she would keep my mother away from that butcher, and she didn't! They gave my other a piece of paper that was supposed to keep my father away from us. The stupid bitch let her take us back to our house. He killed everyone but me!" Doug Shell turned his bleary eyes trying to focus on his torturer.

"Your mother chose to go back there. What do you want with Mrs. James?"

"I lost everyone. Now she needs to feel what I feel. I'm alone and she has those kids. It's not fair! She needs to be like me. I spent all those years in that hellhole, just dreaming of what I could take away from her." Shell started to cry.

"But why give the kids poisoned candy? They weren't even born when your family was killed." Shot needed him to say something incriminating on tape before he figured out he could have a lawyer. They had read him his rights, but Shot wasn't so sure he understood, being as out of it as he was. Just for the sake of the evidence tape, he asked the guy again, "Do you remember us reading you your Miranda rights?"

The guy said yeah.

"So, you do know your rights, correct?"

"Yeah! I can shut up, get a lawyer, and not say anything to make me look guilty of anything. I don't want no lawyer. I need a doctor. I'm hung over, not stupid." He looked at the detective defiantly. That what Shot wanted him to say.

"That woman, Mrs. James, she didn't help us. She let my idiot mother go back to that house. He came the next day! He killed everyone! The cops thought he fell down the stairs, but he didn't. I pushed him. He came for me, and I pushed the bastard! He didn't get me!" He looked please with himself as her stared at Shot with those bloodshot eyes.

"When I got out of the hospital, I found her again. She still had the same house. The neighbor lady told me where she was. I watched that house for a few days before I figured out what to do. If I took those kids away, she'd be alone like me. Now she'll know how I've felt all these years rotting in that hospital. Now it's her turn to feel that kind of pain." His eyes filled with tears. Not for her, but for himself as he retreated into his own head.

"Where'd you get the poison"" Shot screamed at him.

Shell put his hands on both sides of his head in pain. "There's a guy! I got it from some guy! Leave me alone! I'm dying, can't you see?" Shell put his head down on the table, spilling the cold coffee all over the file folder Shot had laid out.

Shot jumped up with the folder, shaking it to get the liquid off. He looked down at the sorry piece of humanity in front of him. "You're pathetic." he said as he gathered his papers to leave. To the guard he said, "Get him booked for attempted murder." He couldn't wait to leave the stench of the room and the man behind him.

"You can't arrest me! I need a doctor. I have to go back to the hospital. The doctor told me. If I got in trouble again, you'd have to put me back there! He said so!" Shell got up from the chair to run to the door. The officer blocked his way stepping in front of the panicked man.

"The hospital released you because they thought you were cured. They said on the record you're not nuts. You go to jail, and then to real live prison. Where I hope they fry your ass. You better hope that child doesn't die. Because if she does, I will do everything in my power to get you the death penalty." Shot told the quaking mass of reeking humanity in front of him. The contempt in his voice was deadly. "Get him out of here." he said to the officer. "Then get this room fumigated."

# CHAPTER 59

SHANA WAS ON THE TREADMILL watching Susan Bakersmith fight with the stationary bike she was trying to program. The woman was joking with the person next to her about how hard it was to ride something that went nowhere. Her bodyguard was watching from her perch near the door to the locker room and trying and failing to look unobtrusive. About fifteen minutes later, Bakersmith headed to the showers. Shana followed, watching how closely the bodyguard kept to her prey. It wasn't going to be easy to separate the two as the bodyguard even stood outside the showers as the woman cleaned herself.

Standing at the sinks applying makeup they struck up a conversation. "You seem to have a shadow." Shana hooked her head at the bodyguard. "You must be pretty important."

"No, I'm not anyone important, except to my kids maybe." the woman smiled.

The bodyguard stepped between them, effectively stopping any conversation. Mrs. Bakersmith glared at her in the mirror, but she didn't seem to care. Shana just smiled as she packed her personal bag. "See you next time." she offered breezily as she left the room.

Two days later, Mrs. Bakersmith and the guard were at the refreshment center when Shana arrived. She sat next to her at the bar and said, "Green can't be good." looking at the drink she was holding.

"My friend here says I should eat more organically. I'm not sure what that means exactly, except everything she suggests is green. Tastes like crap as well. But she insists it's good for me." She sighed putting it to her lips and grimacing.

Shana smiled at her as she ordered a soda. "I saw you here the other day. Do you work out often?"

"I try to come at least three times a week. It doesn't always happen, though. Best intentions and all that."

"I know what you mean by best laid plans. We only can to the best we can. At least we try."

"We have to go, Mrs. B., your mother is waiting." The bodyguard again insinuated herself to stop the conversation.

Mrs. Bakersmith glared at her but got up from the stool. "Next time." she smiled to Shana. Shana stood and took the woman's hand in a handshake, passing her a note in the classic move. Her eyes widened for just a second, and she nodded her head as if to say she understood. The bodyguard had already started for the locker room door and missed the exchange.

In the bathroom stall, the woman opened the note, it read: "I can help you. Call this number 704-777-8686". She flushed the commode after dropping the paper into it.

"You will not speak to that woman again." her bodyguard informed her.

"I will speak to anyone I please. You forget yourself, I think, Cerilla." Mrs. Bakersmith glared at her.

Invading her space, the bodyguard threatened, "I will speak to your mother when we arrive at your home. You know she will agree with me."

Mrs. Bakersmith took a step forward. "Get out of my way."

They stood, nose to nose, for a few seconds before the bodyguard stepped aside. Mrs. Bakersmith had had enough of her mother, her people, and her control. Maybe this stranger really could help. She would see she thought aa she rubbed her bruised cheek.

She was finally alone in her room. Pulling out her cell, she dialed the number the woman had given her. "Who are you really? What do you want from me?" She asked when Shana picked up the call.

"Mrs. Bakersmith, we can help you get away form your mother. We know who she is and what she is doing to you. You would have to do exactly as we say for this to be successful. Do you think you can do this?"

"Why should I trust you? What's in it for you?"

"The only thing we want is justice for the people in those buildings. Your mother ordered that devastation. She needs ot be stopped and punished. You know she's capable of such a thing. You have to believe we know this to be the absolute truth." Shana paused to let this sink in.

"Are you nuts? She's done some terrible things I'm sure. But that? Never!"

"Mrs. Bakersmith, Susan, please don't let anyone hear you. This could be very dangerous, going against your mother." Shana got alarmed for her.

"She...she wouldn't. She couldn't be behind that. I won't believe it." The woman deflated. "Someone's inside the door." Then the phone went dead.

Shana called Fritz Ike to report the conversation. "I made contact. She called a minute ago. We'll see. She's upset, naturally, but I think she might believe it. She hung up abruptly. Does Toney still have eyes on the house?"

"Yes, he does. He's sending feed constantly. Let me get him on the other phone, hold on." He came back on the line. "Shana, he's watching the infrared to ther room. There's one body moving around in there. She looks to be fine."

"I knew Toey was a voyeur!" she laughed.

Toney must have heard her because Ike said "He says he's not. He only watches if the sex heats up the colors." They both laughed at that and hung up.

Shana hoped the woman could do what neede to be done.

# CHAPTER 60

SARAH JAMES DIED EARLY IN the morning. Her grandmother watched from the door of the cubical as the doctors and nurses worked to bring the child back to life. They worked on her little chest for fifteen minutes before calling the time of death. They had tried to get her to leave, but she wouldn't budge. She just stood staring, praying, and crying softly. Even after they had all left the room, she stayed to hold the child's hand until John Shot came to get her. The doctor had called him, he said.

"I'm so sorry, Sarah. She didn't deserve to die. Come on, let's get out of here." He guided the devastated woman out of the area. He had called Washington on the way there, so he knew they were coming back to the house. Mrs. James hadn't said a word since he had picked her up.

They arrived at Washington's house after making a stop for some bakery items. Detective Shot was working on radar. He didn't even know why he had stopped, except it was something to do. Mrs. James hadn't moved out of the car or even acknowledged he had stopped.

Valient had made coffee and served the group in the kitchen. The men didn't know what to do with Mrs. James. She drank her coffee in silence. They didn't thing she even tasted it. After her cup was empty, she took herself upstairs to lie down.

"What's she going to do now?" Valient thought out loud.

"She hasn't said a word. So who knows? There is a sister in Montana. I used to have the number somewhere. I'd better find it." Shot said sadly.

"She was such a cute kid. Irving is going to be beside himself. He already things it was his fault she got so sick because he didn't tell anyone about the candy right away."

"Where is he?" Shot thought the kid would have been up by now.

"He's staying at Cathy's house. I've been busy with the research on the bombings, so I asked if they would keep him for a few days. I'll go get him after we finish the coffee. Not a job I'm looking forward to. You'll stay till I get back, right?"

"Yeah, Sarah shouldn't be left alone."

Valient looked at him questioningly. "Sarah?"

"Yeah, the kid was named after the grandmother. I forgot you didn't know that."

"Why does she go by the formal 'Mrs. James'? I've never known anyone who did that."

"It was something her husband started when they first got married. They addressed each other that way and it just stuck. It was a big joke around the precinct. When he died all her friends just continued it. We even introduce her that way. She doesn't tell too many people to call her anything else. When the grandkids came along, it was joked she was going to be Mrs. Grannie. Little Sarah is the one who stopped that by calling her just Grannie." Shot looked and felt like a stone had been roped around his heart.

Valient and Buddy walked the three blocks to Cathy's house. She knew the second she saw his face that something really bad had happened. Again.

"Mom! Come to the door! Mr. Washington's here." She let him in as she hollered for her mom. "I'll keep Irving busy while you talk to Mom. You don't look so good. Sarah's dead, isn't she?" She said as her mother came up behind her.

"Yes, I'm afraid so. She died early this morning. Mrs. James was with her." Washington felt a tear run down his cheek.

"Come in, Mr. Washington. Can I get you a cup of coffee?" the girl's mother asked, leading the man into her kitchen.

"No, thanks Mrs. O'Neil. I'm fine. Thank you for keeping Irving for us. After everything that's happened, we can never thank you enough for your help."

"How is Mrs. James? She must be beside herself."

"She took herself to her room shortly after getting back to my house. We assume she went to get some much needed sleep. In the whole time young Sarah was in the hospital she never left unless she had no real choice. No one was ever more devoted to a grandchild." Valient said with admiration.

"You can leave the boy here for as long as you need to, Mr. Washington. He's no trouble and the poor thing has been through more than most adults in a lifetime. What's going to happen to him now/"

"I have no idea. His mom is still in the mental hospital. She's getting better, but it's going to be a long road for her. She's in no shape to care for a kid. He's got a few relatives that may take him. It's really too soon to have any idea. None of them are aware of this new problem." Valient felt so old at that moment. "I need to tell Irving. Can you ask Cathy to bring him to me?"

"Mr. Washington, why don't you let Cathy take care of that? He's fine here. If you give him that kind of news then leave, he may feel he's being abandoned again. We can tell him and be here with him for the aftermath."

"I'd feel like a coward, Mrs. O'Neil. I should be the one to tell the kid." Even as he said it, he hoped the woman would insist. In this case, he was a coward. Speeding bullets didn't scare him as much as facing this little boy right now.

"How about we do it together?" She smiled at the man quaking in front of her and took his hand. They walked into the next room where the children were reading a book. God bless Cathy. The book was about a friend who went to heaven. She had already told Irving his friend was dead. Valient approached the girl and kissed her cheek. "You are an angel. Thank you." was all he could say around the huge lump in his throat. Irving reached up to hug Valient.

"Sarah is with Daddy now. Cathy said so. That's a good thing because now they can play together like me and Sarah did before."

Valient picked the boy off the sofa and hugged him tight. "That's right big guy. So we don't have to be too sad now, do we?"

"Who am I going to play with now?" Irving broke down crying. All Valient could do was stroke his back and hold him.

Cathy said, "I guess you'll have to play with me and my mom. That's a good thing, right?"

The child looked up with watery eyes and smiled. "Can I stay here? I like being here."

The older people just looked at each other over his head. "For a little while, kiddo. Until we find out which one of your relatives want you to come play with them, okay?" Mrs. O'Neil assured the child. "We won't throw you out."

Cathy showed the book to Valient. "My dad gave it to me before he died. When he was told he only had a short time to left. He and Mom wanted to make sure I was prepared. I still keep it on my nightstand after all this time. I thought it would be good to read to him."

Valient thought he could see her halo as he smiled.

Valient left a few minutes later. He felt better and worse at the same time.

Mrs. James was back in the kitchen by the time he returned. She had made fresh coffee and arranged the pastries on a plate. She had her phone book out on the table next to the portable phone. The book was open to the funeral parlor she had used before for her family. She was talking to the mortician now. She was back in charge of herself. Her face was set in quiet determination.

Valent left her to her calls after getting himself some refreshments. She only looked up long enough to give him a tight smile.

A few hours later, she walked into the library and sat across from Valient. "Everything's arranged for Sarah's funeral. We'll have a viewing and funeral the same day. Father Tom is doing the funeral Mass at St. Vincent's the day after tomorrow. She'll be buried with her mother in the same grave. I have to go over to the funeral home in the morning to sign the papers and pick out the casket. I thought it was hard when her parents died. This is so much worse." She said as the tears started to fall.

Valient handed her his hankie. At that moment, he was glad his mother always made him keep one in his pocket. "What can I do, Mrs. James?" Whatever I can do to help, I will. I hope you know that. I have become extremely fond of you and Sarah these past weeks. But we could never have envisioned any of this."

"Right now there's nothing I can think of that you aren't already doing. Just being a friend has been the best help you could ever give. Thank you for that."

The next few days went by very quickly. It seemed like a bad dream as the group sat on the back porch sipping spiked coffee a week after Sarah's death. There had been so many people in and out of the house. Valient couldn't remember being this overwhelmed since his dad had died. They we all exhausted.

"I've made up my mind as to what I'm going to do now. My sister and I had a long talk while she was here. We have always talked of moving to Florida, and we have no more reasons not to. She's alone and tired of the weather in Montana. Most of my old cronies have either already moved to Florida or moved on to the great beyond. This week I'm putting the house on the market. One of the ladies who had come to the funeral has a place near the beach outside of Niceville. We'll start there and who knows, we may get used to being beach bums." She smiled at the supporting faces of those she has come to love and depend on literally in life and death situations. "I'll come back for the court case, but we're meeting at the new house at the end of next week. There's nothing to retrieve from the house, thanks to that bastard. It's all gone now. My sister has only a small apartment now, too. Its's a new start for us both."

"Have any permanent arrangement been made for Irving?" Mrs. James looked at the faces once again.

"I'm taking him with me." Ken Stevens looked at John Shot. "Other than Jessie's sister, I'm his closest relative. I've been in touch with my attorney, and the custody is taken care of. I'm going to be named his guardian. I'm going to visit Jessie and her doctor the day after tomorrow. Hopefully she won't think I'm stealing the kid. She never had truly trusted me. Not that any of us can blame her. Just so you know, I've made arrangements with Fritz to move us all to Colorado. I own a large home in the mountains. There's a hospital in Colorado Springs for Jessie and a new life for the whole family to get started on. Dorothy even went along with it. Heaven help Gilliam, her boyfriend and bodyguard. She's a handful." He chuckled and shook his head at the memory of that conversation.

"It seems like the best solution all around." John Shot and Valient agreed. Mrs. James wanted to know where the child would be living. Didn't Stevens travel a lot? Who would be taking care of him on a daily basis?

"I'm hoping Dorothy will step up for that. She agreed but didn't seem too enthusiastic about it. I don't think she takes care of her own kids too well. But I've never been a parent so I'm trying not to be too judgmental. I may hire a nanny. She'd love that I think." Mrs. James seemed to think that was a wonderful idea. Everyone wins so to speak.

"It's been a ride, gentlemen. I don't feel the least bit guilty about getting off." She raised her cup to the group. They returned the salute.

# CHAPTER 61

THERE HADN'T BEEN MUCH TIME to work on the bombing. The rest of the unit and Ken Stevens' people had taken up the slack. Sitaly had cracked the code on the accounting form's bookkeeping. She now had her team compiling the information. The team was confident they'd find the evidence they were looking for. So far what they had proven was that Rolo was not the only shady character in the bunch. The criminals were on both sides of the pencils! Their findings were going to keep the IRS busy for the next century.

Toney had recorded some very telling conversations between Adalaid Ocho and her bomber in hiding. But they still hadn't found out who had actually placed the bombs. She had continued to berate and abuse her daughter. Shana had managed to keep up a relationship of sorts with Susan Bakersmith. Covertly encouraging her to turn on her mother. So far there wasn't much movement in that department. Susan Bakersmith had not called the number again. Her mother had taken her phone.

The unit had people scouring Venezuela for the bomb maker. Ken Stevens' people were expanding that search to Argentina. There had been a bombing in Salta very similar to the Charlotte event.

The company destroyed was also connected to Adalaid Ocho. It was again a tenuous one, but her name came up on th list of clients.

Finally the alphabet soup of government agencies had come around to their way of thinking. Major Crike spent many hours in heated meetings, showing them the error of their ways. Agent-in-Charge Ike put a task force together with a representative from each agency to hopefully become and effective force.

It was time to get back to work.

They were back in the warehouse conference room. A wall-to-wall computer touchscreen was lit up with pictures, flow charts and spread sheets. Various technicians and agents were milling around, touching and swiping things all around it. It looked very impressive. Another wall was now equipped with a huge white board covered with columns and lists of places and names. Valient and Buddy sat at the end of the table, trying to make sense of it all.

Buddy sent Valient a picture of the Ocho woman. "Yup, she's the middle of this mess. We just have to prove it." he said to the dog.

Valient walked to the front of the room. He stood at the podium for minute while the people in the room started to take notice. Under the shelf was a gavel he used to get the attention of those who didn't readily move to a chair. Once everyone was seated and quiet, the meeting began. For the benefit of those who had just joined the group, Valient went through a recap of what little was known for sure, a sequence of events starting from the Rolo embezzlement to the current surveillance of the Ocho woman and a rundown of the suppositions they had come up with. When he completed his introduction, he turned the meeting over to A.C. Ike. Those department heads whose teams had been working on this each gave a report on what they had, or in some cases, didn't have, or thought they had.

When all was said and done, they had more suppositions than facts. That had to be turned around if they had even a prayer of getting Adalaid Ocho. As Valient looked at the various pictures and charts, he sat up suddenly. He was beginning to see the pattern! He just needed a few more pieces.

The three friends met at Micco's after the meeting for a friendly dinner. Buddy was in overload from reading the minds of all the people she had encountered. She didn't understand why she felt so many of them were dangerous, but her friends didn't seem to care. She was distracting Valient by her constant insistence at communication. He tried to show her they were friends, but she wasn't buying it. She got so annoying that Valient gave up and excused himself from the group and took her home.

Next morning they were sitting in the library. Buddy was going over the pictures of the people present at the warehouse one by one with Valient. He showed her pictures of various badges from the internet to let her know the ones who were the good guys. There were a few people he didn't have on his list and couldn't find a picture in his databases. One in particular caught his attention. He had seen this guy before from Buddy. When he communicated that to the dog, he got a picture of the Ocho woman. Valient wasn't much of an artist, so he couldn't sketch himself a picture to show anyone. There would have to go through the security tapes.

The next morning Valient was sitting with Toney in his cave, at least it felt like one. There were more computer screens here than at Best Buy! The room lighting was muted and just enough to keep people from tripping over things on the floor.

Toney had the tapes of the warehouse entrance pulled up on three of the screens directly in front of him. Buddy was staring intently as each one flashed on the screen. After about ten minutes, Buddy barked. She had found the man. Toney looked at Valient for guidance. He didn't know about Buddy other than she was special. It wasn't a very good picture. The guy had kept his face averted from the direct line of the camera. But now they could match with the camera in the meeting room. The current Major Crike had not wanted cameras in that room, he thought it was overkill. Now Valient was glad for them. There was a full frontal of the guy sitting at the table. "Gotcha!" Valient smiled.

The facial recognition software was in full swing. They were running every agency they could find. He wasn't found in any of the local or even national databases. But when they ran Interpol, they got a hit. He was a Brazilian national. He had been flagged only because he had been seen too close to one of the Monacan princesses. It seemed there was nothing concrete in any of the files, but he was in the county each time this princess traveled. What was he doing in their meeting? His name was Raole Houis. He had about a dozen aliases as well. Toney forwarded a copy to each of their people.

Valient called Ken Stevens to see if he had any idea who this guy was and how he got into the meeting. Stevens didn't answer so he left an urgent message. Where was he now?

Next he called Fritz Ike. Agent-in-Charge Ike was very interested in this information. He recognized the guy but thought he was one of Stevens' people. He had seen so many new faces at the meeting it didn't stand out as being strange. But how to find him again?

In the meantime, Shana wasn't having much luck with Susan Bakersmith. The woman was terrified of her mother. So much so that she barely looked at Shana at the gym. It was disappointingly clear that it was a dead end.

One break came from the forensics people. They had found pieces of the paper boxes that matched the color and some parts of the logo from the Pageland printing company. A partial fingerprint had been lifted from a piece of what they thought was a box lid.

It matched a local delivery guy named Terry Hacker. It didn't help much because he had no idea who hired the truck to deliver the paper. He had picked up the boxes at a storage place in Monroe. He gave them the address. There was only the manager at the place to let him into the unit. But at least they knew they were right about the boxes. It was a lead to follow.

# CHAPTER 62

ADALAID OCHO WAS PLEASED. THE Americans were out chasing themselves. They had only suspicion, but no proof, of her involvement in any crimes in this country, that according to her live-in boyfriend who also happened to be number two agent with the Ken Stevens agency. She could leave here and no one could detain her. The flight was scheduled for four days from now. She would have that idiot daughter with her this time. For fifteen years that witch had defied her. Now with her useless husband dead, she had nothing holding her from her homeland. No one kept what she wanted away from Adalaid Ocho, and she wanted her grandchildren with her where they belonged.

Her business with the bomb maker came to a satisfactory conclusion. He had one more delivery. The money was already in his accounts for jobs well done. The last delivery would be in England in two days. Everything was set. He would then take and extended vacation in Australia. She may even join him for a time. Making bombs was not the only thing he did extremely well. The thought made her smile wider.

A.C. Ike and Valient were at the storage unit with Buddy. The manager took them to the unit that had held the boxes picked up by the truck driver, Hacker. They found it pretty much cleaned out. There were six boxes still there, empty. They did see pieces of wire and tape lying on the floor. They waited for the bomb squad people to bring the dogs to check for any explosive residue before they ventured into the space.

Buddy picked up a picture of a man who had rented the space from the manager. It was the same guy who had been found in the printing shop. He wasn't going to be of any help. Valient showed her the picture of the interloper to the meeting hoping she'd pick up something form that. She got nothing.

After a few minutes of A.C. Ike talking to the manager, Buddy got a picture of someone walking away from the unit. Valient asked him about anyone in the vicinity her could remember. He described the man Buddy was showing Valient. He had been in the storage area they were standing in front of. He had forgotten about that. The guy had the key so he must have been with the person who rented it.

They hung around with the bomb squad people long enough for the dogs to detect explosive residue. It didn't take very long. As the forensic arm of the unit came to get working, Agent Ike and Valient went back to Ike's office. They'd only get in the way here.

The preliminary report came late the next afternoon. Swabs showed the presence of C4. They had suspected that but now had proof. They also had the fingerprints of two individuals. One was the dead guy for the print shop. No mystery there. The other was found on a piece of broken plastic tip from a wire nut. One of the boxes had DNA on it! Not just sweat but for sexual activity! Somebody got it on in the storage unit! Bingo! Now all they had to do was match it to someone.

When A.C. Ike shared the information about the DNA, Shana had an idea. If she could get a specimen from Susan Bakersmith, they'd have at least something to try to compare to the one found at the storage unit. It was a start to eliminating suspects. They might get lucky. Ike agreed it was better than nothing.

The next afternoon, Shana found her at the refreshment bar. She was trying to drink another of the green things her shadow ordered for her. Shana didn't a woman could look any more miserable. "Still trying to acquire that taste, I see." Shana smiled at her.

"And failing miserably." Susan gave her a face that 'said this is gross'. She set the glass on the counter.

"We must go, Mrs. B." The bodyguard took her arm to lead her away.

Susan gave Shana a helpless look and let herself be taken. Shana felt bad for the woman. When this was over, she promised herself she would do whatever she could to get her to a safe place. In the meantime, she asked the counterman for a to-go cup and took a plastic bag from her pocket. She collected Susan Bakersmith's glass and the rest of the liquid in it for the lab. Piece of cake she thought. Too easy really. As an afterthought, she did the same for the glass the shadow had been drinking from.

It took until early morning the second day to get the result from the glasses Shana had retrieved. Her hunch was spot on! It showed a familial match to the DNA from the box in the storage unit. They had their first direct link. Now they had to make sure Adalaid Ocho did not leave the United States. All exit lines were pulled closed. Every airport, no matter how small within a hundred miles, was put on alert. Every port was notified. Unless she went via underground tunnel, she would be detained.

The also got a hit from the bodyguard. There was open murder case in Las Vegas with DNA that had been matched to a person. It had been thought a working girl stabbed a john or a lover's quarrel. The guy was a tourist from Asia with triad tattoos. Not one worked the case too hard. Now she could hand them their suspect and get her away for Susan in one shot. Sometimes things just work out.

The Bakersmith children were not happy about leaving their home. At age thirteen and ten, they had school and friends. Their lives were here. Their father was buried here, and they did not want to leave him behind. They did not want to go somewhere they did not speak the language or know anyone, and they didn't like their grandmother one little bit. She was a bully. Their grandmother didn not care for their excuses. She said they were going, and they would do as they were told. Susan had quietly told them they were not going anywhere.

It only made her angrier at Susan that she had not even bothered to teach them what Adalaid had considered their native language. She had hired a tutor to instruct them to prepare for their move to her home. Susan insisted they were Americans and only spoke American. In three weeks, they did not take one class form the teacher. He was turned away at the door each time he showed up. How could she have such stupid children?! They had not even started to pack when their grandmother went to wake them for the trip.

She angrily strode to the hallway and screamed for the daughter. "How can you let them be so disrespectful to your own mother? Tell them to get up and get their things together right now! Or I will have Cerilla pack for all of you! We leave in an hour!" She started to turn toward her own room when Susan quietly said, "No, other we are not leaving our home."

Adalaid Ocho had had enough! She turned on her daughter and slapped her hard enough to knock her to the floor. "Now, to get yourself and your ungrateful children ready to leave this hovel. I will not be patient any longer. You will leave when I am ready. Do you understand?"

Susan pulled herself up off the floor and stood in front of her seething parent. "We are not going. You can kill me as you did all those poor people in those buildings, but my family stays here."

He mother glared into eyes so filled with hate she had to take a step back.

"Yes, Mother, I know what you did. Your greed and power killed not only my husband, but too many others to count. It stops for me right here. We are no longer part of your family. Take your flunkies and leave my home."

The children were in the doorways of their rooms, staring at the scene before them. Cerilla came up behind Susan and reached for her, but a look from her employer stopped her. The kids looked from one woman to the other, holding their breath. They had never heard their mother sound like this before. It scared them more than their grandmother's threats and bullying.

The women stood glaring at one another for what seemed an eternity to the children.

In the end, Adalaid Ocho left the house with only the people she arrived with. Only after she had left the driveway did Susan start to shake and cry uncontrollably. She'd never been so afraid in her life. The kids and she sat holding each other on the sofa. They were too scared to let go. When she regained some control of herself, a much different Susan Bakersmith went to find the telephone.

When Shana answered the burn phone, she couldn't believe Susan really was on the line. The woman she had left at the gym was a scared little mouse with no backbone. This person was defiantly in total control of herself. What a difference a day makes, Shana thought to herself.

Susan Bakersmith gave Shana all the information about her mother's plans to leave the country, when, how, where, and how many in the party. They made and appointment for later in the day for Susan to talk to the team.

Shana was already sending a text to the team to meet at the warehouse as soon as humanly possible. They had work to do and fast!

The members of the unit and, by extension, Ken Stevens' operatives, were back in the warehouse conference room. Seated across from Valient was Raole Houis. Buddy was staring at him and sending bright red auras to Valient. She did not like this guy! Stevens heard Buddy growling low and staring at his man. He knelt and petted the dog. "It's okay girl. He's with me." Buddy looked at him and lay down but was still wary.

Valient called everyone to sit as he began the meeting. Shana gave the briefing this time. "I received a call from the daughter of our suspect. She has given us the date and time of her mother's pending departure. On Thursday, at 6:00PM, she has a charter scheduled to depart form a small airport outside Hendersonville. Ther are eight people in her party, not including the pilots. None of the family are going with her. For now, she has moved from her daughter's home and is staying at a bed and breakfast in Hendersonville. We have been in touch with the owners. They verify the party arrived last night and are paid through tomorrow."

Ken Stevens spoke up. "I'd like to introduce my associate, Raole Houis. He had intimate knowledge of Adalaid Ocho, and I mean *intimate.*" He smiled around the table and got snicker for his troubles. "Raole has been living with Adalaid for two years. He has been part of my organization from the beginning. And, yes, he was recruited for the unit."

Valient was not so sure. Why didn't he show up on the database? This guy was still a question mark as far as Valient was concerned.

He needed to ask more questions before he'd be satisfied. Buddy was still showing the red auras around the pictures of the woman.

Raole gave his insight as to the personalities and fire power of those they would come up against. There was one operative left behind to keep an eye on Susan Bakersmith and her children. It was still in Adelaid's plan to take them with her if possible. One or both children were in danger of being kidnapped and taken to Venezuela with the grandmother or join her at a later date, if that weren't possible. That threat was to be neutralized by tonight by another of Stevens' people. It was suggested there be more than one operative on them. A team of five was authorized. Buddy was showing the man knew there was more than one person waiting at the Bakersmith house. Valient wanted to know why.

When the meeting broke up Valient went directly to Ken Stevens. "What's going on with your guy?" he challenged the man.

"What do you mean? He's been my right hand for the last three years. I trust him."

"Buddy doesn't There is more going on than he's telling you. Ocho has three people still at the daughter's house. Those kids are in more danger than he's telling us. Why?"

"With all due respect to your dog's abilities, the guy is solid. Her so-called insight is wrong here. I think I'll rely on a person rather than a dog, if you don't mind." Stevens never had thought the dog's abilities were real anyway. He really thought Valient was a nut job and needed to be sidelined.

Valient's next step was to report his fears to Fritz Ike. They devised a plan to keep Raole under audio as well as the GPS surveillance. A small transmitter was secreted into his belt loop. Shana had magic hand, he never felt it as she walked by.

Since the flight was scheduled for 6:00 PM, the team would be in place at four. Raole would join Ocho at the bed and breakfast to keep the team up to date on her whereabouts. Toney was monitoring his phone GPS system as well as the transmitter. The audio was also being forwarded to Ika and Washington.

Everything was in place and waiting at the assigned times. The airport had one building and one small landing strip. There weren't too many places to be concealed. There was a golf course about a quarter mile away where they left the cars. The small building held wind comes and other flags, as well as equipment to change tires. Ladders and paint supplies were the only other things in it. There was barely enough room for the seven people waiting for the suspects to arrive.

The small jet arrived about five o'clock. A fuel truck arrived and left, followed by a catering truck a few minutes later. A car arrived to deliver a woman dressed in a flight attendant uniform, who promptly boarded the plane. The nothing for about a half an hour.

At exactly 6:00 PM a small van arrived with the Ocho party. Adalaid was looking around for something. Ike and Washington heard her say, "They should be here by now. Where are they?"

"Where are who, my love?" Raole asked her.

"My grandchildren. I was told they had been picked up and on their way. They should be here by now."

"Don't worry. They'll be here in a few minutes. Things didn't go quite on schedule, but they are on the way."

"You know this how?" She was suspicious.

"I sent my own people to help Cerilla. The kids are five minutes from here. Relax."

Ike asked Toney to check on that last transmission. Toney came back in the affirmative. The children had been kidnaped an hour ago. According to a neighbor, the kids left with a lady and man. The man was carrying the younger one. The team sent to protect them was ambushed enroute to the residence. They were run off the road and not found until ten minutes age. Susan Bakersmith was missing also.

"I told you something was squirrely with this guy." Valient said to Stevens after Ike had relayed the double cross. He just got a dirty look from the man.

As they prepared to leave the shelter, the car with the children pulled into the airport gate. Three agents ran to intercept them while the rest of the team approached the plane.

Adalaid Ocho and Raole Houis made it inside the plane, while the others spread out and started shooting at the team. Two of the suspects fell immediately. The other ran behind the tires and out away from the plane. Three more were hit before they could go more than ten yards. One tried to get into the plane and was taken down. The two who were trying to conceal themselves behind the tires gave up. Two agents were hit but still moving on the tarmac.

The agent approached the plae calling for the occupants to come out peacefully. Valient and Agent Ike could hear Houis and Ocho arguing about where the pilot was. Why wasn't he in the plane? They didn't know he was tied up in the shed where he had gone to retrieve a sack of money his employer had put there to give to Adalaid. The co-pilot had not entered the plane yet. He had been doing a visual check of the outside of the plane when the action started. He was prostrate on the tarmac covering his head in fear.

The car the children were in tried to run the agents over as they stepped in front of it. They held their ground, and it swerved at the last second. The driver lost control, and it careened off the tarmac into the field. They chased it until it came to a stop. The doors opened and the occupants ran from the car and were gunned down. One of them had the fifteen-year-old by the neck as he backed away from his pursuers. The boy was savvy. He elbowed the man in the stomach and then hit him in the face with his fist in a backhand.

The guy loosened his grip enough for the boy to drop to the ground and trip him with a round house sweep of the legs. It was over in seconds as the team moved in to subdue the guy.

The boy got to his feet and raced back to the car to get to his sister. She was still asleep and strapped into the seatbelt. He just held her after releasing it until the agents escorted them to a safer location. The agents were congradulating the boy for keeping his head and being so brave. All he did was smile. He confessed to them he was a black belt in taekwondo, and his sister had a green belt. His Dad had insisted they learn self-defense from the time they were eight. Agent Ike offered him a job.

Valient and Ken Stevens approached the plane with the other agents. Stevens yelled to Houis to come out with the woman. Houis came to the door with his hands raised and a smile on his face. "Well boss, we got it done." he said, trying to be friendly.

"You betrayed me, Raole. You set this up. Not a smart move." Ken Stevens was pissed at his number two.

"I was undercover. That's how it works, remember? Get the mark to trust you. Lie to them."

"Lie to them, not your employer. You went over the edge for a piece of tail. I thought you were smarter than that. You were under too long. You fell for the mark." Stevens raised his weapon toward the man. "You know how it works in this game." He shot the guy between the eyes. "Betrayal doesn't get a second chance." he finished the thought.

They heard a scream and a shot from inside the plane. The agents rushed in to find Adalaid Ocho shot and the flight attendant standing with a gun in her hand, shaking like the preverbal leaf. "She tried to shoot me!" the woman screamed as they disarmed her.

It took another two hours to clean the area of any evidence of the encounter. Pilots from the unit flew the plane out to sea and ditched it. They were picked up by a waiting boat. It was reported to the FBI by the Coast Guard as a plane lost at sea. As far as anyone knew, the occupants all went down with the crashed plane in the ocean. The pilot and flight attendant were threatened and release to tell a story of being replaced by the client's own personnel. They were left stranded at the airstrip to make the story more believable. Any traces of a fire fight were cleaned up by the agents from the unit and Stevens' associates.

The returned the children to their home. They did not find Susan Bakersmith. A canvas of the neighborhood gained nothing. A search of the area around the house and neighborhood found her car on the next block. Her son insisted she would never have left it anywhere. If she were home, it was always in the garage. Her purse was found in her bedroom. The last anyone had seen her was at breakfast. He didn't remember her being there when Cerilla came for them.

Cerilla had drugged the kids in order to get them in the car. The man had injected the boy, but he didn't totally pass out until he was almost in the car. His sister was out before she hit the ground. The man had to carry her, the boy stated. He thought his mom was in the house then, but now he wasn't sure.

Agent Ike called Detective Shot to report the woman missing. The children were taken back to Valient's house. It was reasoned it was the most convenient place since Mrs. James was still there for another day or so anyway. Valient joked he was going to start charging for hotel rates it was so busy there. The kids smiled but were too worried about their mom to see the humor.

Buddy wasn't picking up anything from the kids. Valient thought maybe they had seen something and didn't remember that Buddy could pick up. It didn't happen He wondered once again if Buddy could read the children. She didn't seem to able to read Irving either. Maybe kids were closed to her. He didn't understand it.

Mrs. James left the next day with her sister. She would be returning to testify at the trial of Doug Shell. It should be short and sweet since he had confessed to poisoning Sarah and bugging Valient's house. His confession was the plea deal arranged in exchange for taking the death penalty out of the question. His attorney initially tried to have a diminished capacity defense, but since he had been regarded as sane by the hospital and the court appointed doctor gave a report of knowing his own mind, the Judge denied the request.

The Bakersmith children ended up with an aunt in California. The boy was happy with that arrangement because he always intended to go to college at Berkley.

# CHAPTER 63

V ALIENT AND BUDDY WERE SITTING in the front room watching football on TV. The Panthers were at home, pizza, beer and football, peace and quiet.

The doorbell rang. The dog sent a picture of John Shot. Valient hoped she was wrong.

She was, but she wasn't. It was Shot, Stevens and Ike. Micco was behind them. "This better be a social call." Valient said with a smile. They had more beer and something that smelled great with them.

They spent the rest of the afternoon enjoying the game. The Panthers won! Life was good.

Valient's list was lying on the coffee table. Stevens picked it up. "What's this?"

"In my life, before meeting this group, I was trying to figure out where my life was going. I made this list to get me started. The only things I have done are get my house cleaned and get the dog. I still need a job. But after all the excitement being mixed up with you, I'm not sure I need one."

"How about coming with me? I'm in need of another operative. And you're already trained." Stevens offered.

Micco looked at Valient with a whole new respect. "I thought I knew all about you, my friend. You are more than I ever thought. And to think you came to me for advice! What a joke."

"Sorry to not let you in. But I know you understand why I couldn't." Valient said sheepishly.

Micco shook his head and smiled.

"I think I'm in no matter what I want. Once in, the only way out is underground, right?" Valient looked at the group.

"Welcome back." Stevens and Ike said as they shook his hand.

After they were alone again, Valient said to Buddy, "Life is a series of ripples, one man's actions started a ripple effect that changed everything."